The Chronicles of Valonia

The Jewels of Valonia

Katie Paterson

due for publication later in 2009

The Golden Casket and The Spectres of Light
the second book in 'The Chronicles of Valonia'

THE CHRONICLES OF VALONIA

THE JEWELS OF VALONIA

KATIE PATERSON

HandE Publishers Ltd

Published by HandE Publishers Ltd
Epping Film Studios, Brickfield Business Centre,
Thornwood High Road, Epping, CM16 6TH
www.handepublishers.co.uk

First published in the United Kingdom 2009
First Edition

ISBN 978-0-9548518-7-3

A CIP catalogue record for this book is available from
The British Library

With the exception of the legendary but possible existence of figures
such as King Arthur and the Knights of the Round Table,
all the characters and events in this book are fictitious and any resemblance to
actual persons, living or dead, is purely coincidental.

Copyright © Text Katie Paterson 2009
Illustrations by Charles Tomlinson
Cover design by Ruth Mahoney and Charles Tomlinson
Typeset by Ruth Mahoney

Printed and bound in England
by CPI Bookmarque, Croydon, Surrey

For my long-suffering best friends.
Lisa, Liam, Mags and Rosanna.

BEACH

THE VILLAGE

FARM

THE

Introduction

The sky was dark and dismal and the rain fell gently on the party of mourners standing around the grave, as the minister said the final words. Every villager had made their way to the small churchyard, some carrying small bouquets of flowers picked freshly from their gardens or the surrounding fields, to say goodbye to Celia, the small, quiet lady from the manor. She had never really been one of them; she'd kept herself to herself and hadn't mixed much with the rest of the village. Nevertheless, she had been well liked, as unlike the rest of her family she had a kindly nature. If the truth be told, most of them had felt sorry for her, as it had been painfully obvious that she bore the main brunt of her twin brother's tyranny. His absence from the funeral party compounded the rumour that he had been responsible for her death, not that any of them would dare mention it in his presence.

The funeral over, they laid their flowers by the grave-side and slowly began filing away, back to their cottages, until only one person remained – an old man, with a long white beard, who pulled his thick cloak tighter around him, to keep out the damp chill. He looked sadly down at the coffin, shaking his head. Eventually he motioned to the two men waiting at a discreet distance with their shovels, that he was finished and they could start filling in the grave with the nearby mound of fresh earth. He made his way slowly up the path that wound its way through the graveyard, towards the old stone church. He found a pew half way down the aisle and sat down heavily, staring at the large wooden cross suspended above the altar, still shaking his head in sorrow.

"What to do, what to do?" he said as he leant forward and put his head in his hands.

Years ago he had made a promise, and he had kept it, but had he been right to do so? If he had not pledged his silence, would things have been different, or was he right to still keep his secret? What would happen now? Would matters be taken out of his hands and corrected? What would the consequences of this be?

"Oh what to do, what to do?" he asked aloud, miserably, as the thoughts and responsibilities continued to mount in his wise old head.

He sat back again and looked up at the beautiful arched stained-glass windows that ran down both sides of the church. He stared at the figures depicted in the ancient battle scenes of a bygone age. They were so familiar; he almost expected them to answer him.

His thoughts were suddenly broken by the minister, as he sat down next to him.

"You seem very troubled, my friend," he said.

"Troubled? Yes, indeed. I am deeply troubled," the old man mused, stroking his beard absentmindedly.

"Can I help?" asked the minister.

"I wish you could," was the sad reply. "I am growing old, my friend. I should have known. I should have done something to prevent this. Poor Celia, she didn't deserve to die!"

"You mustn't feel responsible. What could you do? The poor woman drowned! There was nothing you or anyone else could have done to help her. Drowning in the manor lake was no more than a tragic accident."

"I would like to believe that, but you and I both know that nothing is ever as simple as that here," the old man answered with a sigh.

"Even so, you can't be responsible for everyone's actions, however good or bad they may be. Sometimes this responsibility lies with those much greater than us," mused the minister, looking reverently at the wooden cross.

"You're a good man," the old man replied sympathetically. "It can't be easy for you either. Our ways are not of the ordinary. It must be difficult for you, too, to keep the faith here."

"Oh, I don't consider my mission here any different from anywhere else. The fight between good and evil exists everywhere, my friend. Our missions may be different, but they are not that dissimilar."

"No, maybe they aren't," agreed the old man, nodding as he considered this. "Maybe they are very much the same, after all."

"They are indeed, and my advice would be to leave your worries with those higher than ourselves to deal with."

"That is my concern. I know that soon things will be taken out of my hands and there will be nothing I can do to control events. I will have to break a promise and there will be others drawn into this and endangered. Those we have sought to protect."

"Trust, my friend, trust. That is all I can advise you to do."

"I know, and thank you for your concern," the old man answered as the minister got up, laying a hand on his shoulder in a final gesture of sympathy.

He sat for a while longer in the comforting silence of the church before he made his way out, leaning heavily on his stick.

As he reached the path outside, he noticed the tall dark figure of a man standing by the recently filled in grave. He hung back, not wanting to disturb him, and for a moment he felt sorry for the man he recognised as Celia's brother. He had obviously come to pay his respects after all, and the old man felt guilty for misjudging him, until he saw the man throw back his head and laugh as he tossed a bunch of flowers onto the new grave.

The old man's hand flew up to his mouth in horror as he heard the words that followed.

"Celia! Celia. Stupid, stupid woman! All you had to do was go along with my plans, but oh no, you were too good for that. Did you really think you could stand in my way and get away with it? Stupid woman!"

"Stop! Stop! Enough! Have you no shame?" the old man shouted as he rushed towards him.

"You? What are you doing? Trying to catch me out, were you?"

"You killed her, didn't you?" the old man asked, ignoring the angry question.

"I did," he replied with a laugh. "And there is nothing you can do about it."

"But she was your sister – your twin. How could you? Is there nothing you will stop at?"

"Nothing, old man. Nothing at all! But I have what I want now, so there isn't anything or anyone left to stand in my way!"

"Mordred, I implore you – it's not too late! Go back to where you are supposed to be, and live out your life in the way that you should."

"What, after waiting so long?" Mordred answered angrily. "You are even more stupid than I thought. I am the last of the line; there's no-one left to replace me. I'll not give it up now, not after waiting for so long and I'll not be denied it, not by you or anyone else! Do you hear me?" he shouted as he pushed past the old man, almost knocking him over, and strode away towards the jet-black stallion that waited for him by the gate.

"Don't try to stop me, or you will be next!" he shouted, finally, as the great black horse reared up and galloped away.

The old man pulled his hood up and clutched his long cloak tightly around him, feeling chilled to the bone as his worst fears were realised. He walked slowly out of the churchyard with a heavy heart.

"Oh, what to do, what to do?" he asked sorrowfully, as he knew that matters would now be taken out of his old hands.

He walked out of the village and up towards the high cliffs at the top of the hill. He paused for a moment and looked back at the quiet houses and the sea beyond. His gaze fell upon the hedgerows surrounding a small grey cottage, its roof barely visible apart from the thin wisp of grey smoke coming from the chimney. Inside, he knew, were the people who would be most affected by the impending course of events. Should he warn them? No, he decided, best wait and see what happened. It was not up to him any longer.

Maybe those who would determine what happened next, would

still allow his secret to remain undisturbed, as it had already for many a year. Trust, the minister had said. Yes, he would do that, he decided. With another heavy sigh, he started again on his long journey home.

Chapter One
The Grey Bird

In another time and another place, far away in the small town of Chesterton, it was Saturday morning and Rachel Moore pulled the bedcovers over her ears, trying to block out the noise from the next room. Why her brother Gareth had to get up so early on a day when there was no school was beyond her, and why he always had to have the radio so loud was another source of annoyance. She tried to ignore it for as long as she could, but gave up in the end and was eventually tempted out of bed by the smell of bacon drifting through the house.

She threw on some clothes and crossed the room to open the curtains. The sun was already shining quite brightly, and she blinked as the light caught her eyes.

Her attention was drawn to the fence in the garden as there, in the middle, sat the huge grey shaggy bird, as it had so many times before. It stared up at her and put its head on one side, quizzically.

The bird was a bit of a mystery. Rachel had seen it for as long as she could remember, always in the morning, and always sitting looking up at her in the same way, as though it was waiting to see her. Sometimes several months would go by without any appearance, and then out of the blue it would be back again. It was a strange looking creature, almost too big to be a bird at all. It was ungainly, and its feathers were rough and scruffy-looking. It wasn't a bird of prey, as Rachel had looked at pictures of those in the library; besides it didn't have a hooked beak or the sharp piercing look that the eagles and other large birds had.

Neither her brother nor her father had ever seen it, and sometimes she got the distinct impression that they thought she was exaggerating or making it up.

"C'mon, Rach, Dad's got breakfast ready!" shouted her twin brother Gareth, as he clattered down the stairs.

"Okay, I'm coming!" she answered. She looked back briefly at the fence, but the bird had gone.

"You took your time!" said her brother, who had demolished almost half his breakfast by the time she sat down. He reached out to grab the last piece of toast.

"Don't be such a pig!" she said haughtily.

"You don't need to fight over it, there's more in the toaster," said their father, putting a plate of bacon and eggs in front of her.

"You should get up earlier!" announced her brother, his cheeks bulging with the offending toast.

"Don't talk with your mouth full," said Mr Moore automatically and sighed, noticing the satisfied smile on his daughter's face as her brother was told off.

John Moore was a man of routines. He liked them all to sit down to meals together and Saturday morning breakfast was a ritual, and the only day they had a proper full cooked breakfast. Although he was beginning to see the advantage of maybe having his own breakfast in peace, with the morning paper, before they got up, since lately they did nothing but argue over the meal. He appeared strict, but in reality he was a mild, kindly man who had struggled to bring up his two children on his own. He disliked confrontation and sometimes found the two of them a bit of a handful, particularly Gareth who was naturally boisterous and loved to wind up his more reserved sister.

Although they were twins and shared the same golden hair and freckles on their noses, their natures were quite opposite. Rachel was much more sensitive and sensible, and, as the taller of the two, she was often mistaken for the eldest, much to her brother's annoyance.

Gareth was a typical twelve-year-old boy. He loved nothing better than playing pranks, especially if his sister was on the receiving end. He was a natural athlete, good at most sports and generally preferred them to schoolwork, especially homework which he avoided whenever possible. He was extremely popular at school and had plenty of friends. On the whole he and Rachel got on fairly well, even if they didn't care to admit it.

"That bird was there again this morning, Dad," said Rachel.

"It can't always be the same one, you've been seeing it for years – birds don't live that long!" remarked Mr Moore.

"Well, it looks the same, and it always acts exactly the same."

"Acts the same, what are you on about? What do you expect it to do? It's a bird, they all act the same!" said Gareth dismissively.

"I know that, I'm just saying it's strange, that's all."

"You think everything's strange – it's a bird, get over it!" answered Gareth, as he got up to leave the table.

"Yes, but that's what I keep trying to tell you, it's not a normal bird, it's huge!"

"Okay, it's a big bird then, so what?" he answered, pushing his chair in.

"You haven't forgotten the fair today, have you?" said Mr Moore, deliberately steering the conversation away from the argument that seemed likely to erupt again.

"As if! When are we going?" asked Gareth, excitedly.

"I have some jobs to do first, but I thought that if we leave about three o'clock, I'll just have time to cut the lawn as well."

"Yeah, great, I can't wait!" answered his son.

Chesterton was a small country village with one main street and a few shops. It had undergone a slight expansion in recent years, due to the addition of a couple of small housing estates on its perimeter, but essentially it still remained a quiet place to live. The twins had lived there with their father, in the same house, all their lives. The fair was a yearly event and not really much to get excited about, apart from the fact that it was one of the few things that ever happened there, and certainly the only one that interested the twins.

They both headed for the stairs, where they resumed the argument they had started before.

"Why do you always have to make fun of everything I say?" questioned Rachel as she followed Gareth up the stairs.

"I'm not, I was just saying that you find lots of things strange!" he answered.

"No, I don't!" she retorted defensively.

"Yeah, you do! In fact it's you that's strange!"

"No, I'm not!"

"Yeah, you are! You're always saying things that are, well, odd."

"Odd! What do you mean, odd?" she continued, following him into the bathroom.

"Odd, strange, weird, whatever you want to call it. You're always doing it."

"Doing what?"

"You do it all the time. You say things I'm about to say. You mention someone, the phone rings, and it's them! It's weird. Even Rob Bradshaw said you were weird the other day. You asked him if his Mum was better and he hadn't even told us she was ill."

"He must have done, otherwise I wouldn't have asked!"

"Trust me, he didn't."

"Well, I don't remember."

"Well, he does, and he thought it was weird! What about the time I cut my head open on that field trip – you told Dad I'd had an accident before they had even phoned to tell him, how could you know that?"

"Did I?"

"Yeah, you did, and I'll tell you something else, you're always saying you have an odd feeling about things, and do you want to know what the worst thing is? It always turns out that you're right!"

"Am I?"

"Yeah, you are. Now if you don't mind, I would like to have a shower – in fact I'm surprised you didn't already know that, since you seem to know everything before anyone else does!"

"Okay, okay, I'm going," she answered, as he pushed her out and shut the door firmly behind her.

Rachel retreated to her own room to reflect on his words. Did she do that? Maybe she did. On thinking about it, she could recall several occasions when she had known about something before it happened, but she had always put it down to coincidence. Maybe she did it more than she realised. That set her wondering, and she spent a long time sitting on her bed trying to remember exactly how many times it had happened.

"I'm going to the shop, do you want anything?" she heard her brother shouting to her father.

She opened her door and shouted down the stairs, "Hang on, I'll come with you."

"What?" said Gareth. "You want to come with me? Wonders will never cease!"

"All right, you don't need to be clever!" she answered as she joined him, grabbing her coat.

"I'm going on my bike," he stated, still surprised that she wanted to accompany him.

"Well, you can pedal slowly then, can't you," she said as they left the house. He joined her at the gate with his bike, and they turned left into the road leading down to the local shop.

"Now, you asking to come with me," he stated dryly, pedalling onto the road, "Well, that's even stranger!"

"Don't keep saying that, you're really getting me worried now," she answered. "In fact, I've been thinking about nothing else since you mentioned it."

"Oh, you're not still on about that, are you?" he said as he pedalled ahead. "You're weird, just live with it. We have to!"

She broke into a trot to keep up with him, desperately needing an explanation, or at least a discussion to put her mind at rest, but Gareth wasn't interested, in fact he was clearly bored with the subject now.

Rachel spotted Mrs Burton cleaning her kitchen windows, and waved to her as they passed her house. The cheerful lady knew them well, as she had looked after them after school until their father came back from work, for several years. She was always delighted to see them and merrily waved her bright yellow duster at Rachel in return.

At ever-increasing speed Gareth accelerated down the road ahead of her, and Rachel was having trouble keeping up with him.

19

Suddenly there was a rushing noise behind her and she instinctively ducked as something flew past her shoulder. She was amazed to see it was the grey bird that had been sitting on the fence in their garden earlier. It was flying low, flapping its huge wings haphazardly as it flew directly towards her brother.

"Gareth, look out!" she shouted, as the bird's wing made contact with the right side of his head.

"What the …" he shouted, his bike wobbling as he ducked while the bird flew past him.

He regained control of the bike, until the bird turned and flew straight back at him, still flapping its wings frantically, heading straight towards his face.

"Ahhh …" Gareth shouted as the bike skidded, toppled over and landed on top of him on the pavement.

The bird flew upwards past Rachel again, and disappeared.

"Are you all right?" asked Rachel as she rushed over to him.

"Whatever was that?" Gareth asked, dazed.

Before she could answer, there was a screeching noise as a car hurtled towards them from the opposite side of the road, followed by a loud crash as it hit the tree a few feet away from them. It happened so suddenly, they both jumped at the noise and Gareth scrambled up quickly, almost forgetting he'd been hurt.

"Look at that! Look at it!" he said in amazement, staring at the car almost wrapped around the solid tree trunk, a wisp of steam escaping from under the squashed bonnet with a hissing noise.

A crowd was forming now as people rushed out from their houses and congregated around the smashed car.

"Oh my goodness, are you all right?" asked Mrs Burton as she rushed to their side. "I nearly had heart failure then. I thought it had hit you!"

"Yes, I'm okay," answered Gareth. Reminded of his own accident, he looked down at his leg, which was smarting now, and noticed the blood trickling down from a gash on his knee.

"Oh dear, let's have a look, that's a nasty cut on your leg. Come on! Into the house and I'll clean it up for you," said Mrs Burton, taking his arm.

Rachel picked up Gareth's bike and followed them. She could see

20

her father rushing down the road towards them and waited for him, leaning the bike against the wall underneath Mrs Burton's window.

"Are you both all right?" he said worriedly, his face white.

"Yes, we're fine. Gareth cut his leg when he fell off his bike, that's all."

"Oh, thank goodness! I heard the crash from the garden, I came out to see what the noise was and someone frightened me to death by telling me that Gareth had been knocked over!"

"No, don't worry, Dad, he's fine; Mrs Burton's looking after him," Rachel reassured her father as they went into Mrs Burton's house.

"Oh, John, what a to-do, I nearly had a heart attack! I saw it from my window. I thought for a moment the car had hit him after he'd fallen off his bike! Oh dear me, what a shock!" said Mrs Burton, clearly deeply upset.

"What on earth happened?"

"I'm okay, I've just cut my leg and arm, that's all," said Gareth, showing his father the two large plasters Mrs Burton had supplied.

"I'll put the kettle on and make us a nice cup of tea; you look like you need one, John!" said Mrs Burton as she filled the large kettle.

"Oh, thanks, yes, that would be nice," Mr Moore agreed, sitting down. "So what exactly happened, then? You weren't knocked off by the car, Gareth?"

"No, the car crash happened after I was knocked off by this massive bird! It attacked me, it flew at me from behind, and then it flew back again, right into my face! You should have seen it, it was this big!" Gareth demonstrated, holding his arms out. "It was absolutely massive!"

"What?" said his father in amazement, looking first at Rachel and then at Mrs Burton, who left her kettle on the side, completely forgetting to plug it in. "A bird knocked you off?" he repeated, looking stupidly from one to the other. "I'm sorry, but I don't understand."

"Oh John, he's having you on, little monkey!" said Mrs Burton. "There wasn't any bird. I was watching, I'd just waved to you, hadn't I, Rachel? I saw him wobble, and then he wobbled again and fell off. There wasn't any bird!"

Mr Moore looked again from one to the other, not quite sure

what to believe.

"You must have seen it, it was huge. You couldn't miss it!" said Gareth, annoyed.

"No, I didn't see any bird. For heaven's sake, Gareth, your father's had a bad enough fright as it is, without you making up silly stories! In fact you had a very lucky escape there, young man! If you hadn't fallen off when you did, you would have been right under the wheels of that car!"

Mrs Burton's last remark made Rachel suddenly realise what had happened. She knew it was her bird, the one she had seen on and off for years, that had flown at Gareth. She had recognised the scruffy grey bird instantly. What had surprised her so much at the time was that it was flying in a strange, ungainly, un-bird-like way, as though it was a great effort – but she had only ever seen it sitting on the fence before. The thought came to her now that the bird must have deliberately flown at Gareth to stop him. It had caused him to fall off his bike, so that he wouldn't be hit by the car! Even as she thought this, she realised how ridiculous it would sound if she said this out loud, so she didn't, and kept her thoughts to herself while Gareth continued to insist indignantly that he hadn't fallen off, and that he really had been attacked by a large bird.

They got their tea eventually, and while Mr Moore and Mrs Burton discussed how lucky Gareth had been, the twins were temporarily distracted by the arrival outside of police cars and an ambulance to attend to the unfortunate driver of the crashed car. Once the commotion outside had died down, they thanked Mrs Burton and the three of them returned home, wheeling Gareth's bike whilst he limped alongside.

"It sounds to me as though you have been very lucky! What could have happened if that car had hit you doesn't bear thinking about," remarked their father, as they turned into their gate.

"I told you it was that bird," said Gareth sullenly. "Why won't anyone believe me?" He threw his coat onto the peg and marched up the stairs.

Rachel followed him up and just stopped him from closing his bedroom door in her face, by pushing her way inside. "Gareth, wait a minute, I believe you. That was my bird that flew at you – I recognised it straight away, it's the one I've been telling you and Dad about for ages," she said, as he flopped onto his bed in disgust.

"What?" said Gareth, looking up at her in disbelief.

"I've just told you, it was the bird I saw this morning sitting on the fence." She couldn't help sounding excited, now that someone else had seen it, which annoyed Gareth even more.

"Great, so why didn't you say so? Why didn't you back me up and tell Dad and Mrs Burton?" he asked, accusingly.

"They wouldn't have believed me either. Think about it, Mrs Burton didn't see the bird at all."

"She must be blind, then! I can't understand how she managed to miss it; it was like a cat with wings!"

"Exactly. I kept telling you that it wasn't an ordinary bird, but you wouldn't listen," said Rachel, crossly. "How could Mrs Burton not see something that big? The only explanation that I can think of, is that maybe not everyone can. Up until today, I've been the only one who's ever seen it and I can't tell you how pleased I am now that you have as well!"

"Seen it, seen it, it was in my face! I had its feathers in my mouth!" shouted Gareth, jumping up. "It sits there and looks at you, but me, oh no, it attacks me! It swooped down twice and attacked me!"

"You're not getting this at all, are you?" said Rachel, irritated by her brother's attitude. "If the bird hadn't attacked you, as you call it, you wouldn't have fallen off your bike, and you would have been exactly where that car hit the tree. The bird saved you, I know it did – don't you understand?"

For a moment her brother looked at her stupidly, while he digested this last piece of information.

"Oh, that's it, I've heard enough!" he said, grabbing her arm and propelling her towards the door. "This is exactly what I was telling you about earlier! Weird, it's weird! And this is even more weird than before!" he finally shouted, as he pushed her out onto the landing and banged the door shut behind her.

Chapter Two
Madam Katrina

Rachel stayed in her bedroom, not entirely happy with her brother's dismissal of what she thought was quite an important incident with the bird earlier. Fortunately, by the time their father shouted up the stairs to say it was time to go to the fair, she had given up thinking about it. The anticipation of the fair had clearly also made Gareth forget that he was cross with her, as was evident by the way he bounded unceremoniously into her room.

"C'mon, hurry up, aren't you ready yet!" he said impatiently.

"Okay, okay!" she answered, pulling her sweater over her head.

"Are you two coming, then?" called Mr Moore from downstairs.

"I am!" Gareth replied, charging down the stairs, nearly colliding with his father at the bottom.

"Steady on!" said Mr Moore. "It's no wonder you have accidents! I do hope you can manage to stay in one piece when you get there! Rachel, please tell me you'll keep an eye on him."

"You are joking, aren't you?" Gareth replied, as his father pulled the door closed behind them. "It's her that attracts weird things, not me! Anyway, why should she look after me – it isn't as though she's older than me!"

"No, but generally she's a lot more sensible," his father answered,

24

much to Gareth's annoyance. "You will try to be careful, won't you?"

"Of course I will," Gareth said crossly, scowling at his sister. "In fact I'll be fine, as long as she hasn't got any more birds waiting to attack me again!"

Rachel and her father exchanged glances and sighed. Mr Moore had been hoping that the fair would keep the peace between the twins for a short while at least, and Rachel had been hoping that Gareth wasn't going to mention the bird again in front of their father, as she knew what his reaction would be. John Moore didn't like anything strange or odd, and always put everything down to coincidence, generally refusing to discuss it any further.

The three of them walked down the road and turned off into a small alleyway between the houses, leading towards the old church. Although the vicar was a very old-fashioned sort, he had made a special concession to allow this annual event to take place on the land at the back of the church, as the always-busy refreshment tent raised a substantial amount of money for the church funds.

Gareth was getting excited now, his injuries forgotten as the fair came into view. There were a lot of people there already and most of the rides were spinning. The air was filled with screams and laughter along with the drone of motors and loud fairground music.

The smell of candyfloss greeted them at the first stall and Mr Moore promised to buy them some later. They tried their hand at the hoopla and the coconut shy, and the twins both won a prize by fishing out a duck with a lucky number on it at another stall. Rachel chose a pink fluffy dog, and Gareth started the same argument with his father that they had every year when he won, and wanted a goldfish.

Ruefully recalling previous visits and the several goldfish that had died by the time they got home, Mr Moore breathed a very large sigh of relief when Gareth was finally persuaded to settle for a different prize. He steered the twins away quickly in the direction of the refreshment tent, the goldfish thankfully forgotten.

As Mr Moore went off to join the long queue for drinks, Emma and Lucy, two of Rachel's friends, came over, already sipping bottles of brightly-coloured fizzy drinks. Gareth hung back with a bored expression. If there was anything worse than his sister, it was her friends! Their girly chit-chat was something he would normally avoid at all costs.

The girls chattered non-stop about the rides they had been on, and Gareth was eventually persuaded to show them the pack of magic tricks he had selected instead of the goldfish.

"Have you been to Madam Katrina yet?" asked Lucy. "She's the fortune teller in the purple tent next to the sweet stall. Emma saw her first and she knew all about Emma's brother being away, and her aunt's new baby. She even knew about the trouble she's had with her teeth and there's no way she could ever have guessed that! She told me that we'll be moving to a new house and going somewhere hot on holiday!" She paused for a second, to draw breath. "She was really amazing, you've got to go and see her!"

"She sounds really good. I've never been to a fortune teller," said Rachel. "I'd love to hear what she had to say about me!"

"They're not real, they guess – it's all fake," said Gareth condescendingly. "Anyway, don't forget, you owe me. We're going on the dodgems first!"

"What does he mean, you owe him?" asked Lucy. "I thought you said you'd never go on the dodgems with him ever again, after last year!"

"Don't ask!" said Rachel, glaring at Gareth, not wishing to discuss the previous episode with her friends. "It's a long story, and yes, I did say that after the last time. He's an absolute lunatic in those cars!"

"Rather you than me, then," laughed Emma. "I remember the bruises you got last year!"

"Yeah, and no doubt they will be just as bad this year," said Rachel, making a face at her brother. "He does it deliberately; he aims at every car on there!"

At this point they were joined by Mr Moore, who had been patiently waiting in the queue to buy them a drink, and Emma and Lucy went off to join Lucy's parents.

"Can I go on the dodgems next?" asked Gareth. "And Rachel wants to go to see the fortune teller."

"Yes, as long as you're careful," replied Mr Moore. "But I'm not sure about the fortune teller – you know I don't like that sort of thing, Rachel. I'd rather you didn't; there are lots of other things to do."

"Yeah, like the dodgems," said her brother, poking her arm.

"Okay, you've made your point," said Rachel. "I've already said I'll go on them with you, as long as you don't drive like an idiot!"

"Me?" said Gareth in mock surprise.

"Well, I'm going to leave the rides to you," said their father. "Enjoy yourselves; you can meet me back here later. I'm going to go and have a chat with the vicar."

Gareth and Rachel exchanged a knowing look: it was definitely time to go. Although the vicar was a very nice man, he was also very difficult to get away from without seeming rude, so they took their cue and headed for the exit.

After three goes on the dodgems, Rachel finally managed to persuade her brother to get off. To her relief, the rides hadn't been as bad as she had been expecting. She suspected that the fall from his bike earlier had made Gareth a bit more careful than usual. They wandered on and visited the Haunted House, followed by the Hall of Mirrors, where they were fat one minute and thin and bendy the next.

They were still laughing as they left, when Gareth caught her arm. "Look, there's that fortune teller's tent, the one your friends were talking about. Let's go and have a look."

"I don't think we ought to. Dad said he didn't want us to, remember? Anyway, I thought you said it was all rubbish!"

"Well, he won't know, will he, if we don't tell him. Anyway a look can't hurt, can it? I'll go on my own if you won't," said Gareth, dashing off towards the purple, conical tent.

Rachel followed slowly; she was unused to disobeying her father, and she didn't like getting into trouble either. Trouble was generally her brother's domain, something he was often involved in.

By the time she caught up with him, Gareth was already coming back out of the tent. As he emerged, the canvas flap dropped down behind him again.

"You want to see in there!" he said, clearly in awe. "It's really spooky! It's dark, and she's got one of those crystal balls and all of these strange cards with pictures on them. Anyway, she said she'll do your fortune now, if you want. Come on!"

"Oh, hang on! We said we wouldn't," Rachel started, but the words were lost on Gareth, who was already pushing her into the dimly-lit tent, where she found herself in front of a small round table draped with a black spangled cloth. Seated behind the table was a plump, rosy-faced lady in a flowery dress, with a brightly-patterned headscarf tied at the back in a knot, gypsy-style, over a tangle of jet black curls.

"This is my sister, the one I told you about," said Gareth, sitting down on one of the chairs opposite the fortune teller. Rachel sat down next to him rather apprehensively, her eyes gradually becoming accustomed to the dim lamplight, and she found herself drawn to the large crystal ball in the middle of the table. Madam Katrina still shuffled the strange picture cards almost obsessively, and didn't even look up.

"So, young lady, what's it to be, then? The cards, or did you want your palm read?"

Rachel didn't answer. She was fascinated by the crystal ball; she couldn't take her eyes off it.

"I'm Romany, you know," stated Madam Katrina, still shuffling the cards. "The Romanies were the true gypsies with the sight, you know. Oh yes, I can tell you more than any of the others!" she finished proudly, her attention still fixed firmly on her cards.

Rachel continued to ignore her as she stared at the ball on the table, watching a cloud appear inside it like a smoky haze. She watched it, fascinated, as it drifted slowly into a spiral effect, like a small lazily-whirling tornado inside the glass. Madam Katrina looked up at Rachel for the first time, realising that she hadn't had an answer to her question, and she gasped sharply as though in shock. She looked hard at Rachel and then again at Gareth, scrutinising them both very carefully.

"No, I'm sorry, I can't do this," she said. "You'll have to go!" The cards she had been so intent on shuffling were scattered unceremoniously across the table and floor as she pushed her chair back, getting swiftly to her feet.

"But you said ..." started Gareth.

"Never mind what I said," shouted Madam Katrina, her voice taking on a note of panic. "I said I can't do this. Out now, both of you, out!"

Gareth started to get up and looked at his sister, who seemed oblivious to the fortune teller's odd behaviour. She was still staring, completely transfixed, at the globe on the table. The swirling mist inside was changing colour; delicate pinks and purples, violets and blues drifted in and out in a mesmerising haze, one which now seemed to be filtering through the surface of the glass, causing the same smoky haze around the ball. Madame Katrina looked more closely at the crystal sphere and gasped again.

"What are you doing?" she shouted at Rachel. "Stop it now, do you hear me! Stop it!"

Her hysterical behaviour and the panic in her voice were making even Gareth feel nervous, and he nudged his sister. "Come on, Rach, I think we'd better go!"

Rachel completely ignored them both, even more fascinated as she gazed into the swirling colours, watching them clear as a picture began to form at the centre. She craned to see, peering harder into the globe, as the lined face of an elderly man with a long straggly white beard and equally long pure white hair, began to appear inside.

Madam Katrina, almost beside herself now, hurriedly grabbed a red patterned cloth from behind her and threw it over the crystal ball.

The spell was broken, and a dazed Rachel looked up to see the plump form of Madam Katrina advancing round the table towards her. She grabbed Rachel's arm with one hand and Gareth's with the other and propelled them both towards the tent flap, still shouting hysterically: "Out, out, out!!"

Outside in the daylight the twins blinked, and Madam Katrina released their arms, disappearing back into the tent, where they could hear her tugging frantically at the flap to secure it from the inside.

"Wow, what was her problem?" said Gareth, baffled by the gypsy's strange behaviour. "She was all right until you went in!" he added accusingly, his tone implying that Rachel was somehow to blame for the gypsy's hysteria.

Rachel was still in a daze; her mind was as foggy as the haze inside the crystal ball had been, and she couldn't think straight at all. She looked at her brother blankly.

"You okay?" he asked, more than slightly worried by Rachel's ashen face. "I've got to admit she scared me a bit too, ranting on like that. Maybe that was all an act, for effect – what do you reckon? Do you think she was doing it on purpose? Then again she could just be nuts! No wonder Dad said he didn't want you to see her. I hate to say this, but for once he was right!" He took Rachel's arm whilst talking, steering her past the other stalls back towards the refreshment tent, mistaking her silence for fear.

They were almost there when Rachel stopped him, and finding her voice again, said, "Did you see that ball of hers?"

"Yes," replied Gareth. "What about it?"

"No, I mean did you see what it was doing?"

"Well, no, but then I wasn't really looking at it. So what was it doing, then?"

Before Rachel could answer him they heard a shout from behind, and turned to see Madam Katrina rushing towards them. Gareth grabbed his sister's arm, ready to run, but Madam Katrina gasped, "No! Wait, please wait."

She puffed her way up to them, red in the face, "I'm sorry, I need to talk to you, just let me get me breath," she said leaning forward, putting her chubby hands on her thighs, taking in great gulps of air.

"Oh, that's better. Now, I don't normally say nothing you know, 'specially if it's bad, you understand. No, people don't want to hear anything bad, so I only tells them the good things, 'cause that's what they want, you know?"

They both nodded gravely, even though they actually had no idea what she was talking about.

"Well, in your case, it's different and I should've known that, I should! Maybe it's me duty to warn you, maybe you was sent to me, so as I could warn you, I don't know," she said, looking up at the sky almost fearfully as she spoke, wringing her hands.

Rachel gripped Gareth's arm tightly as they glanced at each other in complete bewilderment.

"Anyway, it's me duty, I'm a Romany you know," Madam Katrina said, almost confidentially. "Did I tell you that? Well maybe I did, but I see more than most you know, and it was seeing you two together, that's when I knew. Gave me a right shock, I can tell you! And you," she turned to Rachel, "you should know better than to use someone else's crystal like that. I'll have to cleanse it now, can't use it again like that, it wouldn't be right! Who knows what I'd be seeing!"

"I'm sorry," said Rachel, although she wasn't sure why she was apologising.

"Oh, well, no harm done I s'pose. Anyway, that's not important, but what I'm going to tell you is, and you must listen carefully, do you understand?"

They both nodded, although again, they didn't really know why.

"There's great danger ahead for you!" she said. "Not here, no, but you'll be going somewhere, somewhere you've never been before, that's where the danger is. But if you stay together, that's your strength! All the time, you must stay together. But maybe you would know that already?" she asked, looking at Rachel again.

"They can't harm either one of you, as long as you are together! Remember that and you'll come to no harm! Oh, now, don't look so frightened, me dear, you'll know what to do!" she said, seeing Rachel's alarmed expression. "I told you, this was meant!" she said, rolling her eyes towards the sky again. "So as I could warn yer! Well, I feel better now, I've said me piece and I've done me duty," she continued. "And I'm sorry I shouted at you, but it was the shock, it was. Now you remember what I've told you, won't you!"

They nodded again, in astonishment, and with that Madam Katrina turned and waddled back towards her tent.

"Do you know what she was on about, then?" said Gareth looking questioningly at his sister.

"I have absolutely no idea!" replied Rachel flatly.

"Well, she seemed to think you did," he stated. "But then again I did say I thought she was mad. Anyway, I can see Dad coming. I think we'd better keep quiet about this."

Rachel nodded in agreement, relieved to see her father's familiar face coming towards them, and as soon as he reached them, she put her arm through his and instantly felt safe.

"Well, I don't know about you two but I've had enough now, and I did promise some candy-floss on the way back, didn't I!" said Mr Moore.

"Yes, let's go," said Rachel, and her brother nodded his agreement, both of them more than happy to leave after the strange conversation with the gypsy.

Mr Moore looked at them in surprise. Normally he had to practically drag them away from the fair, and on all previous visits they had insisted on him joining them on the worst ride they could find, before they left.

"Are you all right?" he asked suspiciously, noticing Rachel's pale face.

"Yeah, she's okay, just feeling a bit sick after the rides, aren't you Rach?" Gareth prompted.

Rachel nodded, not saying anything, not wanting to lie to her father.

"Oh well, let's go then. We'll get the candy-floss anyway, and you can have yours later when you're feeling better," said Mr Moore, silently congratulating himself that he had got off rather lightly this year. He hadn't been looking forward to being catapulted up towards the sky and back again on some metal contraption that in his opinion was probably not entirely safe, and he wasn't even going to have to spend the evening nursing a half-dead goldfish. Most definitely an improvement, he thought to himself, and led them away quickly before they could change their minds.

Chapter Three
Aunt Bronwyn

The rest of the weekend passed uneventfully, and soon it was Monday morning, with the usual rush to get ready for school. Rachel couldn't wait to tell Emma and Lucy about the gypsy's warning, as she knew her friends would prove a much more receptive audience than her brother, who had now dismissed the whole thing, declaring the fortune teller a fake.

"Wow!" said Lucy, after she told them what had happened. "Weren't you scared?"

Rachel admitted that she had been, and the fortune-teller's warning became the topic of conversation on and off for most of the day, until they had exhausted all possibilities as to the meaning of it all.

She met up with a very sulky Gareth, at the end of the road, after school.

"Did you have to tell everyone about that gypsy?" he asked in a disgruntled voice, as they walked up the path to the front door.

"I didn't, I only told Emma and Lucy."

"Well, that's like telling the world then, isn't it! I've heard nothing else all day; all my mates have been taking the mickey!"

"Well, I didn't tell them," she answered hotly.

"No, but your friends did. Look, it's bad enough them thinking I've got a weird sister, without you making it worse!"

"I don't care what your friends think. I don't like them anyway!" answered Rachel as she turned her key in the door.

"Well, I do!"

"What are you two arguing about now?" asked their father, appearing from the lounge.

"Nothing!" they replied in unison as they both marched up the stairs towards the sanctity of their bedrooms.

"Hold on, I've got something to tell you," he called after them. "Come back down."

They both walked back down the stairs, glaring at each other.

"I thought you might be pleased to hear that your Aunt Bronwyn's coming to stay with us," he said.

"That's fantastic! When's she coming? How long's she staying?" Rachel asked excitedly.

"Tomorrow afternoon," replied Mr Moore. "She'll be here when you get back from school, and she's staying for a week."

"Oh, I can't wait, we haven't seen her for ages!" said Rachel. "It's a pity we don't start the school holidays until next week though. She'll be going back just as we break up. I wish she was going to be here longer!"

"Don't worry," laughed her father. "You'll see plenty of her."

Bronwyn wasn't really an aunt, she was their mother's cousin, but they had always called her 'Aunty Bronwyn' since they were small, and she was the nearest they had to a real aunt. Relatives were something that were in very short supply in their small family, and Rachel was often envious of her friends when they talked about their cousins, uncles, aunts and grandparents, as the only relatives she could lay claim to, aside from her father and Gareth, were Bronwyn and her sister Catherine, whom they had never met. Her father had grown up in an orphanage and had never known his parents, and her mother had died when she and Gareth were very young. This made Bronwyn's infrequent visits even more special.

She was an unusual woman, attractive, tall and slim, but with a somewhat old-fashioned appearance, dressing in long flowing clothes, almost always black or grey. However, her long, thick, golden hair, which cascaded into waves around her shoulders, and her pale skin, and perfect smile, gave her a striking appearance that made her stand out.

She was a teacher in a remote village in Cornwall, and not often able to make the long journey to stay with the twins and their father, but they treasured the days she spent with them and were always sorry when the time came for her to leave.

Gareth and Rachel rushed home from school the next day, knowing that she would meet them at the door, almost as excited as they were and, true to form, as they turned into the road, they could see her waving to them from the doorway. She greeted them both with a big hug and, once inside, there were the usual presents of hand-made chocolates; and as always, in the kitchen, there were home-baked pastries, bread and cakes.

"Oh, I do love it when you come to stay!" said Gareth, looking longingly at a large chocolate sponge cake sitting in the middle of the kitchen table.

"And I thought you were pleased to see me!" laughed Bronwyn as she cut two pieces of cake, put them on plates, and handed them to Rachel and Gareth.

"Oh, I am! Pleased to see you, I mean," said Gareth as he took a large bite. "But you also make the best cakes in the world!"

"Pig!" said his sister in disgust, as another large bite disappeared. "I wouldn't care if you never brought cakes, Aunty Bronwyn; I'm just pleased you're here!"

Bronwyn laughed and hugged them both again.

She had once explained to them that the village where she lived was so far off the beaten track, that it was almost self-sufficient. All the food used by the villagers was grown or made locally. Home-cooked meals were what Bronwyn was used to, and she always insisted on cooking when she came to stay with the children, much to Gareth's delight.

"Dad's dinners are good," he remarked later at the dinner table, whilst on his second helping of Bronwyn's beef casserole, "but yours are definitely the best!"

"If you eat much more you'll burst, and you certainly won't have room for your pudding!" laughed Bronwyn.

"Oh, I will, you just watch!" said Gareth.

"I'm sure you don't feed him, John!" she said jokingly.

"Oh, believe me he does, Gareth just never stops eating," commented Rachel.

"Well, I don't know where he's putting it then, because he's as skinny as a scarecrow!" declared Bronwyn.

The conversation remained lively for the rest of the night, as it always did when Bronwyn was there, and it was with great reluctance that the twins went up to bed, despite it being a full two hours after their normal bedtime.

After school the next day, Bronwyn and Rachel planned their customary shopping trip. Gareth was invited to join them, but he raised his eyebrows and screwed up his nose at the thought of 'girly shopping' as he called it, quickly declining the offer. Rachel was quite pleased when they left without him, as she enjoyed having Bronwyn to herself for a few hours; being the only girl in the household it was nice to have female company for a change, and for a while she could imagine what it was like for her friends when they did things with their mums.

Two hours of wandering round the shops looking at fashions, without any complaints from her brother or father, was like heaven. Bronwyn treated her to a soft blue jumper and bought herself a new long black cardigan, even though Rachel tried hard to get her to buy a bright green one. She shook her head saying it wasn't appropriate, and paid for their purchases.

"You should have had that green one, it would have looked lovely with your hair," Rachel remarked as they left the shop. "I know you liked it, I saw you pick it up first."

"I know, but we don't really wear anything bright in the village. I wouldn't get any use out of it, nice as it was," she replied with an almost wistful look, not unnoticed by Rachel. She looked at her aunt, puzzled, but before she could say anything, Bronwyn carried on briskly, "Anyway, I think I'm ready for a coffee now – shall we go to that little place we went to last time?"

This idea pleased Rachel immensely, as to her this was another treat. Her father always wanted to rush straight home after shopping and coffee shops were never on his agenda. They crossed over the road to the modern cafe and soon they were chatting over two cups of frothy cappuccinos. The conversation was light-hearted; Bronwyn was easy to talk to and wanted to hear all about Rachel's friends and school, and Rachel found herself confiding things that she wouldn't dream of talking about with her father or brother.

"Gareth keeps saying I'm weird, because I have strange feelings that are always right. He says I know things before they happen, and he's right, I do, but I don't mean to and I can't stop it! Do you think I'm odd?" she asked suddenly, to her aunt's surprise.

"Good gracious me, no, of course not! You're not odd at all!" Bronwyn replied. "Have you told your dad about this?"

"No, he wouldn't understand. He doesn't like to talk about things like that; he always changes the subject really quickly."

"Well, maybe he has his reasons, but on the whole, most men don't really understand that sort of thing. It's called women's intuition, I think."

"Really?" asked Rachel. "Do you get feelings about things, and find they're right?"

"Oh, all the time, most ladies do," Bronwyn answered with a knowing smile.

"Mrs Burton said that as well, when I asked her. She said it was because we were twins, and twins have a sort of bond that other people don't have. But there have been some really strange things happening lately," Rachel admitted, almost wishing as soon as the words came out, that she hadn't said them.

"What sort of strange things?" asked Bronwyn, seriously.

"Oh, nothing really. Just some odd things I can't explain."

"There is always a reason for everything, Rachel," Bronwyn said quietly, sensing her niece's reluctance to talk about it. "Sometimes, there are things that we are not meant to know. There are a great many things we don't understand, and I have always found it better to just accept, because as time goes by their meaning is often explained in ways that you would never expect."

"I knew you would understand. Oh, I wish you were here more often! I can talk to you," said Rachel wistfully. "Dad's lovely, but it's not the same."

"I know, dear. I must try to come and see you more often," Bronwyn answered, laying her hand on Rachel's, and for a moment Rachel thought she saw tears forming in her aunt's big green eyes.

"Gosh, is that the time? We'd better be heading back, they'll be sending out a search party otherwise!" Bronwyn said rapidly, as she motioned to the waitress for the bill.

Eventually they returned home with their shopping, and later on they all went out to the cinema, with Rachel delighted at the opportunity to wear her new sweater. The film was a comedy, with particularly funny bits that were recounted in the car on the way home, making them all laugh again. The mood of hilarity continued at home when they started to play Rachel's favourite board game, 'Treasure at the Manor.' The idea was to pick a route on the board that led to where the treasure was buried, its location denoted by a card chosen from the top of the pack. Each route chosen by the player had several squares which either sent them back or delayed them. Every throw of the dice by Bronwyn consistently landed her on squares that did this, while the others raced across the board, avoiding most of them.

"I don't believe this!" Bronwyn said in disgust as she landed on another one with a question mark and picked up a card from the pile. "You have fallen down the well," she read out. "Miss three goes while you climb out." Everyone laughed at her pained expression.

"It's not funny," she replied. "I've been sent back four times, lost in the maze for two goes, sent to the kitchen to do chores, I even missed a go to help the gardener, and now I've fallen down the well! This is just about the last straw!"

"I've never met anyone who's so unlucky with this game!" laughed Gareth."It must be you, it never happens to us."

"I had noticed that!" remarked Bronwyn, dryly.

They were interrupted by the phone ringing and their father went to answer it, wiping away the tears of laughter as he got up from the table. He returned in a much more sombre mood.

"Whatever's wrong?" asked Bronwyn.

"That was my boss," he answered. "They've got a big contract in Scotland next week. Bill Stone was going on Monday, but he fell off a ladder yesterday and broke his hip, and they've asked me to take over. To be honest, it's one of my contracts anyway, but they don't normally ask me to work away from home as they know my situation here. I can't see any way out of this one though, as there isn't anyone else that can do it. It'll mean being away for at least ten days and it's the start of the school holidays, so I don't know how we're going to manage this!"

"We could stay with Mrs Burton," said Gareth half-heartedly.

"No, she's going away with her son," Rachel chipped in. "Don't you remember she told us the other day?"

"Well, I don't know what we're going to do then!" replied their father despondently.

"They could come back with me," said Bronwyn quietly.

"Oh yes, could we, Dad? Please!" said Rachel excitedly.

"Wow, that'd be great! It's by the sea. It'd be like a holiday," joined in Gareth.

"Oh no, Bronwyn, I don't think so," Mr Moore answered immediately.

"Oh, but why not, Dad? Please, we'd love to go; we've never stayed with Bronwyn before."

"I really would love to have them, John," added Bronwyn.

"No, we'll think of something else," said Mr Moore firmly, trying not to look at their disappointed faces.

"I don't think you have any other options, do you, John?" said Bronwyn. "You know I would look after them, and Gareth's right, it would be a holiday for them."

"I'm not very happy about this, Bronwyn," he said, realising he was already losing the argument. "Couldn't you stay here with them?"

"On no, Dad, that wouldn't be the same at all!" said Rachel. "I'd love to see where Bronwyn lives!"

"Oh please, Dad. Please let us go," begged Gareth. "It'd be fantastic!"

"They're going to be really disappointed, John. It's only ten days, and they will be fine," Bronwyn said firmly. "That's settled then, we'll get two more train tickets and all go back together on Sunday," she finished quickly, before he could object.

"Are you sure?" he said, still looking worried.

"Absolutely," said Bronwyn.

A whoop of joy came from the twins, even though their father still looked as though he was racking his brains to find a reasonable argument as to why they shouldn't go.

They besieged Bronwyn with excited questions about the village. What was there? What could they do? What should they pack?

"Stop!" she laughed, putting her hands over her ears. "You'll be there soon enough, now off to bed with you, or you'll never get up for school!"

They both pulled a face at that, gave her a kiss, and went upstairs.

Later on, Gareth was still wide awake. He decided to go downstairs to get a drink, and maybe even sneak some more of the chocolate cake. Yes, he'd be okay, he decided, reaching the top of the stairs, as long as his dad didn't hear him. He was very strict about bedtimes on a school night.

So he crept into the kitchen and managed to find the cake, without making too much noise. He could hear his dad talking to Bronwyn in the lounge next door. Good! Less likely to hear me, he chuckled to himself. As he made his way back past the lounge door with a large wedge of cake, he caught part of the conversation, which made him pause.

"I'm sorry, but I really don't think it's a good idea, Bronwyn," he heard his dad say. "After all we did agree …"

"I know, but I would love to take them back with me, and it's only for a week!"

"It's ten days, actually."

"Well, all right, ten days! Two of those will be travelling, though."

"I'm still not happy about it."

"Look, it would be good for Rachel, I had a chat to her today, and she's really missing …"

"Her mother, do you think I don't know that? I do my best!"

"I know you do John, I wasn't criticising," she answered quietly. "But it's only a week, and it won't do any harm."

"What about Catherine?"

"Catherine will be all right. Leave her to me."

"What about …"

"It's quiet there; everything has gone back to normal, and if I thought there would be a problem, I wouldn't even have suggested it. Look, I know it hasn't been easy for you, and for once I can do something to help. Please, let me do that."

"It's not as simple as that and you know it isn't. I still don't see how you're going to get round this with Catherine. What does she know, and what are you going to tell her?" He stopped, abruptly. "Wait, what was that? There was a noise in the hall, did you hear it?"

"No."

"I'm sure I heard something."

Gareth heard the chair creak and his dad's footsteps coming towards the door, so he fled back up to his room as quickly and quietly as he could, jumping back into bed with the light off, the cake forgotten. He breathed a sigh of relief when he heard his Dad go back into the lounge and shut the door behind him. Now he was even more awake than before, and he was left puzzling over the conversation he had overheard.

"What was all that about, then?" he asked himself in the dark, and spent a long time lying there trying to make sense of it all.

Eventually he drifted off to sleep, but he relayed what he had heard to Rachel at the first opportunity, which was on the way to school the next morning.

"So what do you make of that, then?" he finished.

"Dad's just being protective; he's just not used to us going away without him, that's all."

"No, you're missing the point," Gareth said crossly. "It's something to do with Catherine. Think about it, she never visits - we've never even met her! And what did Bronwyn mean by saying it's gone back to normal there now? No, there's some sort of secret there. I know there is and it's got to be something to do with Catherine!"

"Like what?" Rachel asked scornfully.

"I don't know, I'm just saying it's odd. Maybe she's mad or something!"

Rachel looked at him even more disdainfully. She was determined that nothing was going to spoil her visit with Bronwyn.

"You must have heard it wrong!" she muttered.

"I didn't! I'm telling you there's something odd, either with Catherine, or something that's happened there."

Rachel declined to reply, and they both went their separate ways as they reached the school.

Chapter Four
Carriages and Cartwheels

Sunday came around surprisingly quickly, for the days leading up to it were spent in a flurry of packing and organising their trip. Rachel and Gareth soon found themselves standing on the station platform saying goodbye to their father, who seemed to have resigned himself to the fact that they were going.

"You make sure you behave, won't you, and have a good time," he said, kissing them both on the cheek. "And Bronwyn, if there are any problems, I'll come straight down and get them."

"Stop fussing, John," Bronwyn replied, shaking her head. "There won't be any problems, and if we stand here much longer the train will be going without us!"

She ushered Rachel and Gareth towards the carriage door, and the goodbyes were all said again as they boarded. The train pulled out of the station, and the twins waved from the window until their father was out of sight, then settled back in their seats to enjoy the journey.

As the scenery flashing past the window changed to a patchwork of fields and hedgerows, Bronwyn told the twins more about her home.

"You'll love it there!" she said. "It's completely different from where you live – it's a very old place. There are no modern houses like yours, but there are plenty of things to do. There's a lovely beach, and if you walk round the pathway on the top of the cliffs, the views are fantastic. The village itself is small; we have a few shops, a church, the village hall and the local farms. I thought that maybe you could have some riding lessons from the Harrrigans at the farm; they keep quite a few horses and I'm sure Abigail would teach you."

"Oh could we? I'd love that! I've always wanted to go horse-riding," said Rachel, her eyes lighting up.

"Of course you can," replied Bronwyn. "I'll get hold of a couple of bikes for you both as well, so that you can explore on those. There aren't any cars in the village, so you'll be quite safe!"

This met with Gareth's approval immediately, as he was never allowed to go too far on his bike at home. Although the roads on their small estate were quiet, the main road past the village green had fast-moving traffic all going to the bigger towns, and he was forbidden by his father to ride on it.

"That would be ace!" he replied. "But no cars at all? How do people get around, then?"

"Horses and bikes, but mostly they walk – the village is only small," laughed his aunt. "You won't have any traffic to contend with there, but you might have to watch out for stray sheep. They can be just as much of a nuisance!"

The journey took a long time, but both the twins were quite happy looking out of the windows and eating the picnic that Bronwyn had brought for them. They had managed to secure four seats with a table in between, something the twins found a complete novelty as this was a luxury not provided by their small local trains. They had not been on many train journeys before, and certainly never one as long as this! The scenery from the window was largely unremarkable until the train got further down the country, and as it glided into the Devonshire countryside the stations became smaller and prettier, decorated with hanging baskets and tubs of flowers.

The train hurtled its way towards Cornwall and eventually to their destination, a small Cornish country station not far past Tintagel, where passengers generally got off to go and see the old castle ruin there, according to Bronwyn. The station was in the typical Cornish grey stone, like the others they had passed on the way. It was well kept, with big stone troughs full of flowers all along the platform.

"It's so pretty," Rachel said as they followed the last few remaining passengers off the train. "Is it like this where you live?"

"Similar," Bronwyn replied. "Most of the Cornish villages are like this one. We'll be there soon and you can see for yourselves. Catherine is meeting us but we'll have to walk a short distance, so I hope you can manage your bags."

"We're okay, we've got Dad's cases with the wheels on," demonstrated Gareth, pulling up the handle.

"Very useful," remarked Bronwyn, picking up her old holdall. "Off we go, then."

They followed the other passengers out of the station, down a short pathway bordered with an array of wild flowers. Hollyhocks, poppies and large white daisies flourished in abundance against the bushy hedgerows, all the way to the end where they came to the road. To their left the road sloped downwards, and Rachel and Gareth could see a small village with pretty grey stone cottages at the bottom. This seemed to be the direction in which all their fellow passengers were heading.

The twins followed Bronwyn as she turned the opposite way to everyone else, leading them up a steep hill away from the village. There were high grassy banks on either side and the trees almost formed a canopy over the road. There were no footpaths and they had to walk on the tarmac, which had crumbled away at the edges, forming a gutter. As they drew nearer the top of the hill, the banks on their side of the road gave way to trees and thick undergrowth. Bronwyn stepped off the road onto a narrow track that wound its way through the bushes and trees. It was so overgrown and the grass so high, that it could have been missed entirely.

"Don't worry," said Bronwyn. "It's not too much further. Catherine will meet us by the pass with the horse and cart; we don't bring horses down into the town."

"Horse and cart!" said the twins in surprise. "Fantastic!" said Gareth. "You didn't say you had a horse!"

"Well, he's not ours, I'm afraid," smiled their aunt. "We borrow him from the farm if we need to travel out of our village, which isn't that often!"

As she was talking, the route was getting darker as the light struggled to filter through the thickening canopy of branches. The pathway narrowed even more, becoming a rough track where the overgrown banks rose steeply on either side, getting denser as they climbed higher.

Further along, the trail began to resemble a stony mountain track, the bushes and shrubbery giving way to boulders and rocks. Rachel was having trouble pulling her suitcase, as it rocked from side to side over the uneven ground. Bronwyn waited for her to catch up, and took hold of one side of the handle to help her.

"Catherine will be waiting for us just round the next bend; the track is wider there so the horse and buggy can turn around," she said, and sure enough, it wasn't long before the light streamed through, as the track broadened and there were fewer branches overhead. They rounded the bend, and there stood a big black horse, harnessed to a green painted buggy.

Catherine was already climbing down and the twins noticed straight away that she was nothing like her sister. She was a good deal older and had dark hair tied back into a knot behind her head. She was wearing the same type of long clothes as Bronwyn, except that Catherine's looked drab and frumpy. She waved, and then looked almost suspiciously at the twins when she noticed them walking behind Bronwyn.

"I thought you were never coming!" she said to her sister. "And who do we have here, then?" she enquired, looking closely at the twins. Her tone was not unfriendly, but, on the other hand, not particularly welcoming either.

"I'm Gareth and this is my sister Rachel," said Gareth warily, scrutinising Catherine carefully for any signs of insanity, remembering the conversation he'd overheard before they left, and was relieved to see that she looked quite normal.

"Well, I'm pleased to meet you. You must be tired after all that walking with those bags. Come on now, you climb up into the buggy and get comfy. We'll get these bags on the back and get home," Catherine said.

Rachel was busy stroking the horse, who snorted with approval as she stroked his neck. "Oh, he's lovely!" she exclaimed as he nuzzled her hand.

"That's our Rufus, he's a gentle giant," said Catherine. "He seems to have taken a liking to you as well!"

Her brother had already clambered up onto the seat at the back of the buggy.

"This is fantastic!" he said as Rachel climbed up to join him.

The two women climbed into the seat in front of them and Catherine took the reins, clicking her tongue. "Come on now, boy!" she said to the horse, which obediently started off down the path.

The twins were really enjoying this part of the journey as the buggy trundled along behind the horse, rocking and swaying. The track was surrounded by huge boulders and high craggy rocks, and was now starting to wind its way downward.

From their bumpy seat in the back they could just about hear Catherine asking Bronwyn about her trip, above the clopping of Rufus's hooves and the noise of the big wooden wheels as they churned over the stony path.

"Why have you brought them with you?" Catherine asked, the sharp tone of her voice catching Gareth's attention.

He nudged his sister, nodding towards the two women seated in front of them. Rachel took no notice, her attention completely taken with the scenery around her, so he craned forward slightly to listen to the conversation.

"You didn't tell me they were twins!" he heard Catherine say disapprovingly. "You should have told me!" she continued. "You told me the boy was older."

He didn't catch Bronwyn's answer as there was a loud rumble of thunder above them, echoing eerily through the rocks. The horse was startled and Catherine pulled harder on the reins.

"Easy now, easy now!" she said in a soothing tone to the horse, steadying him, and the steady clip-clop of his hooves resumed.

The rocks ended and they could see the track ahead of them, winding down into a green valley, and in the distance a cluster of grey cottages surrounded by fields and trees, beyond which a glimpse of the sea could be seen shimmering on the horizon.

"Oh, look!" shouted Rachel. "Is this it, are we here?"

"Almost!" replied Bronwyn. "Look, can you see the sea?"

Gareth was straining over Rachel in anticipation. "Yeah!" he answered excitedly, the overheard conversation temporarily forgotten. "It looks brilliant!"

"Oh, it does! I can't wait to see your cottage," said Rachel.

"Well, not long now, we live this side of the village, so we're nearly there," answered Bronwyn. "I'll show you around the village tomorrow. We'll get a good meal and you can settle in tonight; we've done enough travelling for one day."

The twins looked a bit disappointed at this, but their spirits lifted as they turned into another narrow track and the buggy came to halt outside a delightful stone cottage.

"Oh, this is lovely!" breathed Rachel.

"Here we are, home sweet home," said Catherine. "Now, mind how you get down."

Her instruction was ignored as Gareth leapt down from the buggy, almost falling over in his haste, and Rachel scrambled after him.

Bronwyn pushed open the wooden gate and led them up a stone path, bordered with shrubs and an abundance of flowers. The cottage was very old; the windows had small panes of glass with leading in between, and there was an open stone porch with a solid wooden door that had a huge black door-knocker in the middle.

"Oh, I love your house, Bronwyn!" said Rachel, who had fallen in love with the old cottage as soon as she had seen it. "It's so pretty!"

The heady scent of the honeysuckle and roses around the porch greeted them as they followed Catherine, who opened the heavy door to reveal a hallway with a stone-flagged floor and dark furniture, decorated with vases of flowers sitting on snowy-white lacy doyleys. There was a large grandfather clock ticking loudly on the other side, and as they walked in, there was a cool, slightly musty smell about the place, faintly fragranced by the flowers.

"Well, I'm ready for a cup of tea!" said Bronwyn. "I'll go and put the kettle on. Catherine's going to take the buggy back to the farm, so you two can go and have a quick explore, while I see what I can find as a snack to keep you going till dinner."

The twins didn't need a second invitation, bounding from room to room, until they were satisfied that they had seen everywhere, finally joining their aunt back in the kitchen.

"Wow, is that your cooker?" said Rachel, looking at the huge range with the big metal kettle sitting on it. The kitchen was large with a big wooden table, where there were two mugs of tea waiting for them and a plate of buttered scones.

"Help yourselves," said Bronwyn. "We won't be having dinner until later this evening."

As they sat at the big table munching their scones hungrily, gazing around the homely kitchen, they heard Catherine coming in. She came to sit down with them, chatting comfortably to the twins over her tea, leaving Gareth feeling slightly guilty that he had thought that there might be something wrong with her. He was even beginning to think that he must have been mistaken about the conversation in the buggy earlier.

Catherine got up eventually to start preparing the dinner, while Bronwyn and the twins carried their bags upstairs to their new bedrooms to unpack.

Rachel and Gareth's bedrooms were next to each other at the front of the house. They both had a fireplace and a single bed, with crisp white sheets and a delicate patchwork quilt. Rachel's room had a big dresser with an old-fashioned patterned china water jug on it, and a large wardrobe. Gareth's was the same except that he also had a big three-way mirror on his dresser. There were no carpets in the house; every room had large patterned rugs and wooden floorboards, aside from the kitchen and hall with the stone floors. The twins inspected one another's rooms and Bronwyn left them to sort out their things.

Rachel unpacked quite quickly, hanging her clothes up neatly in the big wardrobe, on padded hangers. She went to join Gareth, who had piled his clothes on the bed and was fiddling with his mobile phone. She sniffed disapprovingly and hung the clothes up for him in his wardrobe, folding his sweaters and putting them on the big wooden shelves.

Later on they went back downstairs and joined their aunts for dinner, around the big kitchen table. Catherine had a lovely meal waiting for them, and Gareth announced between mouthfuls that

48

it was as good, if not even better than her sister's cooking. This appeared to please her, and Gareth and Rachel both left the table feeling full and rather sleepy.

They sat round the fire in the small lounge for a while with their aunts, until their tiredness got the better of them. It had been a long day and with the thought of all the exploring they had in store for them tomorrow, they were quite glad to go to bed; both of them fell asleep almost as soon as their heads touched the pillow.

Chapter Five
Valonia

Gareth woke up with a start. Something had disturbed him. Half asleep, he suddenly realised where he was, and heard the strange noise again: 'Bong, Bong, Bong.' He listened carefully, wide awake now, as the sound echoed eerily through the house. 'Bong, Bong, Bong,' it continued. Then he remembered the old grandfather clock in the hall and realised it was chiming. He had never heard one before, and listened carefully. Sure enough, there was one more chime. Eight chimes, eight o'clock, he laughed to himself, partly with relief.

As soon as the chimes were finished, the house fell silent again; it didn't sound to Gareth as though anyone was up yet. He thought he'd better stay in bed a bit longer, something he always found difficult once he was awake. In the end he gave up and rummaged in his bag for his walkman so that he could listen to the radio for a while with his headphones on and not disturb anyone. He spent a long time trying to pick up a channel, to no avail; all he got was a crackling noise, however much he fiddled with it. Eventually he got fed up trying, and tossed the walkman onto the bed in disgust.

He pulled back his curtains and was pleased to see that the sky was quite clear. He opened the window and leaned out, trying to see as far as he could. He could see the track by which they had arrived yesterday, winding its way down between the hedges and fields, and beyond that, the range of rocky hills. He could hear the seagulls calling to each other and smell the sea on the breeze.

This was really frustrating! He couldn't wait to get out and about. He toyed with the idea of jumping on his sister's bed to wake her up but thought better of it, given that she would probably shout at him and wake everyone up. So instead he put some clothes on, and even went and had a wash before venturing downstairs.

He was pleased to hear noises coming from the kitchen; so he wasn't the only one up after all! He found Catherine with the kettle already boiling away on the huge range, slicing a home-made loaf on a large wooden board.

"Ah, an early bird for breakfast, I see!" she said. "I'm beginning to think you like my cooking! How did you sleep – were you comfortable?"

"Yes, like a log, thanks!" he answered politely, thanking her for the mug of tea she put in front of him. "It was the clock that woke me up; otherwise I'd probably still be there."

"Oh, of course, we don't notice it now, we're so used to it," she responded, taking some eggs out of a large basket on the dresser. "So, would you like some breakfast?"

"Yes, please," he answered quickly, and by the time Rachel and Bronwyn joined them he had polished off a large cooked breakfast and two rounds of toast.

"Gareth, you could have waited!" said Rachel disapprovingly, as she sat down at the table.

"He's all right, nothing wrong with a healthy appetite," laughed Catherine in his defence. "It was exactly the same when Geraint ..." she stopped in mid-sentence, glancing at Bronwyn. "Anyway, I know how you boys like your food," she finished, turning away from them and busying herself with the frying pan.

"Well, I bet you can't wait to explore," said Bronwyn sitting down with them. "I'll take you down to the beach and show you round the village this morning. I'm sure Mr Dregarney in the village will have some bikes we can borrow, and with any luck we might be able to pick them up while we're down there."

"Oh yes, that would be fantastic!" they said in unison.

Later on they walked down towards the village. It wasn't far at all and the cluster of grey stone buildings sat picturesquely against the rising cliffs. To the right of the buildings was a slope that led down to the beach, and as they went cautiously downwards the twins got their first sight of the waves frothing onto the sand.

"What a lot of seagulls!" said Rachel, looking up at the birds circling round above them, making their distinctive calls.

"The tide's in and the fishing boats will have brought in their catch earlier, the seagulls will be looking for anything left over. They do this every morning," said Bronwyn.

They walked to the edge of the jetty where the small boats were all lined up on the beach. Bronwyn waved to a couple of men untangling their fishing nets; the two men returned the gesture before resuming their work. The twins looked down the long sandy beach to their left, and at the high cliffs that sheltered the shops and houses. The beach stretched out a long way, until the cliffs curved out to meet the sea, forming a bay.

"This beach is the safest," said Bronwyn. "The tide never comes right up, and the water's quite shallow. It's safe to swim here, as long as you don't go too far out. The currents are very strong, once you leave the protection of the bay. If you look over this side," she said, pointing down the long beach to her right, "you can see the rocks jutting out into the sea in the distance there. We call that The Point."

"I can see why," said Rachel, as they looked at the jagged rocks stretching out into the sea, forming the bay on the other side. Even from this distance they could see the waves crashing against them.

"It'll calm down a bit there later, when the tide goes out, but it's quite a dangerous area. It's very deceiving as you can climb over the rocks to the next beach when the tide's out, but it doesn't stay out for long there, and when the tide turns it comes in really quickly. Added to which, on the other side of the rocks the beach may look lovely, but there are large areas of quicksand."

"Really?" said Rachel with a shudder. "Doesn't that suck you under if you step on it?"

"Yes, it sucks you under until it buries you alive, doesn't it?" joined in Gareth.

"Well, yes, if you want to be really graphic, that's exactly what it does," replied Bronwyn.

"So has anyone actually died there, then?" asked Gareth, with macabre fascination.

"Well, no-one from the village, obviously, because we know it's there, but there are stories about people having been unfortunate enough to have got into trouble there. The sand looks exactly the same all over the beach and there's no way of telling the difference just by looking at it, that's why it's so dangerous," Bronwyn warned.

"Well, you needn't worry; we definitely won't be going anywhere near it! I'm staying on this beach!" said Rachel, shivering again at the thought of the quicksand.

"I'm pleased to hear that; I'd rather you didn't go onto that beach at all!" said Bronwyn. "The cliff path on that side is worth the walk, though. It's a bit of a climb, and the cliffs are quite high, but there are a few benches here and there. There are some steps down to the rocks that go out onto the point as well, which I've already warned you about crossing, but if you carry on to the top, you can walk right across the cliffs to the next headland. The views are amazing, you can see for miles!"

"Wow, we'll do that!" said Gareth.

"You'll certainly work up an appetite, climbing up there!" laughed Bronwyn. "Not that you need much help with that, Gareth! Come on, I'll show you the village now; I need to pop into a couple of the shops while we're there."

They walked back towards the cluster of pale grey stone buildings, where there was a small row of shops. They went to the baker's first, where a plump, rosy-faced lady was arranging some cakes and pies in the window. The smell of freshly-baked bread hit them as soon as they entered.

"Now then, Bronwyn, how are you today?" the lady said brightly, returning to her counter. "Oh my! Twins!" she added in surprise as she noticed Rachel and Gareth.

"Yes, my niece and nephew; they've come for a holiday," explained Bronwyn.

"Oh, a holiday, twins as well, bless me!" continued the lady as she wrapped up their large loaf of bread. "Well, have a good time," she said as they were leaving.

Their next stop was the farm shop, which was packed with local produce; all arranged in big wicker baskets, up-ended against tables covered in bright gingham cloths. These housed another array of smaller baskets containing different sorts of eggs, butter, and cheeses. The shop was quite busy; there were several ladies in long drab clothes, similar to those worn by Catherine, picking out their purchases and handing them to a tall man who wrapped them in paper. The shop went quiet as the twins walked in and several of the ladies nudged each other and whispered. The tall man swiftly moved across and started chatting with Bronwyn, and gradually the other villagers returned to their shopping.

Bronwyn took them to the post office next, where they were treated to a stern stare from a lady behind the counter, through some extremely small glasses that were in danger of falling off the end of her nose at any moment.

Last, but not least, they went to the hardware shop, to make arrangements for the bikes. Mr Dregarney appeared from behind a big display of old-looking tools as soon as he heard the bell on the door tinkling, as they walked in.

"Ah, Bronwyn, what can we do for you today? Strike me! Twins!" he said peering over his glasses at Rachel and Gareth, who were beginning to feel distinctly uncomfortable at the reactions in every shop so far.

"Yes, my niece and nephew, they've come to stay for a week," said Bronwyn. "In fact we were hoping that we might be able to borrow two bikes for them, while they're here."

"Bikes, yes indeed, bikes," Mr Dregarney answered, still staring at them.

"Would that be all right? Do you have anything suitable?" Bronwyn prompted.

"Suitable? Yes, I'm sorry, of course I have. I have just the thing," he answered, looking flustered. "Yes, you wait here and I'll go and get them."

He eventually appeared at the front of the shop with two rather old-looking bikes, and they went out to join him.

"These should be just the right size I think. Come on, young man, you try this one," he indicated to Gareth, who climbed on to the ancient-looking bike, politely declaring that it was fine. Rachel's bike had a wicker basket strapped to the front, and had the biggest wheels she had ever seen, but she gracefully accepted it, as her brother had done.

"Now, don't you worry," the shopkeeper said to Bronwyn. "They'll be as safe as houses on these! I've looked after them myself. My own children used to ride these. Good brakes, yes, most important, the brakes, I've seen to that myself."

"I'm sure they will be, if you've looked after them. Thank you so much, what do I owe you?" Bronwyn asked.

"Nothing," he answered. "Another brew for Mrs Dregarney from Catherine will suffice. That last one worked like magic, she's been so much better."

"Oh, I'm so glad, and thank you so much," replied Bronwyn.

"My pleasure," he said. "My pleasure, and twins in the village as well, I can't wait to tell Mrs Dregarney!" he said.

As they were leaving, he pulled Bronwyn aside. "You'd best be careful. Does he know?"

"No," answered Bronwyn. "And it's none of his business; I'm quite entitled to have my friends or family stay with me if I choose."

"Well, you be careful, that's all I'm saying, you be careful," he said knowingly.

The twins thanked him again and left, with Gareth riding slowly on the ancient bike, and Rachel pushing hers alongside her aunt.

"We'll go back and have some lunch and then you two can go and explore on your own, as I have some jobs to do this afternoon," said Bronwyn, as they started walking back.

"That'll be good, we'll enjoy that," answered Rachel. "Bronwyn, why was everyone staring at us in the shops? They all seemed to make a very big deal out of us being twins, in fact, I never realised that we must look so much like each other till we came here. No one even mentions it at home!"

"That's scary, do I really look like her?" queried Gareth.

"Well, yes, you do a bit, you can tell you're twins," Bronwyn confirmed, laughing involuntarily because Gareth looked so horrified at this thought.

"But why were they nudging each other and whispering like that?" asked Rachel insistently.

"We don't have any twins in the village, that's why. I suppose they find it a bit of a novelty. We don't really get many visitors either, so everyone is naturally very curious," she added.

When they arrived back at the cottage there was no sign of Catherine. "She'll be working downstairs now," Bronwyn explained. "She works for the chemist's shop in the village and makes a lot of the preparations for them, herbal remedies, that sort of thing."

Gareth noticed a wooden door in the hallway, next to the clock. "Does Catherine work through there?" he asked, looking at the door, intrigued.

"Yes," replied his aunt, "in the cellar, and she doesn't like to be disturbed, so it might be best if you don't go down there, unless she asks you to, of course."

After lunch the twins couldn't wait to go back out again. They decided not to take the bikes, as they wanted to go to the beach. They took off their shoes and walked along the sand, down to the water's edge. The water was cold as the waves splashed over their bare feet, and Rachel shrieked as the second one splashed right up her legs, soaking her shorts.

Gareth was more intent on throwing pebbles, trying to make them skim the surface of the water. He stopped every now and then to gather some more, throwing them as far as he could, disappointed when they landed with a heavy plop and disappeared.

The sun was out, but there was quite a strong wind coming off the sea.

"I'm getting cold," said Rachel. "I'll race you back," and with that, she turned and ran back along the sand. Just as she expected, it wasn't long before her brother streaked past her, and he was sitting on the stone jetty by the time she caught up with him. She had never managed to beat him in a race, but then neither had any of his friends at home. Sport was one of Gareth's strengths, and although they looked very similar in appearance, this was not something they shared. Rachel hated sports, and wasn't particularly good at them.

"Didn't think you'd win, did you?" he laughed, as she collapsed on to the wall next to him.

"No, but I'm used to that," she answered resignedly.

They sat on the wall for a while, the cliffs sheltering them from the wind, and then went off to explore the other side of the beach, eventually reaching the rocks that stretched out to the point. Bronwyn had been right, the waves were no longer crashing against the rocks as they had been in the morning, and they were able to climb onto them and investigate the rock pools that were left.

"There's a crab in this one," shouted Gareth. "Come and look!"

His sister took a look as requested although, unlike him, she had no desire to attempt to catch it.

"We'd better not stay here too long," she said, looking apprehensively at the sea, remembering Bronwyn's warning about the tide.

"Don't be silly, it's miles away yet!" he replied glancing up. "Anyway, let's go just a bit further, if we climb onto that big rock, we might be able to see the quicksand on the other side. He scrambled up onto the rock and Rachel followed. They stood on the top looking over the rocks, to the long stretch of smooth golden sand. Apart from the wavy pattern at the water's edge left by the tide, it didn't look any different from the beach they had just left.

"I'd still like to know if anyone has died in it?" said Gareth. "Can you imagine it sucking you under?"

"No, I'd rather not!" Rachel answered with a shiver. "Come on, let's go back, I don't like it here."

Gareth laughed and followed her back over the rocks. Once back on the beach, they made their way back up towards the jetty, where they could see a slim figure sitting on the wall. As they approached, a tall thin boy jumped down.

"So you are the newcomers then," he said, rather disdainfully.

"Yes, I suppose we are. I'm Gareth and this is Rachel," answered Gareth, good-humouredly.

The boy circled them, looking them up and down, ignoring Gareth's attempt to be friendly.

"And for once the village gossips got it right. You don't look that much like each other, but you are definitely twins!" he said condescendingly. "Why are you here?"

"We're staying with our aunts for a holiday," answered Rachel, taking an instant dislike to the boy.

"A holiday?" he said looking puzzled. "What is that?"

"You don't know what a holiday is?" asked Gareth in amazement, and was treated to an icy glare. "It's when you don't have to go to school or work, and visit somewhere you haven't been before. Don't you do that here?"

"Of course I do!" answered the boy haughtily. "In fact, I can visit places that none of the others can. My father takes me."

"That's nice," said Rachel, lamely.

"So where do you come from?" the boy asked, sounding rather as though he were demanding an answer.

"Chesterton, it's a long way from here," replied Gareth.

"Chesterton, Chesterton?" said the boy, stroking his chin as though thinking about it. "It cannot be a very important village, as I have not heard of it," he finished dismissively.

"Well, we hadn't heard of this place either," answered Gareth flatly.

"Nor should you - you are an outsider," he answered. "We don't like outsiders here."

"Yep, we were sort of getting the feeling that you didn't!" Gareth said sarcastically.

"My father will not be pleased when he finds out you are here. Bronwyn has not asked his permission."

"So who exactly is your father then?" asked Rachel.

"My father is Mordred, he is Lord of the manor and all that you see before you," he answered, puffing out his chest importantly. "I am his son. They call me Theodorus, but you will use my real name, Twedwr!"

"Well, thanks for that, Theo," said Gareth deliberately. "I hope we won't be seeing much of you! Come on Rachel, I can't listen to any more of this!" he added, pulling her arm before he turned his back on the boy and started walking up the jetty.

"You will be sorry you offended me, I will make sure of that!" Theodorus shouted after them.

"Yeah, right, whatever," returned Gareth in a bored voice.

Rachel ran quickly after Gareth as he strode off, and she could see by the reddening of her brother's face that he was about to lose his temper. Fortunately the boy turned away and walked off in the opposite direction.

They carried on back towards the village, with Gareth fuming silently until, at the end of the road, he finally exploded. "I swear, another minute with him and I'd have hit him!"

"That would have gone down well, since we're outsiders, and Bronwyn hasn't asked permission for us to be here," answered his sister dryly. Gareth laughed and sat down on a large stone at the edge of the road.

"If I'd been at home I would have hit him!"

"Yes, I know you would," she answered, sitting down next to him.

"What was all that about? 'You will call me Twed ... whatever his name was, and you'll be sorry you offended me!' What was his problem? I'm telling you, Rachel, this place is weird and the people are weird as well!"

"It's just an old place, that's all, and Bronwyn did say that they don't get visitors here."

"I'm not surprised! They don't exactly make you feel welcome! No, it's more than that, have you seen how they dress? And the way that they were all whispering and staring. We might as well have been a couple of aliens, the way they've all behaved!"

"Well, I have to admit, they have been a bit funny with us, especially him!"

"Oh at last! You're admitting that it's weird then."

"Well, I suppose it is a bit, but I'm sure they are just really old-fashioned," she answered, determined to enjoy her holiday.

"Old fashioned! It's like stepping back in time by a few hundred years," he exclaimed. "No it's more than that, Rachel; this place isn't even on the map. I had a look at Dad's before we came and I couldn't even find it."

"It's probably too small."

"Maybe, but my radio doesn't work here and neither does my mobile. I've tried both, do yours?"

"No, but I'm sure that's probably because of all those hills."

"Okay, but they haven't even got a television."

"Maybe they don't want one, not everyone does."

"Who do you know, without a television?"

"No-one, but that's not the point, it's different here," she answered sensibly.

"You can say that again! I'm telling you, there's definitely something not right about this place."

"Oh, come on, let's go back now, I think your imagination's running away with you! It's just different here, that's all."

"Maybe you're right," he agreed, to her surprise. "Anyway, I'm starving, so let's go back - we'll have a good look around tomorrow and see what else we can find out."

Rachel decided to go along with this, mainly for the sake of peace, and they headed back to the cottage. They banged the heavy door-knocker several times and eventually Catherine answered.

"I'm sorry, have you been waiting long?" she asked as she let them in. "I was downstairs; I can't always hear the door."

As they entered, Gareth noticed that the wooden door in the hallway was now wide open and a strange pungent smell was wafting up into the hall. He couldn't resist peering in. There was a small wooden staircase, but he couldn't see past the turn half way down. Catherine followed him over and closed the door, producing a key from a pocket in her voluminous grey skirt, and locking it firmly. Rachel and Gareth exchanged glances and followed her into the kitchen.

Catherine made no reference to the locked door; instead she asked them about their day as she poured them a large glass of home-made lemonade.

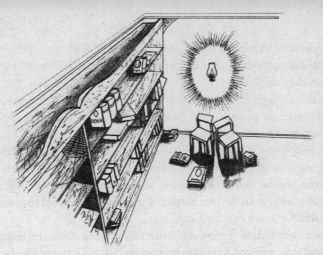

Chapter Six
The Gold Letters

Once dinner was over, the twins found the evening rather boring. There was no television to watch, Catherine disappeared back downstairs to finish her work and Bronwyn stayed in the kitchen to mark a pile of her pupil's books, so they were left to entertain themselves. Gareth had been right when he had said that their radios didn't work, and when he asked Bronwyn, she explained that the hills blocked all the signals. There were no phones in the village for the same reason, she added, and if anyone wanted to use one, they had to travel back through the pass to the next village where the train station was.

"How do they manage if they can't make a phone call?" asked Gareth in amazement.

"Most people here don't need to," Bronwyn answered simply. "They don't have any reason to phone anyone outside the village, their life is here."

This explanation still didn't satisfy Gareth, who waited until he was alone with Rachel in her bedroom later on, before he brought it up again. "I'm sorry, but I don't buy this, it's ridiculous, everything is done by satellites these days! People have radios and televisions all over the world, don't they? We watched English television in Spain with Dad, and that's a lot further than Cornwall! Oh, and then she

61

said that they don't phone anyone outside the village. Now that's really weird, everyone knows someone who doesn't live in the same place as they do!"

Rachel shrugged her shoulders in answer, much to his annoyance, and although she had no better explanations, she didn't really want to accept his criticisms of their aunt's home.

Gareth spent a long time that evening pointing out the strange differences, until Rachel was almost beginning to agree with him, even though she didn't admit it. She was quite relieved when he went off to his own room, except that now she was left to wonder on her own.

Fortunately, in the morning when they went down to breakfast, Bronwyn announced that she had arranged for them to have their first riding lesson at the farm. The excitement made them forget about the strangeness of the place, and after breakfast they joined Bronwyn, who had wheeled out her own antiquated bicycle, ready to ride to the farm.

They cycled through the village and out into the country again. Bronwyn took them up to the farm and introduced them to Mrs Harrigan at the gate. They took an immediate liking to this small, dumpy woman, who led them towards the farmhouse, shooing away several stray chickens in their path.

The cosy building was a very busy place and there seemed to be an abundance of children and animals everywhere. There were two dogs, which jumped all over them as soon as they entered; a couple of cats, several small kittens and another brown speckled hen, pecking at the crumbs around the table legs until it was shooed away by Mrs Harrigan.

"Now then, you sit down and make yourselves at home. Abigail will be back in a minute and she'll take you down to the horses," she said, moving two large piles of neatly-folded washing off the chairs, to accommodate them.

The twins did as they were instructed and marvelled at the way this busy little woman seemed capable of doing a dozen things at once. There was a small toddler in a highchair she was intermittently spoon-feeding, whilst clearing away a mountain of plates and dishes into the big wooden cupboards, then wiping her hands on her apron, she opened the oven to reveal several loaves, all perfectly baked. In between this, several young children came in and looked at them shyly, before their mother handed them three large baskets.

"Now you make sure you get all of them," she instructed a thin boy in dungarees. "And don't go dropping any; we don't need any more smashed eggs, or there'll be none for the market! Dropped the whole lot yesterday, he did!" she said shaking her head as her children left.

The dogs finally left Rachel and Gareth alone, and they watched the comings and goings with amusement as Mrs Harrigan returned to the sink, rinsing and neatly stacking the remaining plates on a wooden rack.

"It's a bit of a mad-house here in the mornings," she said cheerily. "Abigail won't be long though." As she spoke a tall girl with long brown hair in a pony-tail came in. Her trousers were tucked into long black riding boots and she was carrying two black riding hats. "Ah, here she is," announced her mother.

Abigail proved to be just as friendly, and as she led them round to the stables, she told them the names of all the children they passed.

"Goodness!" said Rachel, as a plump little girl with pigtails shyly smiled at her. "How many brothers and sisters have you got?"

"There are eight of us all together," Abigail replied. "Johnny and I are the oldest."

"That's me!" said a tall youth with floppy brown hair, as he joined them. "I looks after the stables and the horses, I do." He gestured with the large broom in his hand. "Miss Bronwyn - she said you've never been riding before!"

They couldn't help but notice that Johnny, who was beaming at them with excitement, was very different from his sister. He was much taller than her, yet he spoke in a strange child-like way. As he brushed his long fringe out of his eyes, they could see a deep scar on his temple and guessed that this might have something to do with it.

"I've got you some lovely horses I have; saddled them up and everything!" Johnny continued happily.

Rachel was thrilled to see Rufus, the big black horse that had been pulling the buggy the day before, standing with a slightly smaller grey horse, waiting for them. She went over to stroke him and he whinnied in response.

"I'm sure he remembers me!" she said delightedly.

"'Course he does. Horses and dogs, they know who likes them, they do," replied Johnny.

The morning turned out to be really enjoyable. Abigail helped them mount and put both of their horses on a leading rein. She swung easily onto her own horse, a chestnut brown, and explained that they would go for a hack around the lanes to get used to the feel of riding, without worrying about taking control of the horses. They ambled along at a leisurely pace, and the twins began to feel quite comfortable with the movement of the horses, although Rachel was still feeling rather high up on Rufus's back.

Abigail explained that although Rufus was the biggest, he was as gentle as a lamb, and the best-behaved horse they had. She taught Rachel and Gareth how to hold the reins properly and how to lean forward and duck as they went under the overhanging branches. Gareth's horse Smokey was a bit friskier than Rachel's and tried to pull away a few times, shaking his head vigorously, nearly unseating Gareth.

"He's got a strong will, that one, but you'll soon learn how to control him," said Abigail. "He's the fastest horse in the stables, and somehow I think he'll suit you well!"

"He's fantastic," breathed Gareth, quite enamoured by the lively grey horse.

They crossed over the fields, where Abigail showed them how to move with the horses, as they broke into a trot. It all passed too quickly and soon they were entering the stable yard again, where Johnny was waiting to help them dismount.

"I knew I'd picked the right ones for you!" the farm boy said with another beam, as they announced how much they had enjoyed their ride. "I just knew it, and Rufus, he really likes you, he does!" he said to Rachel as Rufus put his big head down and nuzzled her gently.

"He's so lovely!" Rachel answered, stroking his nose, laughing when he snorted in approval.

Johnny led the horses away and they followed Abigail back to the farmhouse, where they were immediately invited for lunch. Mrs

Harrigan had already put out big platters of warm fresh bread and wedges of cheese, with salad and homemade pickles.

They sat down at the big table with the others and soon found that their plates were loaded up. The ride had given them an appetite and they tucked into what was undoubtedly the noisiest meal they had ever eaten. Everyone seemed to talk at once, and it was quite difficult to keep up with the conversation, since there were several all going on quite loudly. Little Hannah had secured a place at the table next to Rachel and was still staring at her shyly. Johnny joined them and was promptly scolded by his mother for not washing his hands. He reappeared sheepishly, holding them out for inspection.

Mrs Harrigan, or Betsy as she had told them to call her, was pleased they had enjoyed their ride so much and told them they could come again tomorrow.

"I'll have the horses all ready again for you!" said Johnny, still smiling. "I really likes it when we has new people round, especially twins! Abigail and me, we're twins, you know."

"Are you!" answered Rachel, looking surprised. "You don't look like each other."

"We're not identical twins," said Abigail.

"No, not like you two, you really looks like twins. You looks just like each other," continued Johnny happily. "Abby and me, we never looked the same, and she's really clever, not like me," he added knowingly. "I used to be clever though, before my accident, just like her. Didn't I, Ma?"

"You did, dear, you did," his mother answered, comfortingly.

Johnny leant forward, confidingly, "That's why you needs to be careful, bad things happen to twins here! All of them!" he added resolutely, stuffing a large piece of bread into his mouth. "Yes, you needs to be really careful!"

"That's quite enough of that, Johnny!" Betsy intervened. "Have you finished now? You need to go and see to the horses."

"But I've done that, and I was only saying …" he protested, grabbing the last piece of bread before it disappeared as she whisked his plate away.

"They need to be turned out into the field!" Betsy said briskly. "Come on now everyone, time to get on with your chores. Abigail, take the two little ones out with you, they can help you feed the chickens."

There was a noisy clatter of chairs and a few groans from the children as they all went back to their duties. Suddenly the kitchen was empty and quiet for the first time that day.

"Don't pay any attention to Johnny, he means well, but he gets a bit muddled since his accident," Betsy said sitting down at the table with them.

"Accident?" said Rachel. "Whatever happened to him?"

"Oh, it was a few years ago, Johnny used to take the post from our village through the pass, into the town beyond. He did it every Friday morning, until one day he didn't come back. It started to get dark and we went to look for him, and there he was, lying on the track, by the pass, unconscious, surrounded by rocks, with old Rufus standing protectively over him. He must have got caught in a rock fall and we thought the worst, I can tell you! But, thank the lord, he pulled through. Catherine was a saint; if it hadn't been for her, he wouldn't be as good as he is today. She nursed him night and day!"

"Oh, poor Johnny, that's dreadful," said Rachel. "Did he go to hospital?"

"Hospital? No, we don't hold with hospitals here. Anyway, even if we did, a journey through the pass, and then miles on top of that, would surely have finished him off. No we deal with things ourselves here, and there is no-one better than Catherine for that! If there is anyone that can work magic, she can!" she answered, stacking the plates up noisily around the sink. "His mind isn't what it was, but he's still alive thanks to her. Anyway, like I said, don't pay any heed to what he says. So we will see you again tomorrow? Abigail said how well you did today," she finished.

"Yes, we'll come back tomorrow. Thank you ever so much, we've really enjoyed ourselves," answered Rachel, taking the hint that it was time to go.

They said goodbye and climbed back onto the old bikes and were waved off by all the children at the gate.

They cycled back to the village and stopped outside the shops, where they found a stone wall to sit on. Gareth produced a packet of sweets from his pocket and offered them to Rachel.

"That was a fantastic morning," said Rachel, taking one of the sweets from the packet. "Weren't they all lovely at the farm? I do feel sorry for Johnny, he was so nice – it must be dreadful to have an accident and just not be the same again!"

"Yes, scary, it could happen to anyone. I would have loved to hear what else he was going to say, though!" replied Gareth. "That was a bit weird, when he said bad things happen to twins here, and did you see how quickly she stopped him saying any more?"

"Yes, that was a bit creepy, but maybe he was talking about his own accident, she did say he gets muddled."

"His accident didn't sound strange though, anyone can be hit by rocks, and why did he say we need to be careful?"

"I don't know," shrugged Rachel. "Don't keep on about it; you're starting to really spook me! Let's go and have a look round the shops," she added, trying to change the subject.

"All right, we'll leave the bikes here," replied Gareth, propping them up carefully against the wall. "Do you remember what she said about Catherine as well, working magic?"

"Don't start on that again! I'm sure she didn't mean she was some sort of witch, which is what you're thinking?"

"I didn't say that," he replied evasively.

"You didn't need to!"

They wandered down the street, looking through the small panes of glass that made up the shop windows. The shops at this end were even more outdated than the ones they had been in the day before with Bronwyn. There was a dress shop with an assortment of long drab skirts, shawls and blouses draped in the window, and they could see a long counter at the back of the shop stacked with baskets of wool, behind which the shelves were piled high with bales of material.

"Look, here's the chemist's. This must be the one that Catherine makes those dreadful-smelling things for," said Gareth, peering through the small window. "I've never seen one like this though!" he concluded, thinking of the modern shops in town at home.

Rachel joined him, peering through the small window at the neat rows of shelves all around the walls, holding an array of neatly-labelled, strange-shaped bottles and jars, containing an assortment of coloured liquids and powders. A small man in a white coat looked up from behind the counter, and they quickly moved on.

"Have you noticed all the shops have got black metal plaques with gold letters on, over the doors?" Gareth said pointing to one over the door of the butchers shop. "See, K.O.W.," he spelled out.

"It must be a sort of postcode, like we have at home," she answered.

"Yeah, I thought that, but it can't be because they are all the same. They all say K.O.W."

Rachel walked back a few paces to look at the plaques on the shops they had passed.

"So they do," she agreed, as they carried on walking. "This one's different though, look, its sign says K.O.K.," she said as they stopped outside a book shop.

"Come on, let's go in. We might as well get a book to read, since there's nothing else to do here in the evenings."

Rachel followed Gareth in, rather surprised as this was the first time she had ever heard him volunteer to read anything, apart from his computer magazines.

The bell tinkled as they opened the door and the smell of old paper and dust greeted them. To their surprise the shop was quite big; it went back a long way and was covered from floor to ceiling with shelves full of old leather-bound books of various sizes. There wasn't a paperback in sight.

"Ah! You must be Bronwyn's visitors!" said a voice from the back of the shop.

The owner of the voice appeared, revealing a small, slightly-balding man, with a pale face and small oval glasses, wearing a strange knitted waistcoat over a white shirt.

"Readers, are you?" he asked, peering at them over the top of his glasses. "Well, there's plenty to choose from here!"

"Do you have any new books?" asked Gareth politely.

"New?" the man questioned, with a nervous laugh. "Why would you want new books? These books contain the wisdom of centuries. Some of them have been in our village since it was built, and some are very old, very rare in fact!" he said proudly. "You could consider us to be more like a library really," he continued, ignoring Gareth's disdainful look at the dusty old books. "Take your time, have a good look round, there is a book on virtually everything here. My family have collected these books over eight generations. Just ask for anything, I know every book in here," he continued. "Choose whatever you want, bring them to me and I will sign them out."

They looked at the heavy books in despair; this was not quite what they had been expecting.

"Come on, let's forget this," muttered Gareth under his breath.

"Look, we'll have to pick one now. He's expecting it," said Rachel, nodding at the man who was watching them from behind his small counter.

Gareth sighed heavily, and turned to a section of enormous old books in the next row, leaning down to make out the writing on the leather spines.

"Oh no, not that section," said the man quickly, rushing out from behind his counter. "No, you wouldn't be interested in those, and we don't let them out of the shop, well, not to just anyone," he continued, looking flustered. "I think you will find these much more suitable," he said leading them back to the rows at the front of the shop. Eventually they both picked a book, more out of politeness than anything else, and dutifully took them to the counter.

The small man looked quite pleased with their choices and produced a huge ledger, which he placed on the counter heavily, causing a small cloud of dust to rise. They tried not to cough as he dipped the nib of a long pen in a bottle of black ink, writing the titles and their names laboriously in neat flowing handwriting, patting the entry carefully with a sheet of blotting paper.

"What do the letters on the plaque outside stand for?" asked Gareth, interrupting as the man was writing his name in the ledger.

"Letters?" the man asked, his pen pausing.

"Yes, K.O.K. – the gold letters on the plaque over the door," Gareth persisted.

"Oh, those!" the man answered, looking uncomfortable. "Um, well, they stand for Keeper of the Knowledge. Yes! The books, you see!" he added by way of explanation, noting their blank expressions. "Knowledge, well you can see it, it's all around you!" he indicated with a wave of his pen and resumed his meticulous writing.

The twins thanked him as he handed the books back to them and said goodbye, and the bell on the door tinkled again as they left.

They paused to let two ladies in long black dresses past, who whispered to each other before nodding politely, still staring unsmilingly at them.

"Was that a bonnet she was wearing?" asked Rachel after they had gone.

"Certainly looked like one," remarked her brother dryly. "Bonnets, shawls, aprons, dungarees and shirts on the kids, they're all wearing them! It's like a walking museum here!"

Rachel's heart sank further as they carried on. Some children stopped in front of them staring, they whispered behind their hands and looked almost afraid as the twins drew nearer, and ran away, stopping again to look curiously at them from a distance.

The rest of the shops all proved to be the same; antiquated and rather strange. They found a sweet shop, which they went into next. It contained a huge L-shaped counter, which was stacked with different-coloured sweets in big jars. There were no wrapped bars of chocolate with familiar names to be seen; in fact they all looked home-made. They chose the ones they wanted and a large lady in a striped pinafore with frills around the edges carefully weighed them out on a set of brass scales with weights. She put them into two small brown paper bags, twisting them at the corners, glancing up at them every now and again, in an uncomfortable silence.

Gareth pulled some money out of his pocket to pay and she looked at him strangely when he asked how much they were.

"You're staying with Bronwyn, aren't you?" she asked, producing a pen and notebook from her pocket. "Well, that's all right then, I'll make a note of what you have had," she said, not waiting for an answer.

"Well, this is good," said Gareth, once outside. "No one seems to want any money here, they all just write it down."

"Maybe Bronwyn's said something and she'll pay them afterwards," replied Rachel.

"I don't know. Did you see her pay for anything in the shops yesterday? Because I didn't, now I come to think about it."

"No, she didn't, but maybe they pay for everything at the end of the week or something. Maybe they just do everything differently here. Come on, let's get the bikes and go back to the cottage," she continued despondently. "To be honest I've had enough of this, I'm sure everyone's looking at us!"

"That's because they are, they've been staring at us all afternoon, and I'd still like to know what those letters stand for on the shops!"

"That man in the book shop just told you! It made sense to me!" she replied.

"Yes, it made sense to me as well," said Gareth as they reached the bikes. "Except that the letters over his shop were different from all the others. The other shops all have K.O.W. written on them, his is the only one with K.O.K. on! So, if what he says is right, the others must stand for Keeper of something else."

"Oh, I see what you mean," said Rachel. "They would all be keepers of something beginning with W!"

"Exactly!" Gareth said firmly. "And that doesn't make any sense at all."

They pushed the bikes back towards the end of the row of shops, mulling over all the different words beginning with W that could possibly apply to each one. Some of them sounded so silly they both doubled up with laughter.

"So the post office is 'Keeper of Writing' and the shoe shop must be 'Keeper of the Wellies' then!" said Gareth.

"Don't make me laugh any more, I can't push this bike!" laughed Rachel, collapsing onto the wall by the beach.

"And that strange clothes shop must be 'Keeper of the Woollies,'" Gareth continued, joining her on the wall.

"So what about the butchers and the farm shop and that strange hardware shop we got the bikes from? He's got a plaque as well, I checked on the way past."

"Hmm," said Gareth thoughtfully as he sucked hard on one of the boiled sweets. "Don't know, I'll have to think about those. Come on, let's see where that lane goes to."

The lane had high hedges on either side; it twisted slightly and as they rounded the bend they could see an old church almost in front of them as the lane twisted again.

The small grey stone church looked even older than the rest of the village, if that was possible. It sat at the end of a small winding pathway, surrounded by ancient stones marking the graves of those long gone. It was very quiet and still, apart from the odd irreverent call of the seagulls breaking the silence. They passed under a stone archway and made their way silently up the path, looking at the tombs and gravestones either side of them, many with inscriptions so old they were barely legible. The grass was neat and tidy and as they drew nearer the church, they noticed a figure by a grave at the very back of the churchyard.

"I'm sure that's Bronwyn!" Rachel said, pulling at Gareth's sleeve to stop him going any further.

"Yes, it is. We'd better not disturb her, she's putting some flowers on that grave," he answered, halting as he recognised her.

They turned to go, but Bronwyn straightened up and looked directly at them.

"Too late," whispered Gareth, as Bronwyn walked towards them.

"I'm sorry, we didn't mean to disturb you, we didn't know you were here," said Rachel, feeling rather awkward.

"That's all right, I was about to leave anyway," Bronwyn replied. "It's an old friend, I like to bring some flowers now and again," she said by way of explanation. "We can all go back together," she said brightly, with a subdued smile.

Rachel looked closely at her, and although her aunt was smiling, noted the sadness in her eyes. Not knowing what to say, she just hugged her, tightly.

They walked back to the cottage, pushing their bikes, and they told Bronwyn about their riding lesson and the farm.

"We had a fantastic time there, they were so nice to us, and I've never seen so many children in one family!" said Rachel.

"I knew they'd make you feel welcome," said Bronwyn. "They're a lovely family, and if you think it was busy then, you should see it when they bring the harvest in; half the village goes up to help and Betsy, bless her, has a plate of food for everyone!"

"I bet that's fun," said Gareth as they got to the porch. "It's a shame for Johnny though; Betsy said Catherine helped him get better," he continued, deciding to omit Johnny's strange revelations at the table.

"Yes, Catherine has some remarkable cures," said Bronwyn as she opened the heavy wooden door. "She did her best for Johnny, but I'm afraid he will never be quite the same again. He had a huge blow to the head from one of the rocks; he was unconscious for weeks. He's a good lad, for all his problems. He might be a bit slow but you're quite safe with him, he wouldn't hurt a fly."

Catherine was in the kitchen and she was interested to hear about their day as she peeled the vegetables for dinner. They showed her the books they'd got from the bookshop that afternoon.

"You should have said you liked reading, we've got lots of books in the attic. You could go up after dinner and have a look!" she said.

They didn't like to tell her that they would have much preferred to watch a television for entertainment, rather than finding even more books. Instead they found themselves thanking her politely, assuring her that they would love to.

"There may even be some games up there as well. I can't remember; we don't go up there much these days. Anyway, dinner will be ready soon if you two want to go and get cleaned up."

They said they would, but before they left, Gareth couldn't resist asking Catherine about the plaques over the shop doors in the village. Already half way up the stairs, Rachel paused, interested to hear her reply.

"I have no idea," she heard her answer. "We have some silly old traditions here. I expect that's one of them."

"The man in the book shop said the letters on his plaque stood for 'Keeper of the Knowledge,'" prompted Gareth, undeterred.

"Oh well, there you are then, he should know," answered Catherine, kneading some pastry firmly.

"Yes, but the others had different letters, so they must stand for something else, surely?"

"Maybe they do. I must ask them next time I'm down there," she answered, producing a large wooden rolling-pin, dusting it with flour. "Come on now, once this is in the oven it won't take long; you'd best get cleaned up."

Gareth followed Rachel upstairs. "She works for the chemist

shop, which has a sign saying 'K.O.W.,' but she doesn't know what it means – does that sound right to you?" he asked in a whisper.

"You're not going to leave this one alone, are you?" smiled Rachel.

"No, not until I get some sensible answers!" came his firm reply.

Chapter Seven
The Strange Gift

It had been too dark to go looking for books in the attic after dinner, much to their relief. After breakfast in the morning they left on their own and cycled to the farm for their lesson. There was no sign of Johnny in the stable yard, although the horses were ready for them as he had promised. Abigail told them he had gone up to the far fields to help his father. This time she didn't use the leading rein; instead she took them to the field, allowing them to ride slowly on their own, taking control of the horses under her instruction.

The lesson went really well and they both enjoyed it. Gareth had no fear in the saddle and Abigail declared him a natural. Rachel was just pleased that she didn't have the frisky grey to cope with; she was more than happy on big Rufus, who behaved beautifully for her, as though he knew she was a novice.

The farmhouse was equally as busy as before, and the kitchen was already full when they went in. Johnny was there with his father and two men who had been helping in the fields. He beamed at them as soon as he saw them, but wasn't as talkative as the day before. Rachel and Gareth had a cup of tea and left, agreeing to another lesson the next day.

They cycled back to the cottage, arriving just before a heavy shower of rain. The first drops were starting to fall as they put the bikes away in the shed at the side of the cottage. By the time they reached the porch, it was pouring.

"That was close, we'd have got soaked if we'd stopped to join them for lunch. Look at it now!" said Rachel.

"Great!" replied Gareth. "What on earth are we going to do for the rest of the day?"

"Oh, it'll clear up later!" said Bronwyn, hearing them from the kitchen. "Why don't you go up and have a read for a while."

They went up to their rooms, but it wasn't long before Gareth joined Rachel, complaining he was bored.

"We could go and have a look round the attic, there's nothing else to do, and they did say we should, yesterday," he said swinging his legs against the bed as he sat next to her.

Irritated by the thumping noise and realising that she wasn't going to be allowed to concentrate on her own book, Rachel sighed and closed it up.

"Oh all right, if we must!" she said resignedly, and followed him out of her room to the small staircase at the end of the corridor. The wooden stairs were narrow and turned sharply, creaking loudly as they walked up. At the top there was a small door which creaked even louder as they pushed it open, revealing a large attic with wooden beams that stretched over the whole top floor. There were two small windows where the light streamed in, and the floor was covered in large wooden boxes, most of them looking as though they hadn't been touched in years.

Gareth sneezed loudly as he opened a large case; the dust could be seen rising up in a cloud as the particles drifted across the beam of light from the window. He was disappointed to discover that the case contained a collection of old ornaments, carefully wrapped in paper. He closed it in disgust and started on the next one. He didn't have much success there either, as it revealed layers of old embroidered linen.

Rachel opened one of the boxes and found some old board games, which she left out before putting the box back. She uncovered a smaller box of toys in the next of the big boxes.

"Oh, look at these. They must be very old, they're lovely," she remarked as she produced a wooden train in sections, all neatly wrapped, followed by a wooden sword and a painted shield.

"Strange toys for Bronwyn and Catherine to have," Gareth answered, almost sarcastically. He paused, then said, "Look at these, I've found the books, Huckleberry Finn, Treasure Island, The Pirates of … I can't even read this one it's falling apart …"

"Well, there are plenty of girls' things in the next boxes," announced Rachel, delving deeply into them. "Look," she said, producing an old doll and a wooden cradle.

"Well, I'd expect to see dolls and cradles, but why have they got all of these – they're the sort of toys a boy would have?" Gareth said as he produced a bat and a hard ball, a wooden cart, and some carved figures of knights on horseback.

"Oh, look," said Rachel, ignoring the question, as she uncovered a painted rocking-horse in the far corner of the attic.

Gareth got up and joined her. "These cases look more interesting, I wonder what's in them?" he said pointing to three ancient wooden trunks with black iron strips on their sides and leather straps with buckles holding them shut. He undid the large buckles on one of the trunks, but had trouble lifting up the heavy lid; the hinges were rusty and stiff. His efforts eventually revealed several old, black, leather-bound books.

He lifted one out and opened it up. The paper was thick and yellow with age, and it looked very similar to the dusty ancient books in the bookshop they had visited the day before.

"What's it about?" asked Rachel curiously.

"I don't know, but it's not very interesting, it's a load of lists of names. Page after page of them," he said, briefly flicking through it and reaching for another.

"This one looks the same as yours," said Rachel lifting out another, comparing it with the one Gareth was holding.

"Look, if you wipe the dust off the cover they've got something written on them," she instructed, using her sleeve to clean the dust away.

"K.O.P.!" they both said in unison as the gold lettering became clear.

"I thought they were the same but they're not, yours looks much older. Look at the pages, they're all written by hand in coloured inks. Look at the writing, it's really beautiful," Rachel said, as she inspected the ancient book he was holding. "What else is in it?" she asked, craning her neck to see.

"Pictures, symbols, they look like coats of arms that you see on shields and crests. There are names under all of them, look. Gawain, Bedevere, Medraut, Kay, Bors, Percivale … and look at this one – I'm sure it's the same as the one painted on that toy shield you pulled out, and it says Geraint underneath!"

"I didn't really look at it," answered his sister, as her interest shifted to the heavy black book she was holding. "There are names written inside the cover of this one, look, Bronwyn and Geraint."

"Geraint, there's that name again. It's the same one that Catherine mentioned in the kitchen when we first got here!"

"So who is he, then?" asked Rachel, looking puzzled.

"Search me. What else is in that one?" Gareth asked, and she turned a few more of the heavy pages.

"Oh my goodness, look at this, An Incantation to vanquish thine enemies!" she read out in horror. "It's a spell of some sort! There's another, look …"

"Ah, here you are! I've been calling you, I wondered where you were." Bronwyn's voice startled them; they hadn't heard her entering the attic as they were so absorbed in their findings. Rachel snapped the book shut and they jumped up guiltily.

"Good heavens, I wouldn't have thought you'd be interested in those old things," Bronwyn said, taking the books away from them, placing them back in the old chest. "I'd quite forgotten we still had these. I must take them down to the bookshop. Mr Drevorley would love them, they're so old!" she remarked cheerily as she closed the heavy lid. "Did you not find anything in these boxes?" she enquired, leading them back to the cases they had opened first.

"I did find some board games; I left them out," said Rachel hesitantly.

"Oh splendid, I see you've found the draughts set, and I remember this game, it's rather good. Catherine and I used to play it a lot when we were quite young," she said, reminiscing over the old box in her hands. "Good, we'll take these downstairs; we'll have some fun with these tonight."

Gareth looked at Rachel dubiously before agreeing politely that they couldn't wait, and followed her back down the creaking stairs.

"I was looking for you to tell you that the rain's stopped, if you wanted to go out again. It's lovely now, and the sun's back out," Bronwyn continued as they followed her down the corridor.

The twins decided to take advantage of the sun, which was now streaming through all the windows, and go to the beach. They discussed their strange findings as they walked, once they were out of earshot of the cottage.

"That book has really spooked me! There were spells in it, did you see them?" said Rachel with a shiver.

"Well, only briefly. It's a pity Bronwyn turned up when she did; I'm sure we would have found out a lot more from those books if we'd had the chance. Still I suppose we can always go back to have another look."

"I don't think I want to," said Rachel with another shiver. "I don't want to read books with spells in, I thought only witches had books like that!"

Gareth stopped walking and looked at her, his eyebrows had disappeared into his fringe and his face bore an 'I told you so' look.

"Oh no ... you don't think ...?"

"Well, Bronwyn's name was inside the cover of that book, and I've been telling you ever since we got here that there's something not right about this place. Maybe the whole village is involved in some kind of black magic. It's certainly weird enough!"

"Don't say things like that, I'll never be able to sleep! Anyway, I can't believe that Bronwyn's a witch," Rachel said adamantly.

"Well, they're definitely hiding something. There's also that name Geraint, with Bronwyn's, inside the cover of that book. Catherine mentioned it when we got here and when Bronwyn looked at her, she immediately shut up. Then there's all these letters," said Gareth sitting down on the wall by the beach.

"There's K.O.K., we know what that is, Keeper of Knowledge, but then there's K.O.W. on all the other shops which Catherine claims to know nothing about, even though she works for them, and now we've got K.O.P. on the books, work that one out!"

"I really don't want to. In fact I'm beginning to think I'd like to go home," she answered, sitting down despondently next to him.

"That's another thing; Dad didn't really want us to come. She talked him into it!"

"Bronwyn wouldn't hurt us, and Dad wouldn't have let us come if he thought we were in danger!"

"No, I'm sure you're right, he wouldn't, and I'm sure they aren't going to hurt us either, but I think we'd better keep quiet about anything we find out, just in case. Agreed?"

"Yes," she answered immediately.

"When you think about it, we don't really know much about Mum's family. Apart from Bronwyn, we've never met any of them," said Gareth thoughtfully. "Or Dad's either for that matter; in fact we don't really know anything about any of our relatives!"

"No, we don't, and Dad doesn't ever talk about Mum either. I've always thought that he didn't want to because it upset him, especially since he was brought up in an orphanage and never knew his own family."

"That's probably why. I've never really thought about it from his point of view," agreed Gareth. "It must have been really tough on him when Mum died; he had a family for the first time and then he lost it all again, apart from us!"

"I'm sure that's why he didn't want us to come."

"Yes, that makes sense. Come on, let's forget about all this and just have a holiday. Let's go on that cliff walk!" he said. "Anyway, what could possibly happen to us in a week? Even if there are strange things going on here, they're nothing to do with us!"

They started the climb to the top of the cliffs, and the higher they went the stronger the wind became, leaving their faces tingling from the salty breeze. There was a bench half way up and they could see the steps leading steeply down to the rocks by the point. They sat on the bench for a few minutes, for a brief rest, and then continued upwards, until they reached the highest part of the cliffs, where they looked back to see the whole of the bay on their left. The village looked quite tiny from their high vantage-point and below them they could see the beach with the quicksand, on the other side of the point.

They continued along the cliff-top, the wind taking their breath away, until they could see right across to the next rocky headland. Below were several small beaches, cut off by unmerciful waves dashing against weather-beaten rocks, and across the next bay there were stretches of sand forming further beaches, surrounded by the same black, harsh rocks, making them inaccessible by the tide.

"Gosh, look how high up we are," said Rachel, as the wind caught them sharply again.

"I know, you can see for miles from here! Look at those coves over there, there are loads of caves - I'd love to have a look round them!"

"You'd need a boat to get to those! There's no way down there," laughed Rachel.

They stood for a long time admiring the view before turning back. It was a lot easier going down, and as the bench by the point came back into view, they realised it was now occupied by a hooded figure sitting looking out to sea. As they approached they could see his long brown robes, rather like those of a monk, with some type of walking-stick by the side of him.

Rachel instinctively put her arm through her brother's as they drew nearer, and although he noticed this unexpected action, he said nothing.

The hooded figure turned towards them, revealing a lined, elderly face. A wisp of long white hair caught by the wind escaped from underneath the hood and was brushed back quickly by an old gnarled hand.

"Fine day," said the old man with a smile. "You've been admiring the views across the bay, no doubt."

"Yes, we have, the view's fantastic up there," said Gareth politely.

"It's Rachel and Gareth, isn't it? Bronwyn's visitors. How are you enjoying your holiday?"

"Yes, it's really good, thanks," replied Gareth rather awkwardly.

"Come, sit with me a while. I have been looking forward to meeting you."

The twins looked at each other dubiously, unaccustomed to speaking to strangers, let alone sitting with them half way up a cliff.

"Don't look so worried," said the old man. "I have known

81

Catherine and Bronwyn since they were babes in arms. Come, come, sit next to me, I have come a long way today to meet you both," he said, shuffling up to make room for them, patting the wooden seat next to him.

To Gareth's surprise Rachel sat down, looking quite comfortable with the stranger.

"If you came to meet us, how did you know where we were?" Gareth asked him.

"Oh, I knew!" the old man answered with a laugh.

Gareth sat down apprehensively next to Rachel.

"I hear you have been having riding lessons?" the stranger asked. "And proving to be quite good as well."

"Um, well, yes, we have," answered Gareth.

"Well, it's in the blood, you were certain to be good!" the old man said emphatically.

"Right," answered Gareth lamely, amazed that this man knew so much about them.

"And how are Bronwyn and Catherine, my dear?" he asked, turning to Rachel.

"They're fine, thanks," she answered comfortably, much to Gareth's surprise.

"Good, good, I'm pleased to hear that," the old man mused thoughtfully, stroking his long white beard. "Bronwyn is a good woman, a very good woman; she has had to make the greatest sacrifices of all, sacrifices no woman should ever have to make. It has been very hard for her."

The twins nodded, even though they had no idea what he was talking about.

"And how do you find Valonia?" the old man asked as though he had just returned from his thoughts elsewhere. "Not quite what you are used to, I'll wager!" he chuckled.

"No, no, not really, but it's very nice," answered Gareth, since the question appeared to be directed at him.

"I'll wager you're finding it very strange here," commented the old man, laughing again.

"I really think we ought to be going. Catherine will have started cooking the dinner by now," said Gareth, tugging at Rachel's sleeve.

"Quite so, quite so, mustn't keep a growing boy from his food, must we?" the old man smiled at Rachel. "But before you go I have something for you," he said, delving deep into the folds of his hooded cloak.

"For us?" asked Rachel in surprise.

"Indeed, I have come a long way to give you these," the old man said as he produced two small black leather pouches.

"I really don't think we ought to …" started Gareth, standing up.

"Accept them?" the old man intervened quickly. "Oh, but you must. Listen to me, these are not really a gift, they are your inheritance! You will take them, because I am giving you them as protection. Keep them on you at all times while you are here. They will keep you from danger."

"What danger?" asked Gareth, as the stranger pressed the pouch into his hand.

"Any danger!" he answered, the smile leaving his face. "There are a great many things you do not know about this place, about its people and about their ways. The contents of these pouches will serve you, should the need arise. Keep them on your person at all times."

Rachel and Gareth both held the black pouches, looking at the old man in astonishment.

"Trust me, keep them with you, and stay together, always stay together. No, don't open them now!" the stranger instructed as Gareth immediately pulled at the drawstring to open it. "Look at the contents when you are alone. Tell no-one you have them, and tell no-one you have met me, do you understand? Not even your aunts!"

They both nodded, holding the pouches firmly.

"Now, put them away in your pockets, I trust you have pockets in that modern attire? Ah, yes, you obviously have," he observed as they both obediently stuffed them away out of sight. "Well, now, you had best run along, best not keep Catherine waiting with one of her dinners. I wish I were to be sampling it with you! Oh, yes, I certainly do! But it has been good to meet you, I have waited longer than you can imagine for this meeting, and you will remember what

I have said, won't you?"

They nodded again dumbly, surprised at his warning and still stunned by the conversation they had just had with someone who obviously knew a great deal about them, and yet they knew absolutely nothing about him.

"It has been a pleasure to meet you both," said the old man, shaking their hands in turn, "and for now it will be goodbye, but we will meet again."

They both dutifully said goodbye and started back down the hill, turning back to see the old man waving to them until they were out of sight.

"This place just gets weirder and weirder. I wonder what he's given us?" said Gareth, dying to open the pouch.

"I don't know, but we won't open them till we get home in case he sees."

"He's gone," said Gareth, turning back to see that the bench was empty again and the man was nowhere in sight.

"I don't care; we're still not opening them. We'll have a look in our bedrooms when we're on our own."

"Okay, if it keeps you happy. I have to say, though, I'm amazed that you've just sat and had a long conversation with a perfect stranger wearing a hooded monk's outfit. Especially when we were half way up a cliff with no-one within shouting distance."

"Yes, but he wasn't a stranger, we've met him before," Rachel answered.

"Well, I've never seen him before in my life, so I don't know how you knew him!" stated Gareth, firmly.

"We must have met him before, I recognised him as soon as I saw his face. We must have met him with Bronwyn, the other day."

"Nope, sorry to disappoint you, but I have definitely never met him before!"

"We must have done, he knew all about us."

"Yeah, him and everyone else in this place, we stick out like sore thumbs, being 'outsiders' and all that!" Gareth replied sarcastically.

"Well, yes, I suppose so, but I know I've seen him before!" Rachel said adamantly.

They arrived back in time for dinner and helped Catherine to clear up afterwards, intending to escape immediately to their bedrooms, to look at the contents of the pouches.

However, Bronwyn then produced the board-games they had found earlier. She was so excited about playing them that they followed her politely into the lounge where she set up one of the games on a small table, assuring them that they would really enjoy it. Catherine joined them, placing mugs of tea and biscuits on the small table by the settee. She stoked up the fire, which was crackling in the grate, and sat down next to Bronwyn, looking as pleased as her sister.

"You always used to beat me at this," Catherine remarked, throwing the dice. "Oh, two sixes, maybe my luck has changed!"

The game turned out to be very entertaining; it was a bit like a cross between monopoly and snakes-and-ladders, except that it was built around a castle, and they all had a figure on a miniature wooden horse to move around the board. Certain squares had a flap which opened up to reveal their fate, and the main aim was to finish and rescue the damsel in the tower.

"Oh, no!" groaned Gareth. "Not the dungeons again, miss three goes!" he said as he lifted the flap on the square that he had landed on.

"I don't know what you're complaining about," laughed Catherine. "You've all been round the board three times while I've been in the stocks! If I can just throw another six I can get out."

They all laughed as the dice revealed no more than four, and she shrugged, good-naturedly.

"My turn, five more squares and I'm there!" laughed Rachel.

They were interrupted by a flash of lightning that lit up the room, and the biggest clap of thunder they had ever heard. The candles blew out as the wind whistled through the cottage, and further vivid flashes of lightning were followed swiftly by equally-ferocious peals of thunder.

Rachel let out a scream and grabbed her brother, as they were left with only the glow from the wood burning in the fireplace.

"It's all right, I'll light the candles again," said Bronwyn quickly.

"He's back!" said Catherine, sombrely, the laughter gone now, replaced by a worried look. "You know what this means, he knows," she directed towards Bronwyn.

"Don't be silly, what can he know?" Bronwyn asked as the candlelight was restored.

"Who knows?" asked Gareth. "And what do they know? Who are you talking about?"

"Oh, no-one, pay no heed," answered Bronwyn quickly, looking sternly at her sister.

"It's a warning; the thunder's always a warning. It can only mean one of two things, an outsider has entered the village, or he is back. It always thunders when he enters the pass, you know that!" Catherine said, jumping up. "It's a warning that he has returned!"

"Who's returned?" asked Gareth again.

"No-one, it's just an old superstition, that's all, nothing to concern yourselves with!" Bronwyn answered. "In fact, I think it might be a good idea if we all go upstairs now. It's quite late and if there's going to be a storm, we'd best get some sleep while we can! Come on, I'll come up with you," she said firmly, with a candle-holder in each hand.

They made towards the stairs, leaving an agitated Catherine to sort out the fire and put the game away before she went to bed herself.

Chapter Eight
Secrets

When they reached their rooms, Bronwyn said goodnight and shortly afterwards they heard Catherine coming up the stairs. Gareth waited until he heard their doors close and then he crept back along the hall to Rachel's room. She gasped loudly as he let himself in.

"Shh," he said. "She'll hear you."

"You've just frightened the life out of me," said Rachel, as she jumped up nervously. "I'm scared enough as it is, after all that downstairs!"

"Oh, don't be silly, it was only a bit of thunder."

"Well, apparently not! Who were they talking about? Catherine looked really scared! Whoever it is that's supposed to be back, she's frightened of them! And how can someone coming here make it thunder? Do you think we made it thunder when we came through the pass?"

"No, that's ridiculous, it thunders everywhere, it thunders at home! It doesn't mean anything!" he answered resolutely, sitting down on the bed. "I think that Catherine's completely caught up in all these local superstitions, and she really believes them."

"I don't know, I'm beginning to wonder about everything now, and you've been constantly telling me that there's something not right here. That book frightened me this morning as well."

"It's an old book, someone probably gave it to them, it doesn't really mean anything," said Gareth. "We don't know that they read spells themselves; after all, I've got a book in my room on woodcarving, but I've got no intention of reading it, or doing it! Mind you, that's not to say that other people here don't get involved in spells or whatever else was in those books; I wouldn't put it past some of them, they're a pretty weird bunch to say the least!"

"Oh, thanks!" she said, giving him a shove. "I was starting to feel a bit better till you said that."

He fell sideways, laughing, as she pushed him again, and felt something hard dig into his thigh.

"Ow!" he said loudly and felt in his pocket, pulling out the offending black pouch. "Blimey, I'd forgotten all about this!" he said.

"Oh, so had I! What's in it?" she asked excitedly, as Gareth pulled the drawstring to open it.

He turned the pouch upside down and shook out a perfectly-formed green stone into the palm of his hand. It was heavy and dense-looking, but when he held it up to the light it shone with a beautiful green glow. It was shaped into an oval with cut facets, tapering almost to a point.

"That looks like an emerald. I'm sure it probably isn't, but it looks just like the ones we saw in the Crown Jewels in London."

"Do you get emeralds this big?" asked Gareth, turning it over in his hand. "It'd be worth a fortune, if it were."

"Well, you wouldn't get them that big in the jewellers in town, but those ones in the Tower of London looked exactly like that!"

"Can't be real. Anyway, where's yours – let's see what you've got."

Rachel jumped up and opened the drawer next to her bed, whisked out the black pouch and pulled the drawstring to reveal an identically-cut stone, the same size and weight but a dark rich red colour. When she held hers up, it sparkled with a ruby glow.

They looked at each other in amazement, and then back at the two heavy stones, which when put together under the lamp glistened as a perfectly matching pair.

"They can't be real!" said Rachel as they turned them over. "I'd love to show them to Bronwyn, I bet she'd know if they were."

"Well, we can't do that, the old man said we weren't to tell anyone we had them, remember?"

"I know and we won't, but what he said doesn't make any sense either, he said they would keep us out of danger. I can't see how two stones can do that, can you?"

"No, but he also said there were a lot of things we don't know about this place, and he was right about that! The bit about staying together makes sense; I think we should do that. In fact when he said it, it reminded me of that gypsy at the fair, she said that as well, she also said we were going somewhere where there was danger."

"That's it, that's it!" said Rachel, grabbing his arm. "I knew I'd seen him somewhere before – it was there!"

"Who?" asked Gareth.

"The old man, of course!"

"What, at the fair?" he asked in surprise.

"Yes, well no, not at the fair exactly, in the crystal ball! I told you I saw an old man. It was him! I knew I recognised him!"

"Wow, now that is beginning to sound really weird! Are you sure?"

"Yes, I'm sure, it was definitely him! Gareth, I'm really frightened now. I wish Dad was here. I wish we could just go home. I don't like all this! What are we going to do?" she asked, tears welling up in her eyes.

"Oh, look, don't start getting upset again," he said, putting his arm around her shoulder, rather awkwardly. "We'll put them away for tonight, and tomorrow we'll go back up the cliff and see if we can find him again. I think we ought to give them back. To be honest, we don't even know if we can trust him. They might have some sort of spell on them."

"No, no!" she answered firmly. "We can trust him. I know we can!"

"How do you know?" he asked.

"I just do, don't ask me how, but I know he's on our side. When I saw him in the crystal ball he looked so sad. Something had happened, I know it had, I could feel it. I can't explain how, but I know he's a good person."

"Well, okay then, but I still think we should go and find him tomorrow, and if we can rely on him, like you say, maybe we should ask him the questions that we want answered."

"Yes, yes, we'll do that. I know he'll help us!" she said confidently.

"I still think we ought to have another look in those books in the attic," said Gareth. "I'm sure we'll find some answers there as well."

"All right then," she agreed. "We'll do both."

They had started to put the beautiful stones back into their ordinary-looking pouches, when Gareth let out another shout.

"I don't believe this, look!" he said in disbelief. "K.O.P.! It's engraved on the pouch. I didn't notice it before, it's so faint. Have a look at yours, see if it's on that one as well."

"Yes, it is," she said, with a sick feeling in the pit of her stomach as she ran her fingers over the worn letters. "This is really starting to give me the creeps again, what does it mean?"

"I don't know, but maybe we'll find out tomorrow. Look, we're quite safe. No-one knows about any of this, and we won't tell them."

Rachel nodded, and as soon as Gareth had left for his own bedroom, she pulled the bedcovers up over her ears, nervously.

On his way back to his own room, Gareth heard voices coming from Bronwyn's bedroom. This was becoming a habit, he thought wryly, as he put his ear to the door.

"I don't know what you were thinking, bringing them here," he heard Catherine say.

"It's only for a week, what harm can it do?" Bronwyn answered.

"Supposing he finds out, what then?" Catherine asked, fearfully.

"He won't, and anyway, how could he find out?"

"Don't underestimate him, Bronwyn, you're playing with fire! Anyway, what about them? They're starting to ask awkward questions already. They're bright children, it won't be long before they find out something we don't want them to!"

"No-one here is going to tell them anything," said Bronwyn with a brittle laugh. "After all, keeping secrets is what we do best here! The whole place is built on secrets, hundreds of years of them!"

"You wouldn't have come back, would you, if it hadn't been for …"

"No, I wouldn't!" Bronwyn interrupted loudly. "But then I'm as wrapped up in all of this as everyone else here. There's no escape from it, anywhere!"

"I'm sorry you feel like that. I know it's been difficult for you, but you were warned, you never should have left."

Gareth didn't hear Bronwyn's answer. The door knob turned and he bolted quickly for his bedroom, shutting the door quietly. He got into bed, the conversation he had overheard still ringing in his head.

'Hundreds of years of secrets', 'no escape from it' – what on earth is going on in this place? he thought, his mind filling with even more unanswered questions. Bronwyn had been warned about leaving, why? She'd never told the twins she had ever left; in fact she'd said she had lived there all her life! And what happened there to 'make her go back'? He was feeling quite jittery now, in the dark, and every noise and creak in the old cottage unnerved him even more, until finally, like Rachel, he pulled the covers up almost over his head to shut them out, and eventually fell asleep.

He leapt out of the bed when his sister shook him gently the next morning.

"Shh …" she said. "They're still in bed."

"For heaven's sake, Rachel!" he said, falling back in relief.

"You're jumpy this morning!" she said, surprised. "Anyway, I thought I'd wake you up so we could sneak up to the attic and have a look at those books again. I would have gone on my own, but I didn't have the nerve," she confessed.

"All right, give me a few minutes and I'll meet you by the stairs," he said, and scrambled into his shorts and T-shirt, feeling rather apprehensive about the whole thing. Yesterday it had seemed like a good idea to go snooping around looking for answers, but now he was not so sure. However, curiosity still managed to get the better of him, and he joined his sister. They crept past the other bedrooms and tried to miss out the step with the largest creak on their way up to the attic, where they made straight for the trunks at the back.

"We'll have to be quick!" said Rachel, as Gareth lifted up the heavy lid. "Maybe we ought to take the books straight downstairs and hide them in our bedrooms."

To their surprise, the trunk was empty.

"Try the others," Rachel suggested, but there were no books in those, either. The twins had a quick look around to see if the books might be anywhere else in the attic, and were extremely disappointed when they had to go downstairs empty-handed.

"They've moved them!" said Gareth, once they were back in Rachel's bedroom. "Which can only mean one thing – that they didn't want us to see what was in them!"

"I can't believe it, what could be so important in a load of old books that they would hide them straight away?"

"I don't know, but maybe we ought to stop trying to find out," Gareth answered seriously.

"Well, you've changed your tune!" Rachel said in surprise. "Yesterday you were all for finding out anything you could - it was your idea to get the books!"

"Yeah, I know, but that was yesterday."

"So what's changed, have you found out something I don't know about?" she asked suspiciously.

For a moment he was tempted to tell her what he had overheard the night before, but knowing how she would react, he decided against it, mumbling that he was still tired instead.

"Look, I think we should try and find the old man again later, give him back the pouches and just try and have a normal holiday for the last few days. Let them keep their secrets to themselves," he said.

"What secrets?" asked Rachel, still taken aback by his sudden change in attitude.

"I don't know, whatever secrets they have here. I'm going to go and have a wash before breakfast, I'll see you down there," he said dismissively, shutting her bedroom door firmly behind him.

Rachel thought that breakfast was rather strained. No-one mentioned the thunder or the remarks made by Catherine in the evening. Even her brother was strangely quiet and didn't appear to eat as much as usual, and there was hardly any conversation between Bronwyn and Catherine.

Rachel was relieved when they left for their riding lesson, which at least seemed to lift Gareth's spirits as he galloped across the fields on the lively grey horse. The mood of impending doom that had haunted him since last night began to seem less daunting in the sunlight as he enjoyed his ride. He had successfully evaded his sister's questions on the way to the farm, although he knew that she still suspected that he was keeping something from her, leaving him with the question of 'Should I tell her and frighten her even more, or keep it to myself unless I have to tell her for some reason?' He decided on the latter and put it to the back of his mind for the time being.

Once their lesson was over, they went straight back to the cottage and put their bikes away. They had a sandwich with Catherine and left on foot to see if they could find the old man again, taking the leather pouches with them.

There was no sign of him in the village, so they started up the cliff walk, hoping to find him in the same place as the day before. They passed the empty bench and carried on to the top, where they found nothing more than a stiff breeze and the seagulls circling overhead. They sat down on the grass and Gareth pulled out his pouch. The green stone shone even more brightly in the sunlight.

"I would love to know what these are, and why he gave them to us!" he said wistfully, his earlier thoughts of leaving well alone vanishing as he looked at the perfectly-formed jewel.

"Put it away!" said Rachel, looking around warily. Gareth laughed, but did as he was told, stuffing it back in the pocket of his shorts, before they started on the walk back down.

As the bench came in to view again, they were both excited to see it was no longer empty, but as they got nearer, they realised it wasn't the old man, but a much younger, slimmer figure.

"It's Johnny," said Rachel, half relieved and half disappointed.

"Hello, I thought it was you two!" said Johnny delightedly. "I comes up here a lot and I don't normally see anyone else."

Rachel smiled at him, and they both joined him on the bench.

"I missed you the other day, but I got your horses ready, I did!" he said proudly and took a sweet from the bag that Gareth offered him.

It was easy to see that Johnny was very happy to have their company, and he talked almost non-stop, until he finally exhausted his account of everything he had been doing at the farm and the errands he had been running that day.

"'Course I used to do a lot more things, much better things, before me accident," he finished sadly.

"Do you remember your accident, Johnny?" asked Rachel kindly. "It must have been awful!"

"I does, I remembers it. I still has nightmares sometimes about it," he nodded solemnly, his eyes widening as though in fear. "You see, I remembers the black shape standing over me, after the rocks had come falling down."

"What do you mean, black shape? I thought you got caught in a rock fall in the pass," asked Gareth, cautiously.

"Oh, I did, I did. The rocks started crashing around me and Rufus, and the next thing I was laying on the ground. I couldn't move and then the black shape came. I couldn't see it too well, I was really dizzy and my head hurt, but I heard it laugh before it left and then I listened to the hooves as it rode away. I don't remember nothing after that, till I woke up in bed with Miss Catherine looking after me."

"That's awful!" said Rachel in horror. "Did you tell them what you saw?"

"I did, but Miss Catherine and Mum, they said I'd imagined it, but I knows I didn't, I knows what I saw!" he insisted.

Gareth and Rachel looked at each other wondering what to believe, as he sounded so convincing.

"Well, we believe you, Johnny," Rachel answered sympathetically.

"See, I knew you would. It's 'cos you're twins too!" Johnny said earnestly. "I knew you'd understand. But that's why you needs to be careful!"

"You said that the other day, why?" asked Gareth.

"I told you, bad things happen to twins here!" Johnny said, grabbing Gareth's wrist. "Oh no, I've done it again! Mum said I wasn't to talk about it, she made me promise. She'll be really cross if she finds out I've been telling you again!"

"Don't worry, we won't tell her, it'll be our secret," said Gareth.

"Are you sure? I'll get into all sorts of trouble," Johnny asked, looking worried.

"No, we promise we won't tell anyone, don't worry," said Rachel, feeling sorry for him.

"All right then, our secret," he said, looking satisfied.

"So what did you mean the other day?" asked Gareth. "You said something happens to the twins here."

"It does, to all of them," Johnny answered resolutely.

"All of them?" asked Gareth, looking surprised. "How many have there been?"

"Well," said Johnny thoughtfully, taking his time to answer as though he were having trouble remembering. "Well, there was me! Me and Abby, we're twins. And then there was Mr Mordred's sister, Miss Celia, they were twins too, till she died. They found her floating in the lake at the back of the manor. They said she must have fallen in and couldn't swim! But I knows she could, she used to let me swim in the lake and once when I got there, she had been swimming herself! Mum said I shouldn't tell anyone that though, just in case, you know," he said knowingly, looking up and down the path to make sure that no-one could hear him. "And then there was Miss Bronwyn's twin brother, Mr Geraint. The cliff gave way under him and they found him on the rocks, dead!"

"Bronwyn's twin? You mean our Bronwyn?" Rachel asked in disbelief, even though they both recognised the other name.

"Of course, that's what I said, Mr Geraint! I liked him, he used to take me out in his fishing boat, he did. He was nice."

"So Bronwyn had a twin brother?" Rachel asked again, still uncertain.

"Yes, that's what I said!" Johnny answered. "Mr Geraint, they was twins!"

"That's unbelievable, she's never mentioned being a twin!" exclaimed Rachel.

"So you didn't know?" asked Johnny, looking worried again. "You won't tell nobody I's told you, will you?"

"No, of course we won't, we said we wouldn't," answered Gareth.

"No, our secret, you said, didn't you?" the farm boy said trustingly.

"Our secret," they both agreed, to keep him happy. They left him on the bench swinging his legs, munching the rest of Gareth's sweets, and started back down towards the village. He waved to them until they reached the bottom of the path.

"What do you make of that, do you think he's right?" Rachel asked, still in shock from Johnny's revelations.

"I don't know what to think, except that it's that name again, Geraint! It's the same name that was inside that book next to Bronwyn's!" said Gareth. "It can't all be a coincidence!"

"But why wouldn't she tell us she had a twin brother?" asked Rachel disbelievingly.

"Maybe Johnny's wrong! What did you make of his story about the accident?" asked Gareth.

"For some reason I believe him," she replied. "There are just too many coincidences here, and too many people trying to pass things off as something else. No, I think I believe him!"

They had arrived back at the beach now, and Gareth was looking thoughtfully towards the road leading to the old church.

"I know how we can find out," he said. "The churchyard! If Bronwyn had a twin brother, he'd be buried there. I think we ought to go and take a look at the grave she was putting flowers on, the other day. Maybe it was Geraint's!"

"Surely not! Do you think we ought to?" asked Rachel, as her brother strode purposefully towards the lane.

Gareth didn't answer as he was already on his way to do just that, so she walked quickly after him, despite her misgivings.

They made their way into the quiet churchyard and followed the path round the side of the church, to the back. They stepped onto the grass and walked around the graves. They soon spotted the small posy of blue flowers they had seen Bronwyn place there the day before. Unlike the other graves surrounding it, with their inscriptions weathered away by years of salty winds, it was easy to see that this was a much more recent grave. The words inscribed on the large white stone were perfectly legible and Gareth read them out loud.

"'Geraint Trelawney, aged 28. Much-loved son of Margareta and Cecil and brother to Bronwyn and Catherine. May he rest in peace, as a true Knight of the Ways'."

96

"So it's true!" whispered Gareth, still surprised even though they had both suspected it. "Bronwyn did have a twin!"

Rachel didn't answer; a cold feeling came over her, and she shuddered.

"Which makes you wonder, if this is true, how much of everything else that Johnny said is right?" Gareth continued, still staring at the grave.

Chapter Nine
Dark Encounters

There were no riding lessons arranged for the next day, as Abigail was busy, so instead they decided to take advantage of the warm sunshine and spend the morning on the beach. They spread their towels out on the sand and splashed in the waves, conscious that the pouches containing the stones were hidden in the pile of clothes.

"This is ridiculous!" said Gareth, looking back at them again, even though the beach was deserted. "We can't leave them at home in case Bronwyn finds them, so we've got to bring them with us, and now I'm feeling as though we've got to watch them all the time. It's a nuisance – I wanted to go swimming!"

"I know, but he did say to keep them with us at all times."

"I know that, but we can hardly go swimming with them," he answered. "Oh, I give up!" he said, going back to the towels and drying himself.

"Well, with any luck we might be able to give them back today!" she said, joining him.

"I do hope so; it's a bit of a responsibility carrying them around all day, especially if they're real!"

They sat down on the towels; Rachel lay back in the sun enjoying its warmth after the cold waves.

"Look at that enormous bird!" Gareth said, pointing at the small cluster of rocks nearby. "I don't think I've ever seen a bird that big on a beach, look at it!"

Reluctantly Rachel sat up and saw the huge bird sitting on the rocks looking steadily at them, quite undeterred by their movements.

"What do you reckon it is? It's huge!" he remarked, as the big black bird still fixed its gaze on them intently.

"I don't know. It's certainly big!" she said, lying back on her towel.

"I think we ought to have another go at finding the old man, in fact if we sit nearer the jetty he would have to pass us to walk up the cliff path."

"That's not a bad idea, he would," she answered, sitting up again.

"I tell you what, that bird hasn't taken its eyes off us all the time we've been here."

"Not like you to get spooked about a bird, Gareth," she said sarcastically.

"Yeah, well I didn't until the other week! It is weird though, it hasn't moved, it's looked at us all the time we've been here and if I didn't know better, I'd say it was listening to us!"

"Do you have any idea how ridiculous that sounds?" she laughed as she picked her things up.

"Yes, and I can't believe I said it, but it's no more stupid than you saying that the bird at home saved my life!"

"Okay, point taken!"

"Look, it's still watching us. Even when it's been pecking round the rocks, it's still had its black beady eyes on us, and when we've been talking it stops and stares. Look, it's doing it now!" Gareth said, as he stood up and flapped his towel towards it, an action that would have sent most birds into the air, but not this one. It spread out its huge black wings and leant forward, hissing menacingly, still gazing intently at them.

"Come on, let's go, I've had enough of this!" said Gareth nervously, as the bird made to move forward off its perch on the rock, hissing again through its hooked beak.

They walked back along the beach to the jetty, where Gareth looked back to find that the huge bird had gone.

"Finally, it's disappeared," he said as he sat down on the wall. "I know it sounds daft, but there was something about it that didn't seem bird-like, in fact, it reminded me of that bird of yours! It was about the same size as well!"

"My bird wasn't like that one, at all," said Rachel indignantly. "My bird was nice, that one had a sort of nasty look about it!"

"I'm so glad my mates can't hear this!" said Gareth wryly, "and if I have to write an essay on 'what I did in the holidays,' I certainly won't be including any of this!"

"No, wouldn't do your cool image much good, reading all this out, would it?" laughed his sister.

They were interrupted by the arrival of a tall dark figure, walking towards them down the jetty. He was a striking man, striding purposefully with his long cloak flowing behind him as the sea breeze caught it. His whole attire was black, a colour favoured by most of the village, but his was more extravagant-looking than their simple clothing. Under the cloak he wore a black shirt and tailored tunic, with black trousers fitting snugly into a long pair of highly-polished boots.

His tanned face was framed by a neatly-trimmed dark beard and jet black hair; his eyes were dark and deep-set, and his nose was slightly hooked. He greeted them with a thin smile, revealing a perfect set of even white teeth.

"Ah, you must be the twins my son told me about!" he said, pausing when he reached them.

They didn't answer; instead they stared rather uncertainly at this imposing figure.

"Theodorus was right, you are both very much alike" he continued. "He said you are staying with Bronwyn, some family members I believe."

This was definitely a statement, not a question, and neither of them felt obliged to reply as there was something in his manner that unnerved them, even though he continued to smile.

"Hmm, interesting, very interesting," the dark-haired man continued, looking hard at Rachel and Gareth, undeterred by their silence. "Did Theodorus tell me Bronwyn was your aunt?"

"She isn't a real aunt, we just call her that," replied Gareth.

"Really," he replied, looking hard at Rachel. "Yet such a strong family resemblance," he said, reaching out to touch her hair, an action she recoiled from, stepping back quickly.

"And how long might you be staying? Theodorus did not say," he continued, ignoring her discomfort.

"Another couple of days that's all, we're here for a holiday," answered Gareth, taking an immediate dislike to the man.

"A holiday, yes, my son did mention this, something I find rather strange. Valonia is not a place where people come to take holidays!" He smiled again, but his eyes were dark and cold, and he looked expectantly at Gareth as though commanding an explanation.

He didn't receive one, as Gareth was more concerned with an acute burning sensation on his leg. He shifted uncomfortably as the man, not receiving any answer, turned his attention towards Rachel. Gareth put his hand in the pocket of his shorts and found the cause; the leather pouch was radiating such a heat that it was burning his leg through the thin fabric. He shuffled again uncomfortably, wishing the man would go, since he couldn't take the pouch out in front of him.

"We normally go on holiday with our father, this is more of a visit really, to stay with Bronwyn and Catherine," said Rachel defensively, realising the stranger was obviously still waiting for an answer to his question.

"Ah, so would Catherine be an aunt as well?" asked the man.

"Well, sort of," Rachel answered, glancing at Gareth, still silently shifting around awkwardly next to her. "But she's not a real aunt either."

"Hmm, interesting, well I shall not detain you any further," the stranger said pompously, with a swirl of his black cloak as he turned to walk away. Gareth was just breathing a sigh of relief, when the man turned round sharply and asked, "You said you go away with your father – is he accompanying you?"

"No," answered Rachel.

"And your mother, does she not holiday with you?"

"No, she's dead," replied Gareth, almost rudely, ignoring Rachel's look of surprise at his curt answer.

"Oh, I'm sorry, is this recent?"

"No," answered Gareth flatly again, wishing the man would leave as the burning against his thigh was so bad that he was now trying to hold the pocket away from his leg without drawing attention to it.

"Well, recent or not, you have my sympathy: I lost my own sister but a few months ago," said the man. Not receiving any answer from the twins, his false sympathetic smile quickly vanished. "Well, I shall bid you good day then." He finished abruptly and continued back up the jetty.

Gareth waited for as long as he could and then grabbed Rachel's arm, pulling her towards the beach.

"Quick, down behind those rocks by the cliff!" he said dragging her with him.

"What on earth is the matter with you?" she asked, as he ducked down behind a large rock onto the sand.

"Has he gone?"

"Yes."

"Thank goodness, I thought he would never go!" Gareth answered, throwing himself down on the sand, against the bottom of the cliff, tugging frantically at his pocket, while his sister stared at him in amazement.

"Oh, thank goodness!" he repeated in relief as he pulled the pouch out, dropping it unceremoniously on to the sand. "Any longer and it would have burnt a hole in my leg!"

"What on earth are you talking about?" asked Rachel incredulously.

"Feel it! It's red hot!" he answered, pointing at the offending pouch. "Where's yours?"

"In my bag, but I still don't understand."

"Well, get it out, and see if it's like this one?" he said crossly, explaining what had happened, as she looked in her bag for her stone.

The pouch she produced proved to be as cool as it had been when she put it in there. Gareth gingerly tipped his jewel out of its pouch, as it was still too hot to touch, and they noticed it was glowing strangely, its colour blazing brightly in the sun.

"That's amazing, how's it got so hot?" Rachel asked, prodding it quickly with one finger, "and why? When did you notice it?"

"As soon as that man started talking to us, it just got hotter and hotter!"

"So the old man was right, these stones really do something after all!" she carried on in amazement. "Maybe it was warning you. I had a really dreadful feeling as soon as he came up!"

"Do you know, that's the first time I've heard you say that here! At home you have bad feelings about things all the time, but here, it's been me telling you that things aren't right!"

"Weird, actually," she commented. "In fact it's been your favourite word since we've got here! You're right though; it's strange I haven't had any awful feelings here, well until we met him, that is! I've almost felt sort of comfortable here, as though we belong, even though there are so many odd things here, they almost don't feel odd! I can't explain it! It's like the old man who gave us the stones, I know that he is all right and we can trust him, but the man we've just met, he's different. There's something … evil about him."

"Evil, that's a bit strong isn't it? I know he was unpleasant, but evil?"

She didn't answer for a moment; she looked at the glowing green stone, which had cooled down sufficiently enough for her to hold, and stroke it absentmindedly.

"No, he's evil. He's cold and hard, he's killed people. He's the one they're all frightened of. He's the Black Knight," she said quietly, her eyes staring at the stone with a glazed expression.

"What are you on about? Here give that to me, I'm putting it away, you're freaking me out now!" her brother said taking the stone from her, putting it back in the pouch drawing up the string tightly. "What was all that Black Knight stuff about?"

"What?" she enquired, blinking rapidly.

"The Black Knight, you said he's the one they're frightened of."

"Did I?"

"Yes you did, don't you remember?"

"No I don't, and I'm feeling a bit dizzy now," she said sitting down again on the sand.

Gareth tried to push her for more answers, but she didn't seem to remember anything she'd said. He decided to leave her alone as she looked quite white, even though he was dying to find out what she'd meant. He had been quite concerned by the strange way she'd spoken when she was holding the stone, almost as though she was in a trance.

Rachel sat on the sand, leaning against the cliff, turning her face to the warmth of the sun with her eyes closed. Gareth sat quietly next to her, keeping a watchful eye out for the old man in case he passed on his way up the cliff. Some answers from him would be helpful, he thought wryly.

The peace was shattered by the arrival of the same large black bird again, which flapped down and took up residence on the rocks in front of them.

"Oh no, not you again!" said Gareth as the bird looked menacingly at him.

"What's the matter now?" asked Rachel quickly, opening her eyes.

"It's that damn bird again," he answered, as the bird cocked its head to one side, never taking its eyes of him, staring down at them unblinkingly from its high vantage point.

"That bird's giving me the creeps!" said Rachel eventually with a shudder. "I'm starting to get the same feeling I had, when that horrible man was here! It almost reminds me of him in some way."

"Come on, let's go before it starts hissing like before," he said crossly, and they left the bird sitting haughtily on its rocky perch and made their way up the jetty towards the village.

"I've never thought much about birds, till that grey one of yours knocked me off my bike, now there's this nasty black one! I'm beginning to think there must be some connection; other people don't meet up with weird birds wherever they go!" said Gareth thoughtfully.

"Don't be silly!" retorted Rachel. "My bird back home can't be connected to this place; it's miles away, it's just a coincidence."

"I didn't say it was!" said Gareth crossly. "I'm sure it is a coincidence, I was only saying that since that grey bird appeared at home, there have been a lot of strange things happening, that's all!"

They arrived back at the cottage to find it quiet. They shouted a loud 'Hello' as they went into the hall, but there was no answer.

"I wonder where they are?" said Gareth. "Look, Catherine's

door's open, the one down to the basement."

They peered through the open door, but all they could see was a small wooden staircase, which turned sharply, blocking out any view of the room below. Instead they were greeted by a strong overwhelmingly pungent smell that wafted up the stairs.

"That's really disgusting!" said Rachel, holding her nose.

"Come on, let's go and have a look!" said Gareth, starting down the steps.

As usual Rachel was hesitant, but found herself following him. She was just as curious as him really, but she didn't like the idea of getting caught.

"It's all right, she's not here," he said as he reached the bottom.

They found themselves in a large stone cellar, with an uneven slabbed floor. The walls were shelved and filled with an array of pots and jars, similar to those they had seen in the chemists. There was a big wooden table in the middle and in the corner a wood burning stove similar to the one in the kitchen, with a huge black pot bubbling away on it. The steamy vapours got stronger as they approached, and Rachel held her nose again.

"Well, that's obviously where the smell's coming from," she said pulling a face. "What on earth is she cooking?" she said, peering into the pot which contained a brown bubbling substance, with a grey film frothing on top.

All around the room there were herbs and leaves hanging upside down, neatly tied into bunches, and as they examined the many hanging objects they came across a dead rabbit and several black bats, neatly hung on metal hooks.

"What on earth does she do with them?" Rachel asked with a shudder.

"Search me," replied her brother, busily examining the piles of papers on the table that were surrounding a large wooden chopping board and several knives. Next to it were more jars half filled with strange coloured liquids and even stranger objects floating in them. Rachel looked warily at them, relieved to find that most contained herbs or leaves, but shuddered and stepped back when she noticed some more with beetles or insects floating in their murky depths. All were neatly labelled and dated.

"I hope this isn't what she sends to that chemist's shop, have you seen these?" she said, pointing to a jar with a large stopper, containing a green liquid. "There's a dead frog in this one!" she exclaimed in disgust.

Gareth was too preoccupied to answer; he had picked up a large, worn and slightly tatty black book.

"This is like the ones we found in the attic," he commented, as he turned the thick pages.

"What's in it?" enquired Rachel, trying to look over his shoulder.

"Don't know, it looks like a hand-written recipe book."

"Here let me have a look," said Rachel impatiently, pulling it away from him.

"Wait a minute, what's that on the cover?" she said noticing the worn gold letters.

"K.O.W.!" they both read out in unison.

"And look, there's a list of names inside, Catherine's is written at the bottom, underneath Margareta Trelawney, that's the name that was on Geraint's grave!" said Rachel. "She must have been their mother."

"Yes, I thought that, but I still think it's very strange that Catherine didn't know anything about the letters on the shops, even though they are exactly the same as the ones on the cover of her book," answered Gareth suspiciously. "Let's have a closer look at those recipes!"

"These aren't recipes; they're potions of some sort. Look at the ingredients, bark of elm, twisted barley, root of chestnut, cloves, dandelion leaves, root of primrose, belladonnas. That's deadly nightshade, it's poisonous!" said Rachel in horror. "Look there's laburnum and hemlock in these, I'm sure they're both poisonous as well!"

"Really, how do you know all this?"

"Well, you obviously weren't listening in biology, when we did plants!" she replied haughtily.

"So what are they for then? What does she do with them?" he asked.

"An infusion for hysteria and fits: A poultice for infections,

106

swellings and wounds," she read out solemnly. "They do sound like cures I suppose, hang on though! Listen to these at the back! A potion to induce obedience: A potion to induce a trance like state: An infusion to induce memory loss, to impair the nervous system, to induce vomiting, fitting and certain death!" she went pale as she read the last ones in horror. "These are spells! They aren't cures at all, they're spells like witches use!"

"Well, if they are, then I must be the witch!" said a loud voice behind them. They jumped guiltily as Catherine swept over to them.

"I knew this would happen," she said taking the book away from Rachel. "I told Bronwyn, but she wouldn't listen! I told her it wouldn't be long before you both started meddling in things that don't concern you. You were told not to come down here!"

"We're really sorry Catherine, we wondered where you were and we came down to look for you," said Gareth lamely.

"Were you, or were you not, told not to come down here?" she asked again, her face red with anger. "I hope you haven't touched anything."

"No, no we haven't, honestly," said Rachel, imagining a black pointed hat on Catherine's head, thinking it wouldn't look out of place at all with the rest of her long black flowing attire, and for a moment the strange ingredients in the black book rushed into her mind. Was Catherine a witch? she wondered, shrinking away from her nervously. Gareth must have been thinking the same, she deduced, as he had gone very quiet and was shuffling nervously next to her.

"Why oh why, couldn't you just do as you were told and leave well alone?"

"What are you going to do with us?" asked Rachel in a small voice, as she glanced towards the wooden door, which she noticed that Catherine had closed.

"Do with you?" said Catherine in surprise. "Do with you? What on earth do you think I'm going to do? On the other hand, I suppose I could always turn you both into a couple of toads, or bats, bats would be quite good!"

"Oh no please don't do that, we won't tell anyone about what we've seen!" pleaded Rachel, now completely terrified.

"Oh, for heaven's sake you don't really think I'm a witch, do you?" answered Catherine.

There was no answer from the twins and she sighed heavily. "You two have got the most vivid imaginations!"

"Well, what about all of this?" said Gareth pointing at the array of strange potions. "And these?" he continued, pointing to the strange ingredients all around them. "What are we supposed to think?"

Catherine sighed again. "I suppose you'll be looking for my broomstick next!" she declared. "Oh for goodness sake I was joking! I don't have one, and I don't have a black cat either!" she continued as she noticed Rachel looking fearfully around her.

"All right, I knew it would come to this, what do you want to know?" she said, pulling out a stool from under the table, sitting down on it with another heavy sigh, motioning for them to do the same.

"All this is weird," said Gareth with a sweep of his arm, "and you've got a book of spells here with your name inside the cover."

"It's not a book of spells; it's a book of cures, it's very old, and has been passed down from generation to generation. The cures would be referred to where you live as homeopathic, in other words they are all natural remedies, made from herbs and plants, and they have worked for generations here to heal the people of this village. It's a knowledge that has been passed down from mother to daughter for hundreds of years."

"So how do you explain the ones at the back of the book?" asked Gareth. "They don't sound like cures at all, quite the opposite in fact."

"No, I don't suppose they do, but with all medicines, if not used correctly, they will cause harm. Your medicines are exactly the same; do they not have warnings on the labels?"

"Yes they do, but we don't have instructions on them, telling us how to make them do the opposite," declared Gareth adamantly.

"As I said the book is hundreds of years old and as to whether the remedies are used for good or bad, well, that's down to the person who is administering them! Everyone who's used this book has added their own remedies, ones they have found to work."

"So if there had been a witch using the book, she would have written down the ones that caused harm?" asked Rachel.

"If she wanted to, or she may have included them as a warning. Similar recipes and plants have been used for centuries, and I'm sure there may have been times when they have been used inappropriately. There was also a time when many women were branded as witches and burnt at the stake, for using these plants to heal people."

"Witches?" asked Rachel, in a small voice. "Here?"

"I'm talking generally, not so much here, but all over the country, you have to understand that through ignorance, anything that people didn't understand was deemed as magic," replied Catherine.

"You sound as though you're defending them, the witches I mean?" said Gareth suspiciously.

"I'm not defending anyone, I am merely explaining how things got misconstrued in the past!" she answered coolly.

"So what about the letters on the front cover, K.O.W." interrupted Gareth, steering the conversation back to the answers they had been looking for.

"K.O.W. stands for 'Keeper of the Ways,'" she replied. "We keep the ways here, our ways, the old ways, and the old traditions. The plaques on the shops are the same. They keep to our ways. They grow our food, they bake or cook for us, they make, build or repair things for us, in the same ways that they have since our village was built! We don't get involved with the rest of the world, with cars, televisions and phones, we have no need to. We choose to live this way, and this is why we don't like strangers here, we don't want to change, do you understand?"

Gareth and Rachel nodded silently in reply.

"But what about the letters, K.O.P. on the books in the attic then, what do they stand for?" asked Gareth suddenly remembering them.

"No, they would have had the same letters, K.O.W. for 'Keeper of the Ways,' you must have been mistaken," Catherine replied firmly. "The light in the attic isn't that good and the books are very old and worn. It would be an easy mistake to make."

The twins looked at each other but Gareth didn't challenge their aunt again.

"All right, we'll say no more about this then," Catherine concluded getting up.

Dismissed, the twins crossed the room towards the door, but Gareth turned back again still determined to find out more.

"So who is Geraint then?" he asked. Rachel froze and Catherine went white.

"Who told you about him?" she gasped, sitting back down on her stool again.

"There was a boy by the beach," he mumbled, feeling slightly uncomfortable now as he didn't want to involve Johnny and get him into trouble.

"Oh, Theodorus no doubt?" she immediately surmised, without him saying anything else. Gareth shuffled and nodded, ignoring his sister's raised eyebrows. Well, let the obnoxious Theodorus take the blame, they didn't owe him anything anyway, he thought, feeling relieved that Catherine had jumped to this conclusion.

"Geraint was my younger brother and Bronwyn's twin. He died very tragically in an accident on the cliffs. We don't talk about it, and I would rather you didn't mention this to Bronwyn, she gets very upset about it," she said sadly. "Geraint's death was a tragedy to us all. Bronwyn misses him dreadfully, she wasn't here when it happened and she somehow blames herself. Maybe she thinks she could have prevented it in some way, I don't know, but nevertheless I would like you to respect my wishes and not talk about it. As for Theodorus, that boy is nothing but trouble; stay away from him."

"Who is he?" asked Rachel.

"Twedwr or Theodorus as he is known, is Mordred's son, they live at the manor."

"I think we may have met his father today by the beach," said Gareth.

"You met Mordred, did he speak to you?" asked Catherine, going even whiter, if that was possible.

"Yes, he asked a lot of questions, I didn't like him," said Rachel.

"What sort of questions?" Catherine asked immediately.

"Why we were here, how long we were staying, that sort of thing," answered Gareth. "Oh, and he was very interested as to whether you and Bronwyn were our real aunts."

110

"What did you tell him?"

"The truth of course, that you weren't," replied Rachel.

"Mordred is a very powerful man, he has a lot of connections outside the village and he is also particularly unpleasant. I would suggest that you stay well away from him and his son while you're here," said Catherine.

"That's fine by me, I didn't like either of them," said Rachel as they continued up the stairs. It wasn't until Gareth's bedroom door closed behind them a few minutes later, that Rachel breathed a big sigh of relief.

"Whatever possessed you to ask her about Geraint, did you see how white she went? Still, I suppose she has at least cleared up all the mysteries here," she finished.

"Oh, no she hasn't," he replied firmly. "There's no explanation as to why we're walking around with two enormous gems in pouches that have K.O.P. written on them, given to us by a total stranger to protect us from something! One of which glows and nearly gives me third-degree burns, as some sort of warning when we're talking to the very man that she is telling us to stay away from! And that business about us making a mistake about the letters on the books in the attic, well I know what I saw, bad light or not! No, none of it makes any sense at all! She's definitely hiding something!"

Chapter Ten
Quicksand and Lightning

When they went down to dinner, it soon became apparent that Catherine had told Bronwyn she had found them in her room and they were treated to mild reprimand again over the dinner table. However, it was also apparent, that Catherine hadn't told her sister about the whole conversation, as Bronwyn made no reference to her brother, or the fact that they had thought Catherine a witch, although she did reiterate her sisters warning about staying away from Mordred.

The evening became more relaxed over several board games, and when they eventually went to bed, Rachel went off to sleep quite quickly, relieved that peace had been restored. Gareth however, tossed and turned for a long while, remembering the day's events, and the more he thought about it, the less convinced he was by Catherine's explanations. After all, why would she deliberately lie about the letters on the books upstairs? She was very defensive about the subject of witches as well, he decided, as he heard the old clock downstairs chime again. He finally went to sleep, still unconvinced and still undecided as to whether it would be a good idea to try and find out more, or to play safe and just try to ignore it all for the last few days.

The following day their morning ride took his mind off things.

Abigail let them take the horses down to the beach where they had an exhilarating ride, splashing through the gently rolling waves, cantering along the sand right to the end of the beach and then back again to the fishing boats, where there was a long queue of ladies haggling over the mornings catch.

They were both in high spirits afterwards when they walked down to the village, where they met Johnny outside the sweet shop, looking very pleased with himself. He told them he had finished his chores early so he could have the afternoon off.

"I likes to get up really early and get everything done, so as I can go up top and look at the boats sometimes," he said, motioning towards the high cliffs. "It'll be a good day for boats, today; I likes to see the boats I do! I've got these!" he showed them an old pair of binoculars. "I can see for miles with these, I can! You can borrow them if you likes, if you're up there."

"Thanks, we might see you up there later," said Gareth, as Johnny headed off, proudly clutching his sweets and his binoculars.

They wandered round the village for a while: it was very quiet and a lot of the shops were closed. They walked along the beach and then headed towards the cliff path. The sun was warm now and Rachel was regretting wearing her denim jacket as they started on the incline.

"Race you to the top!" said Gareth sprinting off.

"Oh no, I can't be bothered, you always win anyway!" she called after him, and carried on at a leisurely pace, watching her brother disappear round the bend in the path.

As Gareth got further up, he realised how far behind she was; he grinned and ducked down behind some large bushes. He hid there, chuckling to himself when he heard his sister plodding past, knowing that she would carry on right to the top, thinking she was following him, and have to come all the way back when she found he wasn't there. He waited long enough for her to be out of sight, and then came out of hiding, sitting down on the grassy bank to wait for her. He chuckled again, knowing how cross she would be when she got to the top and realised he wasn't there.

Boy was she going to be mad, he thought, as he leant back on the grassy bank. Eventually he started to get bored: she was taking an awful long time, and he'd been there for ages! Even at her slow pace, she ought to be back by now.

Eventually after what seemed like an eternity, he could hear footsteps. He leant forward in anticipation and was surprised to see Johnny coming towards him.

"Is Rachel still up there?" he asked.

"Rachel, no I haven't seen her. I've been on me own up there. Saw lots of boats though, I did!" he grinned, gesturing with the binoculars. "You can borrow them if you like. I said you could, remember?"

"You must have passed her on the path, are you sure you haven't seen her?" Gareth asked incredulously.

"No, I just told you, I was on me own!" replied Johnny thrusting the binoculars at Gareth. "Here, you borrow them, I don't mind, honest!"

Gareth took them absent-mindedly. He still couldn't believe that Rachel wasn't at the cliff top; there was nowhere else she could have gone. The path only went one way.

"You're sure you didn't pass her anywhere?" he asked disbelievingly.

"No, I said didn't I? Last time I seen her, she was with you by the sweet shop! Better go now, still got some chores to do before tea. I'll see you tomorrow," Johnny said, as he started to walk down the hill.

Gareth stared up the path, a feeling of panic creeping over him. Where was she? She had to be up there: he'd seen her walk past. He looked down and realised he was still holding the binoculars, they would have to wait, he had to go and find her. He started up the path in the direction she had gone, with all sorts of thoughts racing into his head.

Had she fallen off the cliff? Had Johnny pushed her off? No, he wouldn't do that! He was being stupid, but where was she? He was really worried now, and started calling her name. The thoughts got worse; if anything had happened to her it would be his fault for playing his stupid prank. Suddenly he remembered the gypsy's warning, telling them to always stay together, reinforced by the same message from the old man, and what had he done? He'd hidden and let her wander off on her own! As he rushed up the path, calling her frantically now, Johnny's warning sprang to mind as well, 'bad things happen to twins here,' he had said. Oh, why had he been so stupid?

Gareth reached the steps leading down to the point and stopped, out of breath. Surely Rachel hadn't gone down there! It was the only other place she could have gone if Johnny hadn't seen her on the path. He deliberated as to whether to carry on up to the top of the cliffs or go down the steps to the point. He called out again listening carefully, scanning the rocks below for any sign of her. He thought he heard something and remembering he was still holding Johnny's binoculars, he quickly held them up to his eyes and scanned the rocks again. He still couldn't see her, but for some reason he felt compelled to go down there, even though this was probably the last place she would go on her own. He started off down the steep steps, almost missing his footing in his urgency.

Halfway down he thought that he could hear something again, and quickened his pace, shouting her name. He scrambled on to the rocks and heard it again.

"Help, help, oh please help me!" It was very faint, but it was definitely Rachel! But where was she? He clambered across the rocks in the direction of the next bay, but he still couldn't see her.

"Rachel, where are you?" he shouted frantically. "Rachel?"

"Gareth, oh thank God! I'm over here, quick, please hurry! I'm over here!" she sobbed.

"Where are you, I still can't see you?" he shouted, scrambling over the rocks as fast as he could. "Where are you, are you hurt?" he shouted in the direction of her voice.

"I'm stuck! Gareth I'm in the quicksand!"

Finally he saw her as he climbed over the last rock.

"Stop!" she yelled, halting him, just as he was about to jump on to the sand. "Don't come any closer, you'll get stuck as well, that's where it starts!" He peered over and could see that the sand was up over her knees and she was terrified.

"Oh get me out, please get me out, I can't move!"

"Keep still! I'll have to get help!"

"There isn't time!" she cried. "It's sucking me under, every time I move! You've got to get me out now!"

"All right, all right, keep as still as you can and I'll try to reach you," he shouted back, knowing she was too far for him to reach her without stepping onto the sand himself.

He got as close as he could and stretched out his hand, but he was nowhere near close enough. He tried to lie across the rocks, edging out as far as he could, but he was still a long way from her.

"Gareth please?" she sobbed again, as the sand crept up further.

This was hopeless, he thought and looked around the rocks frantically for a piece of driftwood, or anything he could reach her with, but there was nothing! So he lay down again on the rocks and slid forward as far as he could again, stretching out his arm towards her. To his dismay he still couldn't get close enough.

"It's no good," he said. "I just can't reach you; I'll have to get help!"

"No, no, don't leave me!" she begged, as she slid further in, the tears running down her cheeks. She was so upset and frightened that every movement she had made had sucked her under further, She was so distressed by the quicksand that she hadn't even noticed the burning sensation against her chest, until it became so strong that she automatically put her hand up to her top pocket and felt the hardness of the stone, its heat blazing against her.

It was only then that she felt a pulsing sensation coming from the jewel and she pulled it out. As she held the pouch, a feeling of calmness came over her, and the fear left. She knew then, with a strong certainty, that she was going to get out.

Another thought came into her head as she held the pouch tightly in her hand. It was as though someone was saying 'Use the stones! Use the stones!' over and over again. Mesmerised, she took the bright red gem out of the pouch and suddenly she knew what to do.

"Gareth, quickly, get your stone out!"

"What?" he asked incredulously.

"Just do it, just do as I say," she said with a note of authority in her voice.

For a moment he looked surprised, but when she shouted again, he quickly fumbled shakily with his own pouch, even though he had no idea why, until he was holding the green jewel. He looked back at her dumbly for more instructions, to see she was holding her own stone with her arm outstretched, the tapered end pointed directly at him.

"Now, hold it out and point it at me!" she commanded. "Try and point it at my stone!" He did as she instructed, trying to line up the tapered end towards hers, he felt the emerald starting to pulse in his hand and stretched out his arm as far as he could. As he lined it up, the pulsing becoming so strong he had to hold it with two hands, then suddenly, what looked like a bolt of lightning shot out from both the stones, sparking as it connected in the middle, causing a sound like a fire cracker going off. They were both immediately enveloped in a bright white light, connected by a silver beam that shone like a laser between the two stones. Gradually the silver beam solidified, becoming a thin, hard, shining metal rod, which they were both holding.

"Pull!" she screamed at him.

He did, as hard as he could! He pulled and pulled with a strength he didn't know he possessed, until the sand parted in ripples like water in a pond and he could feel her being dragged towards him. He pulled relentlessly until he had hauled her as far as the rocks, where she heaved herself to safety, collapsing onto the rock next to him. There was a loud crack like a firework, which threw them back, as the white light seemed to explode all around them and in another bright flash the rod they were holding disappeared leaving only the two glistening stones in their hands. The rod was gone, the light was gone, and they were left on the rocks with only the sound of the waves and the seagulls.

Rachel was sobbing and shaking violently, and he put his arms around her instinctively, something he wouldn't normally do, under any circumstances!

"Thank God you're all right!" he said, with relief.

"Oh Gareth, I thought I was going to be swallowed up by that sand until I died!"

"I know, I'm sorry it was all my fault!"

"No it wasn't, it was that blasted bird's fault! Gareth I really thought I was going to die there, in that sand. Thank goodness you came to look for me, otherwise …" She started crying again, the sobs racking her body.

He looked at his tearful sister, still trembling from head to foot, the muddy residue of sand all over her legs, with one shoe missing, and the reality of what had just happened hit him.

"I don't believe what I've just seen!" he said in amazement. "The stones, they saved you. I would never have got you out otherwise!" He looking down at the cool unassuming gem he was holding, in disbelief. "How on earth did that happen, and what was that light? Where did that come from?"

His sister was far too distraught to answer, so he put his own stone back in its pouch, safely restoring it to the depths of his pocket and then prised hers out of her hand and did the same, putting it back in her top pocket.

"I'm really sorry," he said shamefacedly. "I hid from you, it was meant to be a joke! I thought you'd go up the cliff and come back again when you couldn't find me, but when Johnny said you weren't there, I was worried sick! I'm really sorry!" he confessed miserably.

"It wasn't your fault, it was Mordred and that awful bird. It hissed and pecked at me. I was so frightened!" she started crying again.

"Mordred! The bird?" he said not understanding.

"Yes, that nasty black thing, it flew at me and pecked at me until I went back and back over the rocks until I was in the quicksand. I was trying to get away from it!"

This was all too much to take in. Gareth had no idea what Rachel was talking about, and decided not to pursue it, as he was still trying to get to grips with what had happened with the stones. Suddenly there was a crash behind them and a sprinkling of cold salt water rained down on them, as a large wave boomed against the rocks.

'The waves!' thought Gareth in panic, remembering Bronwyn's warning about the tide there. He turned sharply to see that the waves were much closer than before and the pointed edge of rocks had already disappeared in a deluge of foaming spray. Even the rocks behind them were covered in froth as another wave splashed against them.

"Rachel we've got to start back, the tide's coming in!" He said in

118

a panic. She didn't appear to be listening, so he grabbed her arms and pulled her up.

"Rachel come on, we've got to go!" she was still trembling but he managed to get her to start climbing back over the rocks. It was slow going as she only had one shoe and some of the rocks were sharp. He kept glancing round fearfully as the waves were getting closer all the time and even lapping around their feet occasionally, when particularly large waves sent the water rushing through the crevices between the rocks. Eventually they reached the safety of the beach, but Gareth still wouldn't stop until they reached the steps where he finally breathed a big sigh of relief.

"Come on, let's go, you can rest on the bench," he said. Rachel was still looking shaken and dazed; she had been limping along with him, clutching at him for support, the tears still pouring down her cheeks. He was still worried that if she stopped now, he wouldn't be able to get her up the steep steps. It took him a long time to get her up to the cliff path, as she was still shivering violently. Eventually they reached the safety of the bench where she collapsed, crying again.

He sat down next to her with a shudder, realising the danger they'd been in, first from the quicksand and then from the tide, lapping at their heels as he had urged her across the rocks. For a short while they sat in silence getting their breath back, each reflecting on the unbelievable events of the last hour.

"I know I was wrong and I shouldn't have hidden from you, but whatever possessed you to go down to the point, and what were you thinking about going on to the next beach? I can't believe you'd forgotten what Bronwyn said about the quicksand!" said Gareth eventually in disbelief.

"I didn't forget about it, I only went because Mordred told me you'd gone down there, and I was worried that you'd forgotten about it!" she replied indignantly.

"Mordred said I'd gone there?" he questioned, astounded. "I haven't even seen him since yesterday! I don't understand any of this, what exactly happened after I left you?" he asked.

"Well, after you disappeared like a marathon runner, I walked up the path after you. I got as far as the steps to the point where

Mordred was coming down towards me. He was blocking the path and I didn't want to talk to him on my own!" she said tearful again. "He frightens me!"

"So what did he say?" Gareth urged.

"He asked me why I was on my own, and I said I was following you, up to the top of the cliffs. He said he'd spoken to you, and you'd asked him to tell me you were going to the beach past the point."

"He's a liar, I didn't even see him, let alone speak to him!" Gareth said raising his voice in anger.

"Well, I didn't know that, but since there's only one track there, if he was coming down he would have had to have passed you, so I believed him. Anyway, I was worried to death, and I asked him about the quicksand. He told me it was safe for quite a long way along the beach and the quicksand was right out where the waves were. He said it was safe by the rocks and on the sandy part by the cliffs and that you'd asked him the same thing before you went down the steps."

"He was lying! I was never up there: I was by the big bushes, right by the first bend. I didn't even go any further than that!"

"Anyway, I went down the steps and on to the rocks," she continued half sobbing in between breaths. "I climbed right over the rocks and looked down the beach, to see if I could see you, but I didn't want to go on to the sand, I was still frightened about the quicksand. There was no sign of you on the beach, so I turned back and was crossing the rocks again, when I saw this huge black shape flying towards me. I'm sure it came straight off the cliffs! It hit the side of my face, flew round and came at me again and again. It pecked at my arm each time it passed, look!" she said, showing Gareth several rips in her jacket sleeve, which were tinged with blood.

"I couldn't go back, it wouldn't let me, in the end I was forced right to the edge of the rocks, where I lost my balance and stepped onto the sand. It came down once more, and I stepped back several times to get away from it, then it stopped, and sat on the rocks, just looking at me, before it eventually flew off across the sea. I was so relieved, but then when I tried to go back towards the rocks, I couldn't, I was stuck, I couldn't move my feet at all, and the more I tried to move them I sank down even further! Oh Gareth, I really thought I would be swallowed up and I would never go home, I thought I'd never see Dad or you again!"

She started crying and the violent shaking started again, as she relived the horror of her experience.

"Look it's all right, you're safe now," Gareth said.

"I know," she said with a big sniff, "but if you hadn't come when you did, I would never have got out!"

"Well, I couldn't have got you out, if it hadn't have been for the stones," said Gareth quietly. "How on earth did you know what to do with them?"

"I don't know," she said, calming down instantly at the mention of them. "Something told me. Something inside me told me exactly what to do, and once I was holding it, I wasn't frightened any more, I can't explain it!"

"How strange, but thank goodness for the jewels!" he said firmly. "I still can't work out this Mordred thing though. He would have had to pass Johnny or me, at some point. It's a single narrow path there, and he didn't! I didn't see him and Johnny didn't mention him, he said there was no-one up at the top of the cliffs. He would have had to pass one of us somewhere on the path, and why did he lie about seeing me? It's almost as though he sent you down there deliberately, but why would he do that?"

"I don't know, I don't even want to think about him," said Rachel in a tired voice.

"There must be some connection between Mordred and that awful bird. If you think about it, we've only ever seen it when we've seen him. That seems odd, maybe the bird belongs to him," he murmured thoughtfully.

"Belongs to him?" asked Rachel.

"Yes, you know how people train hawks and kestrels, maybe the bird is Mordred's, and he can get it to do things?"

"What, things like attacking me?"

"Possibly, it's just an idea and it would make sense. Mordred lies to you, says I've gone down there, knowing you would go to look for me, then he sends the bird down to attack you, so you fall into

121

the quicksand!"

"I hope you're wrong!" she answered, the tears starting again. "That would mean he was trying to kill me!"

"Well, it was only an idea, take no notice," Gareth said, concerned as she started shaking again. "Come on, do you think you can make it back to the cottage?" he asked, realising again that he still had to get her back, and for once, he would be quite happy to hand the responsibility over to his aunts.

Rachel nodded, and they started walking slowly back down the path again. She seemed to get whiter and shakier with every step they took, and by the time they reached the jetty, Gareth was beginning to wonder if she would get as far as the cottage without passing out on him.

When they reached the wall she sat down again to rest and Gareth noticed a buggy pulled by a big black horse trotting past the last shop.

"I'm sure that's Rufus, pulling that cart," he said. "Yes it is, it's Johnny too. I'll get him to help us!"

Gareth dashed over and jumped out in front of the big black horse waving his arms frantically.

"What's the matter?" asked Johnny, pulling the horse up quickly.

"Oh I'm so glad to see you, could you take us back to the cottage?" asked Gareth.

"Course I can, climb in, what's the matter with Rachel?" Johnny asked, jumping down in concern when he saw her dishevelled appearance.

"She's had a bit of a fright, she got caught in the quicksand, and I've got to get her back," replied Gareth.

The farm boy helped Rachel into the buggy, and produced a blanket, wrapping it round her shoulders gently. It smelt strongly of horses and was covered in bits of straw, but she clutched it round her gratefully and sat back in the seat.

Gareth climbed up next to him in the front, and Rufus started off at an even, slow pace, his big hooves clopping reassuringly.

"Johnny, did you see Mordred on the cliff path?" asked Gareth quietly.

"No, there was no-one up there I told you that, the only person I seen was you."

"Has Mordred got a big black bird?"

"Black bird?" said Johnny as they pulled up next to the cottage. "So you've seen it as well!"

"Yes, why, what do you know about it?" Gareth asked.

"I'm not supposed to talk about it, but I saw a big black bird just before I had me accident. It kept flying at us, me and Rufus that is. That's why we stopped, old Rufus, he was getting right upset by it he was. So I pulled him up and we stopped under the cliff, that's when the rocks started falling on us."

"Was that the black shape that you saw, after the rocks hit you?"

"No, the shape was a person, I thinks, but I don't really know, I couldn't see too well, but I knows it wasn't the bird I saw before!" Johnny answered adamantly.

"Thanks," said Gareth as they helped Rachel down. "Look, do me a favour, don't tell anyone else about this."

"No, no, course I won't. Our secret!" he said touching the side of his nose.

"Yes, and thanks again," said Gareth, as the farm boy climbed back up into his seat.

"Listen," said Johnny, leaning down, "I knows everyone thinks I'm stupid and slow, but I tried to warn you before. Bad things happen to twins here, or one of them at least, and if you've seen the bird, then Mordred is out to get you. He won't stop at that. Your sister's lucky to still be alive, like me!" he added chillingly.

"Thanks for the lift – and the warning," said Gareth solemnly, grateful that Rachel hadn't heard it.

He waved to Johnny as he left, and turned his attention back to the cottage doorway, where a worried Bronwyn had seen the state of her niece and was obviously going to require an explanation of some sort.

Gareth took a deep breath and followed them in, deciding that maybe it was best to tell them the truth this time. Well, most of it, anyway.

Chapter Eleven
Flickering lights and black silhouettes

Bronwyn called Catherine and helped Rachel into the cottage, and even though she was still clutching the blanket round her, Bronwyn noticed the mud and missing shoe straight away.

"What on earth has happened?" she asked Gareth.

"We had a bit of an accident, Rachel was attacked by a bird and ended up in the quicksand by the point," he told his astonished aunt. "Well, it's a bit of a long story really," he added awkwardly, wondering exactly how much he should tell them.

Catherine appeared, and the two women fussed around Rachel, taking her into the kitchen, where once the blanket was removed, the ripped, blood stained jacket immediately caused them to question him again.

"How's she done this?" asked Bronwyn, sounding unintentionally accusing.

Gareth explained briefly about Rachel's meeting with Mordred, after he had hidden from her, and that he had told her to look for him down by the point, where the bird had attacked her. He finished by telling them that he had gone to look for her and had dragged her out of the quicksand. He decided not to complicate things further by mentioning the stones, and the part they'd played in her rescue.

There was a silence as Rachel removed her jacket, revealing

the wounds on her arms and shoulders where the bird's beak had ripped through the material, leaving long wounds in her skin, which fortunately, had already stopped bleeding.

Catherine went back down to her room to get some of her remedies, while Bronwyn sat her down at the table, administering a cup of warm sweet tea. Gareth sat down next to them, feeling slightly redundant, and he noticed that Bronwyn looked almost as shocked as his sister. He was quite relieved to be back in the safety of the familiar kitchen, with his aunts taking the responsibility away from him.

Bronwyn replaced the jacket with a soft shawl, and Catherine reappeared with two bottles and some cotton wool. She poured one out onto a spoon which Rachel swallowed dutifully, the other she poured onto the cotton wool, which she applied to the livid red wounds.

"I will take her up for a lie down," said Catherine. "The draught I have just given her will help the shock, and the antiseptic will stop any infection," she said, as she led Rachel upstairs.

"Thanks Catherine," said Bronwyn. "No, you can stay here!" she finished sharply, as Gareth made to follow them. "I want to hear exactly what happened again!"

"Don't be too hard on the boy, he looks as though he's had quite a shock as well," said Catherine, pausing in the doorway. "Besides, if it's anyone's fault it's yours, not his!"

Her last remark, as she led his sister away, silenced Bronwyn, who busied herself making another cup of tea, leaving Gareth feeling very awkward.

"What did she mean?" he asked eventually, as Bronwyn put two mugs down on the table.

"Maybe she's right, maybe I shouldn't have brought you here!" Bronwyn answered thoughtfully, ignoring his question. "I just thought you could have a holiday, I didn't think that a week here would be a problem."

"I don't understand. Why shouldn't we come and stay with you, what's wrong with that?" asked Gareth.

"Well, there isn't anything wrong with it, apart from the fact that people here are a bit strange in their ways and don't encourage visitors. They like to keep the village hidden away from the outside world. We lead a very different life here, and they are very protective about it."

"But most of the people here have been really kind to us, especially Abigail and her family at the farm. We did have a lot of strange looks at first, but after that it's been fine, in fact the only people who haven't been nice, are Mordred and his horrible son!"

"Well, Mordred's the problem really, but I didn't think he would even be here."

"Well, I think he sent Rachel down to the point deliberately, and I think he's got that bird trained to do things for him," said Gareth, recounting the story again.

"I don't know anything about any bird, I'm sure that was just a coincidence," answered Bronwyn. "I'm sure Mordred didn't mean for her to go that far, he knows about the quicksand, there must have been a misunderstanding of some sort," she finished looking uneasy.

Gareth looked at her astounded. He couldn't understand why she appeared to be so reluctant to accept Mordred's part in it, even though Catherine had implied that he was someone to be frightened of, when she warned them to stay away from him.

He looked at his aunt suspiciously and noticed that her hands were shaking as she lifted her cup to her lips.

"Bronwyn, Mordred lied, he told Rachel he'd spoken to me, and I hadn't even seen him!"

"I'm sure there were crossed wires somehow. The main thing is that you're both all right," Bronwyn replied firmly, much to Gareth's amazement. "You've only got another couple of days here, and I'll make sure that I come everywhere with you. It'll be fun, I had intended to spend the next two days with you anyway, and you can still go riding, we'll have a nice time and make up for today," she replied with an unconvincing brightness, and for a moment Gareth saw fear in her eyes. He knew in that instant that she was as frightened of Mordred as his sister was.

He didn't say anything, but he was convinced that she was still covering something up. It dawned on him that she probably did believe him after all but wasn't going to admit to it, in case she had to divulge their secrets. The ones that everyone seemed so hell bent on them not discovering.

After all, why would Mordred want to try and kill Rachel? None of it made sense, but Bronwyn was right, they were due to go home soon, and they ought to be safe enough if she was with them. He was about to ask her some more questions when Catherine reappeared and announced that Rachel was having a nice hot bath followed by a sleep.

"She'll be right as rain when she wakes up," she finished.

Rachel reappeared rather drowsily before dinner, and seemed to have recovered from her earlier ordeal completely. They all sat down to dinner and the subject wasn't mentioned again, in fact it appeared to Gareth that the conversation was deliberately steered away from it, even though it must have remained on everyone's mind.

Afterwards, Catherine produced a pack of playing cards and taught them how to play several games, other than their usual snap. Again, it all seemed slightly false to Gareth, it was almost too light hearted after their revelations, but Rachel looked quite unconcerned, as she and their aunts laughed over a particularly bad hand. Everyone seemed to be enjoying it apart from him, so he decided it was best to say nothing and join in the charade.

They finished the game of cards and Bronwyn went into the kitchen to make them all some cocoa.

"What's that noise? It sounds like the church bell, can you hear it?" Gareth asked, listening to the slow monotonous 'dong, dong, dong,' in the distance.

"Yes it is!" said Catherine jumping up, the cards scattering everywhere.

"It's a bit late for church isn't it: it's almost dark?" he asked surprised.

"No, it's not for the church; it means we have to go to a meeting. I must tell Bronwyn, she can't have heard it."

Bronwyn obviously had, as she entered the room, the cocoa forgotten, looking extremely agitated.

"He's called a meeting, we'll have to go," stated Catherine.

"Yes, I know," her sister answered, as the bell continued ringing in a tuneless, steady monotonous tone, drifting eerily on the breeze.

"What meeting?" asked Gareth. "Have we got to go as well?"

"No you can stay here, it's only for the villagers, they ring the bell to tell us there's an emergency meeting, so that we can all attend," answered Bronwyn.

"What even at this time of night?" asked Gareth, feeling yet another mystery unfolding.

"Oh, they ring the bell at any time, so the whole village is present if an important decision has to be made; it's just the way we do things here," she said calmly, even though Catherine was looking nervous and her own face had paled significantly.

"Don't worry, we'll go down to the village hall, it'll be a fuss about nothing as usual, and we'll be back before you know it. You'll have to finish the cocoa yourselves though I'm afraid; I should take it up to bed with you."

There was a loud knock at the door, which almost made them jump out of their skins.

Catherine looked nervously at her sister.

"I expect that'll be Betsy, bless her, they always stop off with the buggy and pick us up when this happens," said Bronwyn.

"I'll go and see," Catherine replied apprehensively.

They heard Betsy's loud cheery voice as Catherine opened the door. "The buggy's outside, we thought you'd like a lift."

"Thanks we're just coming," they heard Catherine answer. "I'll just get Bronwyn. We'd better go," she said handing a long black cloak to her sister.

"We won't be long, lock the door after us and don't open it to anyone," Bronwyn said as she put the cloak on, pulling the hood up as she left. "This is very good of you Betsy," they heard her say to the homely farm lady in the hallway.

"Well, I said to Jim, they won't want to be walking all the way up to the pass at this time of night. Lord sakes! What on earth does he want at this hour? Jim's got to be up at daybreak to see to the cows! Mighty inconsiderate I'd say!" they heard Betsy continue as Catherine followed her sister out, in an identical, long flowing black cloak.

"Oh I know, we were just about to go to bed! And you're quite right; I wasn't relishing the idea of trekking all the way up there!"

128

Bronwyn answered, as she shut the heavy door behind them.

"What on earth is going on now? What do you make of it, it sounds a bit odd to me meetings at this time of night?" said Gareth.

"Who knows, it was nice of Betsy to stop and give them a lift though," answered Rachel.

"Hang on a minute; didn't Betsy just say they wouldn't want to walk all the way up to the pass?"

"Yes, she did, we'd better make sure the doors are locked like they said," answered Rachel, going into the hall, pulling the heavy bolt across.

"I'm sure Bronwyn said they were going to the village hall."

"Yes she did," answered Rachel, oblivious to the significance of her words.

"Well, the village hall is nowhere near the pass, so where exactly have they gone?"

"I don't know, does it matter?" she answered calmly. "I think we should do what they said and just go up to bed."

"Rachel, are you feeling all right?" asked Gareth as she turned off the lantern in the kitchen.

"Why wouldn't I be?" she answered, closing the door.

"Well, you were in a right state this afternoon, yet since you've got up, it's almost as though it never happened!"

For a moment she looked confused. "I had a sleep this afternoon, I can't imagine why, I don't think I've ever done that in my life!"

"Don't you remember what happened this afternoon, with quicksand and the stones?"

"I sort of remember something, but I'm not sure what, it's very hazy, in fact I thought I'd dreamt it," she answered, looking slightly dazed.

Gareth stared at her in horror, Catherine had given her one of her potions; he remembered her saying the brown liquid was for shock and that it would help her sleep. What on earth was in it? Surely she hadn't given her a potion from the back of the book they'd seen? What did it say? He thought hard trying to remember the passage his sister had been reading out loud. 'To induce memory loss,' that was it! He looked worriedly at his sister, since she certainly didn't seem to remember much about the afternoon, had Catherine given her something to make her forget it altogether? The thought sent a chill through him.

He took the mugs of cocoa upstairs, as Rachel had already gone up, intent on doing as they had been instructed. He found her in her room looking out of the window.

"That's strange, come and have a look," she said. "There are loads of flickering lights all up the track to the pass."

He put the mugs down and joined her at the window.

"Look at the top of the pass, it looks as though it's lit up, you can see an orange glow up there!" she said.

"Strange," he answered, straining to see where the glow was coming from. "Hang on, I've just remembered I've got Johnny's binoculars in my room, I'll go and get them."

He raced off to get them, and returned, to take up his position back at the window, with the old binoculars focusing on the flickering lights.

"They're lanterns, there's a stream of people carrying them. It looks as though the whole village is going up to the pass," he announced peering through them. "Take a look," he instructed, handing them to her.

"So it is, I can see them. It's like a procession, there are so many of them! Look they're on horses, bikes, and the rest are walking and that orange light seems to be coming from those big rocks at the start of the pass. That must be where Catherine and Bronwyn have gone!" she answered. "So they haven't gone to the village hall at all. They've gone up there with everyone else, why didn't she tell us that?" she asked, handing the binoculars back to her brother.

"I don't know, maybe she thought we would ask questions if she told us they were going up there," he answered, "and presumably, there's something going on, they don't want us to know about! I thought it was a bit strange, Betsy bringing the horse and cart to pick them up, when the village hall's only round the corner!"

"What on earth can they all be doing up there?" asked Rachel.

"Well, there's only one way to find out, isn't there?" he answered.

"You don't mean go up there?" said Rachel in horror.

130

"You don't have to come, if you don't want to!" said Gareth. "You can lock the door after me and stay here, you'll be quite safe!"

"Oh no you don't! I'm not staying here on my own!" said Rachel even more horrified.

"No, it's probably best if I go on my own, I'll just have a look to see where they've gone, and I'll come straight back, I'll take the bike as far as I can."

"I'm not staying here on my own," she replied adamantly. "If you're going, I'm coming with you!"

He was about to argue with her, when the warnings about staying together sprang to mind again. Maybe he shouldn't leave her on her own, after all, and he found himself saying, "you'd better put something dark and warm on then. I'll see you downstairs."

She hurriedly put on some trousers and a dark jumper and met him, apprehensively, in the hall.

"I've got the bikes out and I've taken the lantern out of the kitchen, just in case we need it," he said.

She nodded, and they left the safety of the cottage, pushing the bikes onto the road where they mounted them in the half-light and rode towards the track.

They started pedalling up the road to the pass, puffing as they attempted the incline. By the time they were half way there the sun had gone completely and they headed towards the orange glow in the dark. They slowed up as the slope got steeper but they almost made it to the top, before their legs gave out, and they abandoned the bikes leaving them behind the last bit of shrubbery and continued on foot towards the orange light which they could now see was pouring out from between the two huge rocks.

They were still out of breath from the steep climb by the time they reached the pass, where the source of light became evident. Burning torches illuminated an entrance between two massive boulders, revealing a tunnel entrance that led into the rocks themselves.

There was no-one around, so they walked cautiously towards the entrance. The stone walls were ablaze with light, from the many flaming torches, flickering in black conical brackets set on the cave walls. Further inside, a large underground passageway hewn out of the rocks, its destination obscured from view by a sharp right turn, led downwards into the bowels of the mountains themselves.

"I don't think we should go any further, this is really scary!" said Rachel with a shudder.

It was quiet and still, apart from a murmuring from deep below, echoing eerily into the tunnel entrance. They both listened carefully, realising this was a mixture of voices and echoes, but were unable to make out its contents.

"I really think we ought to go back," stated Rachel nervously again, as Gareth ventured further inside.

"Look we've come this far it would be silly not to go a bit further. We won't find out anything from here!" he added, heading towards the bend in the passage, curiosity taking over. "I really want to see what's going on at this meeting; we're quite safe, Bronwyn and Catherine are down there anyway," he said as he continued down the steep slope.

Rachel followed him uncertainly, not because she shared his overpowering desire to find out what was going on, but because she didn't want to stay on her own in the entrance.

The fiery torches became further apart and the light dimmed, as they continued downwards. Eventually they turned another bend where the voices became louder and the light became bright again, the tunnel ended abruptly, and they were bathed in the glow, from more blazing torches that were illuminating a huge cavern below them. They immediately stepped back, pressing back against the stone wall, in case they were seen.

From their high position on the parapet they could see a steep flight of steps leading down into a vast cavern. As they leant cautiously forwards they caught a glimpse of a sea of black hooded figures below them seated in two semi-circles facing a stone platform. There was an aisle between the two sets of seats leading towards the steps. It looked like a huge stone, underground amphitheatre, deep in the bowels of the rocks.

They both immediately dropped down into a crouching position as they stared down into the huge, torch-lit cavern.

"Wow, how weird is this?" whispered Gareth.

"I don't like it," stated Rachel, looking at the undistinguishable black hooded figures below them. "They all look like witches!

They're all dressed the same, in those long black cloaks. The whole village must be here, there are so many of them!"

"Yeah, it looks like one of those meetings of the coven!" said Gareth remembering a particularly scary film he had watched at home, although he never dreamt that he would ever see anything like it in real life.

"Don't say that, you're frightening me!" whispered Rachel.

Neither of them moved, even though they both knew the most sensible thing to do would be to get back to the cottage, but they were both transfixed by the unreal spectacle beneath them.

The stone platform at the front almost resembled a stage, where two figures, like players, were holding the hooded audience's attention: their argument dominating the cavern.

"It's time you all realised, I am in control now!" the black-cloaked figure shouted menacingly towards the assembly in front of him. "I alone am Keeper of the Power; I will not be challenged by anyone here. I will make the rules and you will obey them! Do you all understand?"

There was a silent, resigned nodding and a small murmur of reluctant acceptance from beneath the black hoods below.

"I will not tolerate anyone disobeying my rules is that clear?" said the commanding voice on the stage, as he paced up and down, his cloak swirling as he turned, revealing a highly polished pair of long boots below it.

"That's Mordred! I know it is!" whispered Rachel. "I'd know his voice anywhere; it sends cold shivers down my spine every time I hear him!"

"I thought it was, but who's the other man?" Gareth whispered back.

"I don't know I can't see. He's still in the shadows, but he looks slightly familiar."

"My family has had to wait centuries," continued Mordred, pacing up and down the stage as he spoke, "for the inheritance they were cheated out of, denied, by every pair of simpletons, every pair of village idiots that could lay claim to being the next in line. Well not any more, there is no more line! There is no-one left to lay claim to what should have been mine years ago!"

"I think you may find that is not entirely correct," said a quiet, elderly voice from underneath the brown cloaked hood, as he stepped into the limelight. "The Power cannot be manipulated, by destruction of its descendants. The Power will always transfer to the next in line."

"There is no next in line, you old fool. I have made sure of that!" snarled Mordred, a cruel smile illuminating his face. "Step back, old man, there may have been those that sought your ancient wisdom in the past, but I have no need of it, and if you try to stand in my way, I will destroy you as well!"

"I don't think you quite understand, you are not the last remaining descendant, and you are not the Keeper of the Power!" continued the elderly voice, undeterred. "The conditions of the Power are not met; the conditions, you know full well, are that the Power is held by two, always two, never singularly: always by twins, one male, and one female!"

"The end of the line stays with me, old man!" continued Mordred angrily. "There are no other twins; I have made sure of that! I am the last remaining descendant, so therefore the Power will have to stay with me!"

"The Power doesn't have to do anything, and certainly, it would not remain with a man who would kill his own twin sister to keep it to himself!" the elderly voice said, becoming stronger.

There was a loud gasp from the hooded spectators at this statement. The elderly figure took command of the stage, unafraid of the large, aggressive Mordred.

"The Power does not work like that," he continued standing his ground. "Oh you may have held it for a short while, after you destroyed one of every twin in line to get it, but the day you killed Celia, your own twin sister, is the day that you lost it."

"Lost it, lost it?" shouted Mordred. "I have not lost it! I cannot lose it; it has to transfer to a new set of keepers. A new set of inheritors, twins in the line of Arthur, and there are no more!"

"I'm afraid you are wrong again," the older man replied calmly. "The Power left you when you murdered your sister. It has been with its new set of Keepers since that day."

Mordred rushed towards the elderly, brown-hooded figure, his own hood falling back to reveal his angry red face.

"There are no twins, there are no descendants! I am the last, the very last. What say you old man?" he said, putting his face up close to his. "Give me your descendants; give me your new Keepers. I would say you can't, because there are none!" he finished with a cruel laugh and a swirl of his black cape, as he stepped back into the centre of the stage, satisfied that the old man wouldn't have an answer for him.

The old man didn't reply straight away, and for a brief moment he looked up towards Rachel and Gareth, revealing a glimpse of white hair and long white beard underneath the brown hood.

"It's him; it's the old man who gave us the stones!" Rachel gasped.

"I'm sure he looked at us then?" answered Gareth, worriedly. "Do you think he saw us?"

She didn't have time to answer, as the argument below heated up again.

"As I said the Power is already with its chosen Keepers. I do not have to defend this, nor prove it. The Power goes freely to those deserving of it. You are but one now; the power will not serve you, nor stay with you after what you have done," the old man continued calmly, facing Mordred, who looked fit to attack him at any moment.

"You seem to forget I have this!" Mordred sneered, holding up a round shining object, and a gasp ran through the previously-silent assembly when they saw it.

"It looks like a gem, like the ones we've got!" gasped Rachel.

"It's much bigger than ours!" replied Gareth. "It's massive, it looks like the biggest diamond in the world!" he added as the light caught it.

Mordred waved the large jewel triumphantly at the crowd, tossed his cape again and leaped up onto another raised platform at the back of the stone stage.

"Ah, the missing centrepiece," the old man answered, unperturbed. "That will do you no good either!"

"I will show you! You old fool! You'll regret this, you'll all regret this!" Mordred shouted as he turned to the large rock on the platform in front of him, on which a golden cross stood in the middle. He climbed up, poised to do something, and then turned back looking towards the old man again, his fury evident, even from their high vantage point.

"Where are the others? They are missing!" he screamed at him, jumping off. "Where are the other pieces?"

The crowd started to murmur again, as heads turned to one another, the old man stood his ground watching Mordred calmly, refusing to be browbeaten by his anger.

"This is your doing! Where are they?" he bellowed at the old man again, his temper fuelled even more by the lack of response. "What have you done with them?"

Again, there was no answer, causing his anger to turn to a boiling fury.

"Your time has run out old man! I won't have you standing in my way any more. I should have got rid of you years ago!" Mordred shouted angrily, leaping back to the rock, clamouring his way up to the top of the cross, where he pushed the shining gem into the middle and twisted. He grabbed both sides of the cross and pulled.

"What's he doing?" whispered Rachel.

"I don't know, it looks as though he's trying to pull it off the rock!" Gareth answered, craning forward to see.

It became evident that whatever Mordred was trying to do wasn't working, as he grappled irreverently with the golden cross, swearing and snarling, like someone possessed. Eventually, he gave up and jumped down again.

"You have done this, this is your doing, you meddling old fool! I will kill you for this!" Mordred screamed as he reached under his cape and drew out a long shining sword, which he pointed at the old man, launching himself towards him.

The old man didn't move or flinch he simply raised his arm and pointed at him. In a second, a beam of blue light shot from his finger and hit Mordred, enveloping him, freezing him, still leaning forward in a running pose, his arm and sword outstretched.

The old man walked past the motionless Mordred towards the front of the platform ignoring him completely and faced the astounded audience: their speculative murmurs washing through the crowd.

"Good people, this has been a revealing night for us all, but there is more I fear, there is more that you must know!"

The audience fell silent again.

"Mordred has had a hand in many deaths," he motioned towards the frozen figure behind him. "Too many, and I cannot allow this to happen any longer, I have to reveal something, something I have kept a secret, for many a year."

"No, no you can't do this!" a lone hooded figure stood up in the assembly confronting him. "You promised!"

"That's Bronwyn!" whispered Gareth, recognising her voice.

The old man raised his hand, silencing her. "I'm sorry, but I have to, I have kept this secret for as long as I can, but now I have to break my promise. There are descendants, true descendants, that none of you know about. They are the true Keepers of the Power, they hold it in innocence, and they alone can prevent Mordred from any more of his evil pursuits."

"No, no, please don't do this!" shouted Bronwyn, struggling past the seated figures towards him.

"Who are these descendants?" asked a man, voicing the question that everyone wanted to know.

"They are here with us," answered the old man, looking directly up at the high parapet the twins were crouching on. "Come down my children, join us; do not be afraid!"

The twins froze in fear as the black hoods below them all turned, and were replaced by a sea of faces, looking up at them.

"Please, come down, come down and join us," he said reassuringly.

"What are we going to do?" Rachel asked terrified grabbing Gareth's arm.

For a moment he was tempted to say 'run' but there was little point, as where would they run to? The whole village was there in front of them, and the old man was approaching the bottom of the steps.

"Come, come," the old man said again cajolingly. "Take up your rightful place, here with us!

"Gareth?" questioned his sister again, clutching his arm harder.

"We'll have to go down, just play along with them," he gulped, in answer, wishing he felt as confident as he sounded.

The old man smiled as he watched them walk down the steps, and when they reached the bottom, he took their hands and turned them towards the crowd.

"Good people of Valonia," he said clearly to the hooded assembly. "I give you your descendants. I give you Bronwyn's children!"

Chapter Twelve
The Passage of time

The murmurings of the hooded audience reached their highest level that night, at the old man's words, and the twins stood rooted in fear as they faced them, not understanding any of it themselves, and more to the point, they were terrified at what would befall them as they joined the strange assembly they had been watching so intently, hidden from view.

The old man led them swiftly through the whispering black figures towards the platform at the front. Rachel was so frightened by now, she felt sick, and her legs were weak. Gareth's bravado had left him completely, and he was now wishing he had never suggested that they try to find out what was going on in the cavern, and by the time they reached the stone stage, he was shaking as much as his sister. They stepped timidly onto it, glancing nervously at the frozen figure of Mordred, behind them. There wasn't a flicker of movement from the large dark figure apart from his eyes, which followed them, and they could sense his burning hatred as he glowered at them.

They were so terrified that the full impact of the old man's words hadn't really dawned on them, until they saw Bronwyn pushing her way through the crowd, with another black-cloaked figure close behind her, who they guessed was probably Catherine.

"Please, please don't do this!" she cried again, as she ran into the aisle. "They mustn't find out like this!"

"What did you mean 'Bronwyn's children'?" asked Gareth nervously.

The old man didn't answer as Bronwyn joined them on the platform and hugged Rachel and Gareth tightly saying, "I'm so sorry, I never meant for any of this to happen!"

Her anguish did nothing to make them feel any better, in fact it made them feel worse, confusing them even more.

"It's too late, I did try to warn you!" said Catherine as she reached them, pulling her sister away gently. "You will just have to let matters take their own course now."

"What did you mean 'Bronwyn's children'?" asked Gareth again.

"I'm truly sorry Bronwyn; it pains me greatly to have to break my word to you," said the old man sympathetically. "The people here have a right to know the truth, and so do Gareth and Rachel, they are part of this and have been denied something great and wonderful: their inheritance. They have to know!"

"I don't understand," said Gareth, looking at Bronwyn. "He must have made a mistake, tell him! We don't even live anywhere near here, we're not related, and we're nothing to do with anything that's going on here!"

"I'm afraid that's not true, he's right," Bronwyn answered quietly. "You are a part of all this, you just don't know about it, because you haven't been told. We've kept it from you," she said with a sob.

Gareth and Rachel looked at her, stunned. How could they be? And were they really suggesting that she was their mother? How could he even think that? Their mother had died a long time ago when they were small!

"Please trust me: all of your questions will be answered, I promise!" interrupted the old man, conscious that the murmurings from the crowd were getting louder, as they all turned to each other, voicing their own concerns.

"Please leave this to me, you have never had any cause not to do so before, have you?" said the old man to Bronwyn, who shook her head in answer.

"Then let me do what I have to do here first," he said to her.

"I want to go home!" said Rachel tearfully. "I want to go home to Chesterton, to Dad."

"And go home you shall!" said the old man. "Tonight I will explain everything to you, and afterwards you can choose what you want to do. You won't understand until then, no harm will come to you, but you must trust me! Do you think you can do that?" he asked her quietly.

Rachel nodded, still frightened, but felt somehow comforted by the old man's words.

"Good," he said. "We have matters to attend to here first, and then I will tell you the story, a long and ancient story!"

"Good people," he said holding his hands out, silencing them immediately, and it was obvious from their response, that they all held him in high regard, and were prepared to listen to whatever he had to say.

"Good people of Valonia. You have all been faithful to the ways, and have struggled to uphold them for many a year. You have all had your fears about Mordred, and the way he has acted, but I promise you this will not continue. He is not the Keeper, and he has no hold over any of you. The rightful Keepers are here with us now; they are the next in succession and twins as the condition states. They have been holding the Power in their innocence, oblivious to its very existence."

"That's all very well," said the man who had questioned him before. "We have all kept to the ways, all of us, but Mordred has powers. We have seen them; we have all had to live with them! He is from your time, not ours. He should not even be amongst us, yet he is! How do we stand up to him, when he has the power to do this?"

"Mordred's family have always had powers from another source, we know this and there is nothing we can do about it, that is why he has been so intent on possessing the only remaining Power that is pure. His mother and younger sister are both sorceresses, be thankful he does not possess their powers!"

"We know this, but how is he to be stopped?" came another voice from the assembly.

"He will be stopped, make no mistake about that, but it will not be instant my friends! This will be a battle that will be fought over and over. Mordred will not relinquish his position easily, and I have to ask you to rely on us to put things right!"

The crowd murmured again, as they turned whispering to each other, finally the first man stood up again.

"We trust you, we have always taken our direction from you, this must continue for us all to keep our role here!" he finished, speaking for all of them.

"Well, there are some things we can put right, here and now, and put them right we shall!" answered the old man resoundingly, as the audience fell silent again. "Do you have the stones with you?" he asked quietly, turning to the twins.

Gareth nodded, unable to speak, as, although they had been listening to the conversation, none of it made any sense at all.

"Good, then this will be your first task; you shall restore them to their rightful place. Could you get them out please?"

Gareth nodded again and they both fumbled in their pockets, producing the old leather pouches holding the stones.

"Prepare yourselves, this may not be easy, but I want you to go and place them in the spaces either side of the centrepiece that Mordred has put back in the sword."

"Sword?" questioned Gareth. "I thought it was a cross, on the rock!"

"No, these are the jewels that belong to a great and ancient sword; the sword you see before you, its tip is buried deep in the rock," answered the old man. "This is probably the greatest and most famous sword in history, the sword of many legends, and the sword that has only been drawn out and used by King Arthur himself!"

"What?" exclaimed Gareth, and as he looked at it, he slowly began to understand, it was like pieces of a jigsaw, starting to fit together. "Are you telling us that this is Excalibur, King Arthur's sword?" he asked, in sheer amazement.

"The very same!" replied the old man.

"And Mordred, you called him the Black Knight, the other day, Rachel! He can't be the same Black Knight that was with Arthur at the Round Table surely?"

"I'm afraid he is," answered the old man.

"I don't understand, that was hundreds of years ago. He can't possibly be the same person!" replied Gareth, astounded.

"These are all the things that I have to explain to you later," answered the old man patiently.

"Well, if the sword is Arthur's, and Mordred is one of the knights, who are you?"

"I think you already know the answer to that question," the old man answered smiling.

"Not Merlin, the wizard? You can't be Merlin, surely?" Gareth asked, the words sounding even more unbelievable as they left his mouth.

"I am indeed, the very same," Merlin answered, his smile getting broader.

"I don't believe this!" Gareth said dumbfounded. After all, these were people that existed in myths and legends from a bygone age. The thought was too impossible to take in, let alone believe!

"Maybe this will help you," said Merlin removing the long brown cloak, revealing a strange long flowing purple garment studded with jewels of every hue, sparkling from top to bottom, in intricate scrolling patterns. His snowy white hair fell down over his shoulders and his long white beard reached almost down to his waist.

Rachel gasped as he suddenly became the exact picture that anyone would imagine that the ancient wizard Merlin, to look like.

"But you can't be! That would make you thousands of years old!" Gareth said, unable to take all of this in.

"Time is a strange thing," laughed Merlin, "and some of us are lucky enough not to have to worry about it. Now, the stones?" he reminded them.

They looked uncertainly at the sword, standing upright on the rock at the back.

"Place your stones each side of the centrepiece, push it in and twist," he prompted patiently.

The twins went over nervously to the rock, where the great golden sword stood majestically on top. They were aware that all eyes were on them, including those of the dark, frozen figure to the side of the rock.

Rachel went first and Gareth helped her up. She balanced precariously, and pushed her gem into the hole, next to the shining white stone in the middle. It fitted neatly, and she twisted it clockwise, until it felt firm. She scrambled back off the rock just before a strong wind blew fiercely across the platform, and a low deep rumbling shook the cave.

Gareth climbed up and inserted his gem on the other side, this time the rumblings were immediate, and the cave shook as he twisted it firmly into place. There was a flash of white light, and for a moment the deep rumbling became so loud and the cave shook so violently that Rachel was frightened it would collapse on them all. There was another explosion of illuminating radiance, like fireworks, and Gareth, still clinging to the rock, felt his hand gripping the sword involuntarily.

Things happened very quickly as the dazzling white brightness disappeared as quickly as it had come, and Mordred's roar filled the cavern as he came out of his frozen pose and leapt into action. The hatred in him burned furiously and the sword still in his hand was now pointed directly at Rachel, as he rushed forward, his argument with Merlin forgotten in his intense desire to destroy one of the new Keepers.

Rachel screamed as she saw Mordred coming towards her. In a second, the ancient golden sword in Gareth's hand came alive; it slid as smoothly out of the rock, as though it was drawn from a scabbard. Excalibur in his hand, Gareth leapt down from the rock pushing his sister behind him, challenging his dark opponent.

"Don't come any closer!" shouted Gareth, holding the sword with two hands, pointing it at Mordred. The evil man stopped, suddenly unsure, as he faced the great sword. He was unnerved by the apparent ease with which Gareth had drawn it out of the rock, and memories of the magic surrounding it flooded back to him, and his own sword lowered instinctively.

As if by magic, Gareth found himself in front of Mordred, with his sword pressing against his throat. He had no idea how it had happened, but he stood his ground firmly, as the big man leant his head back to relieve the pressure, and a faint trickle of blood ran down his neck where the sharp point dug into his throat. Mordred dropped his sword and stepped back. His eyes glinted with pent-up fury at the humiliation of a mere boy opposing him in front of the entire village.

144

Another gasp went round the assembly as Mordred turned and ran to the edge of the platform, leaping into the aisle with another angry roar. He ran half way up the aisle, pushing people out of his way as he went, then stopped and turned.

"You will regret this, boy!" he shouted, pointing at Gareth angrily. "You've just made a big mistake; you should have killed me when you had the chance, because, when I raise my sword to your throat, I will slit it like that of a squealing pig!"

"Get out of my way!" Mordred snarled, pushing another couple of figures deliberately as he strode towards the steps. He ran up them two at a time, until he reached the platform at the top. "Remember what I have said, boy!" he shouted, his voice echoing round the cavern. "I will destroy you and your snivelling sister!"

Mordred's words and the reality of what he had just done suddenly hit Gareth, his knees buckled and he almost dropped the sword. A great cheer echoed round the cavern from the watching crowd, and Bronwyn and Merlin rushed forward to Gareth's side. Merlin relieved him of the sword and Rachel and Bronwyn rushed at him, practically smothering him as they hugged him.

"I don't believe I just did that!" Gareth said weakly, trying to push them away.

"You were so brave!" exclaimed his sister.

"I don't think it was me, it was that sword: it sort of took over!" he said, looking in awe at it as Merlin placed it back on top of the rock again.

"No, no, Excalibur recognises bravery and acts alongside it," said Merlin stepping down from the rock. "The sword recognised that your main desire was to protect your sister, and that is what it helped you do!"

"You make it all sound very simple," said Gareth, still shaking from his ordeal.

"That's because it is," replied Merlin, and turned towards the black-hooded audience.

"Good people," he continued. "Go back to your beds, where you may sleep easy tonight in the knowledge that the great Mordred has just encountered his first defeat! May God protect you all and keep you safe until we meet again!"

The crowd nodded and reverently murmured their thanks as they all filed out, streaming up the steps like black shadowy silhouettes, their identities still unknown, until the cavern was finally empty, apart from the echoes of their voices as the villagers still murmured their concerns as they walked through the tunnel above.

Their small party was left alone on the platform. Bronwyn's face was white, and her sister put her arm round her in silent support. Gareth leant against the rock as his legs had turned to jelly and were having trouble supporting him, and Rachel, as pale as the others, was still clutching at him in shock.

"Well, I'd say that went particularly well, wouldn't you?" said Merlin rubbing his hands together with a satisfied smile, as they all looked dubiously at him.

"In fact, I'd go so far as to say, spectacularly well, and Gareth, such bravery, you did your ancestors proud!" he said gleefully patting him heavily on the shoulder, almost knocking him over in his excitement. "Oh, that was so satisfying, to see the great powerful Mordred run from you!"

They all stared at Merlin, still reeling in shock, and no-one replied.

"Now then, there is much to be done tonight, yes, much to be done!" he continued excitedly. "We must start on our journey, 'tis but a small distance, but we must make haste."

"Journey, where are we going?" asked Rachel, worriedly.

"To the beginning, the very beginning, where you shall learn of your inheritance," Merlin answered, immediately silencing Bronwyn's protests. "Don't worry, I will explain everything to them, they will understand."

"Understand what? And where are you taking us? We're going home tomorrow; Dad will be waiting at the station for us!" interrupted Gareth.

"And you will be there!" he answered. "You will be back in plenty of time for your train, but tonight you will come to the place where everything will become clear."

"Is Bronwyn coming with us?" asked Rachel, looking nervously at her aunt.

"No, but she will be here waiting for you when you get back,"

Merlin answered firmly.

"I will, I promise," said Bronwyn tearfully. "I will always be here for you, I always have been!"

"Well, now that's all settled," answered Merlin, ushering them towards the back of the platform. "Come, come, there is much to do, yes, and much to tell! Oh yes, so much to tell!"

They walked with him into the dark shadows at the back of the platform, towards another small opening, looking over their shoulders at Bronwyn, who waved them on tearfully. As they picked their way carefully down some steps, they could see there was another much smaller tunnel ahead.

The tunnel was in total darkness, but once inside it, Merlin waved his hand and the passageway lit up immediately as torches on the walls either side of them blazed into life. He walked ahead of them, his pointed shoes made no noise, but his long robes swished and rustled as he walked. He continued a flourishing motion with his hand as he walked, and more torches lit up in front of them. As they passed the flames they flickered, dimmed and the tunnel behind them was plunged into blackness again.

"How on earth does he do that?" whispered Gareth to Rachel, as another set of torches lit up.

"I don't know, and I don't really care," answered his sister. "I'd like to know where we're going, it must be nearly midnight, and we're wandering around underground passages!"

"Yeah, and there's a whole lot more that I want to know," replied Gareth, as they stepped up their pace to keep up with their elderly host, who despite his age was striding out purposefully in front of them.

"All of your questions will be answered in due course," Merlin said, making them jump, as they hadn't realised he could hear them.

"Well, I'd like some answers now, otherwise I'm not going any further!" said Gareth obstinately, sounding much braver than he felt.

Merlin turned and walked back to them. They expected him to be angry, but he smiled sympathetically.

"You said a lot of things in there that we don't understand," stated

Gareth.

"I know that," the wizard answered, "but you will understand when I have told you the story. It is a long story, too long to be told here."

"You said, we've inherited something, some power, whatever that means," said Gareth, undeterred. "You told them we were Bronwyn's children, and I asked you what you meant, but you didn't answer me, so what did you mean?"

"I admit I was avoiding an explanation of this now, as it would be like reading the end of a book before you have even looked at the first chapter," he answered with a sigh.

"I don't care. What did you mean?" asked Gareth adamantly.

"I told only the truth to the keepers in the cavern. You are Bronwyn's children, Bronwyn is your mother," he answered quietly.

"She can't be, our mother died in an accident," insisted Rachel. "Bronwyn's a sort of aunt."

"No my dear, that is what you have been told, and that is what you have believed for all of your young lives," replied Merlin gently, "but it isn't the truth. Your mother didn't die, Bronwyn is your mother."

"She can't be!" said Gareth adamantly. "Why would they tell us she'd died, if she was Bronwyn, and then pretend she was our aunt when she came to visit? There has to be some big mix up or mistake. You must be wrong!"

"There is no mistake, Bronwyn is your mother," repeated the old man.

"That means that they've told us lies for years, even Dad!" Gareth questioned angrily. "Why?"

"They kept it from you, and everyone else, for your own safety," Merlin answered sadly, looking at the two astonished, disbelieving faces in front of him. "Years ago, your mother and father made a decision to keep you away from all of this, with good reason. They decided it was best that you knew nothing about it, and kept you a secret from the people here. They decided you would live in safety with your father in Chesterton. Bronwyn loved you both very much and it was because of this that she left you. She led the villagers to believe that her marriage hadn't worked out and she had come back

148

to the place she belonged. No one ever questioned this, as it is not their way to make a life outside Valonia, and no-one ever suspected that she had any children."

"So why didn't she just stay with us, if we were all safe with Dad in Chesterton?" asked Gareth, an angry note creeping into his voice. "Why did she leave us and get Dad to lie and say she was dead?"

"Bronwyn made a huge sacrifice, it broke her heart to leave you, and your father, when she loved you all so much, but she had to for your safety," repeated Merlin.

"I still don't understand, if she was our mother why would she leave us?" asked Rachel.

"No doubt it's something to do with this Power and this inheritance, whatever it is!" interrupted Gareth sarcastically.

"Unfortunately it is," answered Merlin. "It is very late, we must continue! Walk with me and I will explain as we go."

They resumed their journey through the vaulted passage, at a slower pace, and Merlin kept his word and continued his explanation.

"I know this is difficult for you to understand, but you must not blame her. Bronwyn was born here, she had a twin brother called Geraint, and when your grandmother died, the Power automatically passed to them. The Keepers of the Power have always been twins and Geraint and Bronwyn were next in succession. Bronwyn left the village to go to university and become a teacher. It was unusual for someone to leave for the world outside Valonia. No-one really understood why she did it, and she was warned by everyone that it would lead to no good. She was insistent that she left to gain more knowledge to pass on to her pupils. I think this was the excuse that she used but I am more inclined to think that she had some other calling. Anyway she went to university and this is where she met your father."

The twins nodded, they knew this bit of the story at least.

"Your father and Bronwyn married and continued their life away from here, where you were born. They were very happy and Bronwyn never had any intention of ever coming back here, until she heard that her brother Geraint had died in an accident on the cliffs. She returned for the funeral, where she learnt that his death was suspicious, and may not have been an accident at all. She had been told that the cliffs to the right of the village had given way under him and he had fallen to his death, but Geraint knew the land around here well and there was a mystery as to why he was there, and how it had happened. Everyone in the village presumed that the Power transferred to the next set of twins in line, which was Abigail and Johnny, and within days, Johnny met with his accident at the pass, which you know about. This led everyone including Mordred to believe that, as the only twins left in the village, he and his twin sister Celia were now the new Keepers of the Power."

"I still don't see what that has to do with us," said Gareth.

"The whole point is, that Johnny and Abigail, and Mordred and Celia, were never the next in succession for the Power, and they were never its Keepers. You were the next twins in succession, but no-one knew of your existence. Bronwyn told Catherine that she had two children, but she didn't even tell her that you were twins! She kept that a secret even from her sister."

"So she wanted to keep us a secret from this Power, whatever it is?" asked Gareth, still not understanding.

"No, she kept you a secret from Mordred," answered Merlin firmly. "If Mordred had known about you, he would have destroyed one or both of you, the same as he did with Geraint, Johnny and lastly Celia, his own twin sister, who he drowned in the lake at the manor, thinking he was already the Keeper and that there were no more twins to succeed. He wanted the Power to himself for his own ends! Bronwyn denied herself her own children and her life away from here, to make sure that Mordred never knew about you, to protect you from him."

"So did Mordred cause Johnny's accident? Johnny said he heard someone laughing as they rode off and left him there!" said Gareth disgustedly. "Was Mordred the black shape he saw?"

"I'm fairly sure it was!" Merlin nodded, sadly. "Johnny is a good person and so is Abigail. Mordred thought the Power had transferred to them, and for that reason, I think he caused the rock fall."

"But Johnny wasn't killed? So why didn't Mordred think they still had this Power?" asked Rachel.

"Johnny survived, against all odds, but his mind was impaired after the accident, and Mordred knew the Power would pass on because of this! The awful thing is, that they may never had the Power, but it was naturally assumed that they were its Keepers since no-one knew about you. It was Geraint's accident that made Bronwyn realise that you would never be safe from Mordred, and that is why they made their decision for you to stay with your father away from all of this!"

They walked silently behind him, both shocked by his answers. The tunnel twisted and turned, and the torches still blazed and then flickered and died, but after Merlin's revelations, they hardly even noticed them.

"So, if they all went to such great lengths to keep us a secret, why did she bring us here, now?" asked Gareth eventually. "And what is this Power, that we have to have whether we like it or not?"

"Don't blame Bronwyn, it's not entirely her fault that you are here," answered Merlin, noticing the angry tone in Gareth's voice.

"Well, she brought us here, if it wasn't for her we wouldn't be caught up in any of this," he returned swiftly.

"Circumstances were organised. Bronwyn was put in a position that we knew she would not turn down, as she has always been desperate to have any time she could with you," said Merlin.

"What do you mean?" asked Gareth stopping again. "What circumstances?"

"I know what he means," said Rachel. "He means that when that poor man was injured and there was no-one else to take his place, Dad had no-one to look after us, and Bronwyn automatically stepped in and offered to bring us here!"

"Precisely my dear, precisely!" agreed Merlin.

"You mean you brought us here then?" asked Gareth.

"Oh, no, not me," laughed Merlin. "Even my magic is not that strong."

"Well, who and why?" asked Gareth. "Why are we here?"

"You are here because it is your destiny. You are here because without you Mordred cannot be stopped, and it takes a force far greater than any of us to organise the events to ensure this. Now we must make haste," he concluded, resuming his brisk pace down the tunnel, leaving them no option but to follow, or return into the blackness behind them.

Chapter Thirteen
The Hall of Memories

Their footsteps echoed as they walked on and on down the long narrow tunnel, until eventually it widened and the domed ceiling rose dramatically, as they entered a network of caves, with more dark tunnels leading off to the left of them.

"I'm sure I can hear the sea!" said Rachel listening carefully.

"Yes you can," answered Merlin breathing in deeply. "The tunnels lead down to the beach you probably saw from the cliffs, they're rather like an underground maze."

"Is it much further?" asked Rachel, stifling a rather large yawn, as the day's events were catching up with her.

"Oh you poor things, you must be very tired, it's been a long day for both of you!" answered Merlin sympathetically, slowing his pace again for them. "We're nearing the end of the passages now, we're almost there, but there is something I need to warn you about, before we go any further," he continued seriously, and Rachel glanced apprehensively at her brother.

"Don't be surprised by what you find when we leave these passages. We have passed into a different time, the time where your inheritance began, and the time where my home is," he said, before resuming his stride slightly ahead of them, satisfied that he had prepared them, for whatever it was they were to meet there.

"What is he on about now?" whispered Rachel anxiously, as they glanced at each other again, struggling to comprehend his last words.

"Search me," shrugged Gareth in reply, as they followed the purple swishing gown in front of them, towards the opening at the end of the tunnel.

A cold breeze chilled them and Rachel shivered, as they left the brightness of the torches and emerged into the dark night air, through a large opening surrounded by rocks. When their eyes had adjusted to the darkness they realised that Merlin was walking towards a man, standing a small distance away, with four horses behind the large boulders.

"Ah, Percivale, I knew you wouldn't let me down!" Merlin said clasping his arm.

"'Tis my pleasure, m'lord," the man answered, stepping forward, where the last of the torchlight illuminated him against the blackness.

Gareth and Rachel stared in amazement as they noticed that underneath his long cloak, was the full attire of a knight! They stepped back in shock hearing his chain mail clinking as he walked towards them holding out two thick cloaks.

"'Tis, cold, you might be in need of these," he said, offering the cloaks to them.

They continued to stare slightly rudely, not answering, taking in every detail of his strange attire, from his round metal helmet, to his shirt and red tunic, emblazoned with a large gold crest. His chain mail leggings reached his ankles and were crossed at the bottom by the laces of his flat slightly pointed leather boots. Hanging at his side was a long sword. His shoulder length hair curled out from underneath the helmet, and he had a slightly scruffy looking beard, but his smile was kind, and he obviously held Merlin in high regard.

"Thank you Percivale, so thoughtful! Yes, 'tis a cold night and no mistake! They will be most grateful of these," Merlin interjected quickly. "Come now, put these on, t'will guard you against the cold night air," he said, draping one around Rachel, as Gareth took the other one gingerly from the knight, muttering his thanks.

"We have a short ride," said Merlin, wrapping his own brown cloak tightly round him, before he mounted a large dark brown horse.

They had been so busy staring at Percivale, they hadn't taken much notice of the large black and grey horses, until he led them out from behind the boulders and handed the reins to Gareth.

"Rufus!" exclaimed Rachel as soon as her attention went to the big black horse. "Gareth, look – it's Rufus, and Smokey too! How on earth did you get here?" she asked the big horse, as he nuzzled her and snorted gently when she stroked his nose. "Don't you look lovely!" she said, admiring the long cream blanket under a small flat saddle. There was a crest embroidered on the side and red and white tassels hanging all around the edges. His reins had matching tassels dangling from them, and he had a leather head-piece over his brow. For all his fancy attire she was pleased to see he was still the same old Rufus, snorting again when she stopped stroking him, pawing the ground impatiently.

"Come, come now, let's be getting along," said Merlin, anxious to get moving again.

"Let me help you miss," said Percivale politely, stepping forward to help her mount. Gareth had already scrambled up into the saddle, perched on a dark blue, equally-ornate blanket adorning Smokey's back.

"I thought you would prefer to ride the horses you are used to," said Merlin by way of an explanation as Percivale swung easily into his saddle in one swift movement, and led them across a grassy valley into the moonlight, with the twins following behind.

"'Tis only a short ride to the castle," said Merlin over his shoulder.

"Castle?" queried Gareth. "Are we staying in a castle, a real one?"

"You most certainly are," replied Merlin, before he turned back to his conversation with the knight riding at his side.

"How weird is this? Do you think he's real, the knight I mean?" whispered Gareth, his tiredness forgotten at the thought of staying in a castle.

"It's weird all right!" answered Rachel dryly, "and he looks real

154

enough to me, have you seen his sword?"

"Merlin said we've gone back in time. Do you think we really have? We could be back to the time of the knights!" he asked excitedly.

"We can't have, we only walked through that tunnel. It's not possible," Rachel said sensibly. "Anyway, Rufus and Smokey are here, and they didn't go through the tunnel, in fact Rufus was outside the cavern with the buggy, after they gave Catherine and Bronwyn a lift, if you remember!"

"So how did they get here then? Can you think of a better explanation?" Gareth asked crossly. "You said yourself the knight looks real, and Percivale was one of the Knights of the Round Table. I remember his name! That sword in the cavern wasn't just a normal sword either. It went for Mordred all on its own! I was only holding it, and if the old man is really Merlin, like he said, then the sword must be Excalibur!" he finished, flushed with excitement.

Rachel said nothing; if she could have come up with any sort of sensible answer she would have done, but she couldn't. She didn't share her brother's enthusiasm at all, and the more she thought about the whole situation, the more worried she became.

The twins followed in silence, entering a wood, where the horses picked their way carefully in the dark, the branches scratching them occasionally as they were caught unawares. When they emerged from the narrow paths and tangled branches, they could see across a sloping plain, surrounded by woods and deep valleys. The moon shone brightly across the grassy area, turning it into a silvery pathway, at the end of which they could see a castle in the distance, set high on black rocks, silhouetted against the moonlit sky.

"Wow, look at that, is that where we're going?" breathed Gareth, in awe.

"It is indeed," replied Merlin proudly, drawing up his horse for a second, alongside them. "Welcome to Tyntagyle, the great fortress and home of the good Knights of the Round Table and the great King Arthur himself!"

"Really, is it really Arthur's castle? I can't believe this, it's so fantastic! Will he be there?" asked Gareth, hardly able to contain his excitement.

155

"Sadly no, Arthur died several years ago in his last great battle at Camlann. Some of the younger knights still remain at the castle though. Percivale, here, Galahad, Bors, Kay, Tristram, and the others that are left, still return to meet at the Table. Arthur's traditions still live on with those who are willing to still maintain them."

"So Arthur's dead, then?" asked Gareth disappointedly. Rachel looked at him, amazed at his easy acceptance of all of this.

"He is, and a great tragedy it was to all who followed him. But there are still those who are committed to his cause. His death was a huge loss, he was a great leader!"

"Aye, that he was," agreed Percivale, enforcing the enormity of his leader's death, in his few, short, sombre words.

The horses, started off into the moonlight again, and the twins rode in silence as the strangeness of their situation became more and more evident with every thud of their horses hooves, across the silvery plain.

They reached the end of the fields to see a long stretch of causeway leading towards the castle, which now loomed majestically tall, and imposing, jutting out into the sea. The ground fell away either side of the causeway, into deep, dark, wooded valleys, eventually meeting the craggy rocks with the sea beyond. As they looked up at the castle in awe, they could see the great stone walls and turrets towering up against the sky and in the distance they could hear the pounding of waves as they crashed against the jagged rocks.

They crossed the causeway in single file, the drop becoming even deeper either side as they approached the high stone walls and arched gateway. The horses moved slowly, and Rachel couldn't help looking down nervously as Rufus plodded on sure-footedly.

When they reached the enormous wooden door in the gateway, a flurry of activity could be heard from behind, as it slowly swung open to allow them to file through.

They found themselves in a long courtyard, surrounded by small buildings with wooden roofs, enclosed by stout, impenetrable walls with parapets. Three men secured the great door behind them with a huge beam of wood, levering it down with a heavy rope. They shouted a greeting, and Merlin and Percivale answered jovially.

They continued on horseback, through the long outer courtyard towards another archway, which seemed to form the only entrance through the thick exterior walls that surrounded the main castle buildings. They passed through it and dismounted in a large area in front of the main entrance to the castle.

Percivale led the horses away and they followed Merlin through a small wooden door into one of the lofty towers at the side.

They stepped inside and Merlin took a torch off the wall, passed his hand over it and it slowly came to life, illuminating the round stone passage, with a small winding spiral staircase. He shut the door and led them upwards, round and round, up the small steps that were so narrow at the inner edge there was no room for their feet. They passed a couple of small wooden doors, but continued upwards, their legs aching as they followed the sprightly old man.

Eventually they reached a bigger door which Merlin opened and they followed him into a room, which even in the torchlight they could see was rich in colour and warmly inviting.

"Welcome, welcome," he said throwing his cloak over the back of a heavy wooden chair. "Make yourselves at home."

"Wow, now this is really amazing!" breathed Gareth.

"I'm glad you like it my boy!" answered Merlin.

"Like it, it's fantastic!" Gareth enthused, gazing around in wonder.

Merlin lit several lamps and the room glowed. The wooden furniture was heavy and solid looking, but was padded with richly coloured cushions. The stone floor had thick fur rugs strewn about and there were big carved cabinets lining half of the walls. They were full of strange looking objects, piles of scrolled papers and carved wooden boxes.

In the middle was a huge table, piled high with parchments and a disarray of more strange objects.

"Mmm, maybe not as tidy as I remembered, but it's home!" he mused, sitting down on a large chair by the window, plumping the cushions around him. "Ah, that's better. I'm far too old to be out wandering through time, late at night," he said, gesturing for the twins to join him on the large wooden seats.

Rachel and Gareth sat back, finding the soft cushions comfortable.

"Did we really, pass through time?" asked Rachel in a small voice, already knowing what his answer would be.

"Look around you, my dear, does this look like your world, or your time?"

She shook her head, surprised that she didn't feel more frightened.

"Then there's your answer," said Merlin. "Now I think, tonight we will have some food and a good night's sleep."

"Sleep, I couldn't sleep, even if I tried! This is far too exciting," said Gareth. "This is real isn't it; this really is Arthur's castle, isn't it? Will we see the knights as well and the Round Table? Will they be there, all of them? Will we see them tomorrow? Oh, I can't wait!"

"Calm yourself," laughed Merlin. "Tomorrow is another day."

"But I still don't see how we could go back thousands of years when we only walked through those passages, it's just not possible!" insisted Rachel, ignoring her brother's excitement.

"In your world that sort of thing certainly wouldn't be possible," laughed Merlin. "But, those were no ordinary passages, and Valonia is no ordinary place."

"What do you mean?" asked Rachel, confused.

"Valonia may look like an ordinary Cornish town by the sea, but it isn't, it isn't even in your time. Valonia is a sort of half-way place between your world and this one."

They were interrupted by a knock at the door. Merlin opened it and a young girl carrying a tray entered the room. She looked shyly at them as she set the tray down on the table.

"Thank you, my dear," said Merlin, as she bobbed a small, respectful curtsey and quickly left.

"My, my, look at this! I don't know about you, but all that walking has given me quite an appetite," said Merlin, their previous conversation completely forgotten by him, as he put out the plates and lifted the lid off a large pot, the meaty vapours wafting into the air. "Oh now that smells good, come on now, tuck in, tuck in!" he instructed, spooning the steaming broth into three bowls with a large ladle. They tore off big chunks of bread from a large uneven-looking loaf and settled back on the seats, finding they were as hungry as their host. The broth was thick, and had large chunks of meat and vegetables floating in the slightly grey-coloured liquid. It was warm and extremely tasty; they ate it with a spoon and followed Merlin's example, dunking their bread in it.

"Oh, that was good, that was good!" said Merlin, wiping his mouth on his sleeve. "All we need now is a nice warm drink to follow," he said, filling three large goblets with a warm, purple, frothing liquid from a large jug.

"What is it?" asked Rachel, savouring the spicy aroma as Merlin handed her the goblet.

"A very old and special recipe, my dear, full of beneficial herbs," said the old wizard, settling back comfortably on his chair. "Just what is needed, right now."

"Merlin, you were telling us about Valonia," prompted Rachel, anxious to hear more.

"I was, yes, so I was," he mused, taking a sip of the fragrant brew. "Do try your drink, while it's still hot," he urged. "Rest for tonight, let us worry about the explanations after a good night's sleep."

Realising he was not going to elaborate any more on his earlier statement, Rachel sipped the warm drink and sat back. It smelt wonderful and tasted sweet and fruity. By the time she had finished it, she felt warm and comfortable, and her eyes started to close. She curled up on the big padded seat, sinking back into the soft cushions.

The next thing she knew, the light was streaming through the small oblong windows of the tower room. She sat up stiffly, noticing that Gareth was still fast asleep on the other end of the settle. Merlin had piled thick covers over them; they must have both fallen straight asleep, as she couldn't remember anything else.

She got up quietly, stretched and went over to the window. Standing on tiptoe she could see the sea stretching out, shimmering in the morning sun. As she leant forward and looked down, the waves below were crashing ferociously against the jagged black rocks. She watched them for a few minutes and then went across the room to another window.

She gasped as she took in the view below her. The window overlooked the courtyards, which may have been quiet when they rode in the night before, but they were far from that now; they were a hive of bustling activity. The courtyard was now alive with the people of a bygone age, men, women, children, all dressed in the costume of their era, all going about their daily business. She watched them, fascinated; she could see the stone buildings where the workmen were going about their trades. There was a clink of the blacksmith's hammer as he was shoeing a horse; there was a clopping of hooves as several men walked their horses past, and the children's voices and laughter rose up as they tended to the animals that were roaming freely all over the place. There were chickens and geese, which the children were feeding with grain from wicker baskets, scattering it on the floor where the birds flocked around them, squawking loudly, pecking at the food. There were a couple of large pigs feeding at a trough, and some goats, which a young boy was tethering to a post.

The whole scene was like a history book coming to life in front of her and Rachel watched, absolutely amazed by what she was seeing. Three men were talking directly below the tower window; she craned forward as far as she could to see them. She wasn't to be disappointed; they were dressed the same as Percivale, with tunics and chain mail. They held long pointed lances and shields with painted emblems. Another man joined them, leading their horses. She thought he might be a servant until the men bowed and slapped him jovially on the back, taking the reins from him. He looked much younger than the other men and his attire seemed more casual. He wore a loose-fitting shirt, open at the neck, under a sleeveless open tunic, and instead of the heavy chain mail worn by the other men, he wore hose that were tucked tightly into his long flat boots. He had no helmet and his long dark hair waved in an unruly fashion onto his shoulders.

The other men mounted their horses sedately: the younger man leapt onto his horse, which was clearly spirited, as it reared and danced backwards, shaking its head. He pulled up the reins immediately bringing it under control with a laugh, and as they turned to ride out he looked upwards at the tower, meeting Rachel's stare. She stepped back quickly, not wanting to be seen leaning out of the window watching them, and collided heavily with Gareth.

"Wow, have you seen this?" he said, pushing her out of the way,

160

unceremoniously. "This is so amazing!"

"Well, I did, until you shoved your way in!" answered his sister crossly.

"What? Oh, sorry, but I just can't believe this, we've definitely gone back in time, and we're really in Arthur's castle, this is just too incredible for words! Have you seen this down here?" he said leaning so far out, he was in danger of joining the people below.

"Yes I have, and I keep hoping that I'm going to wake up and find this was all a bad dream!" said Rachel despondently.

"How can you say that?" asked Gareth, turning momentarily away from the scene below. "This is so brilliant!"

"Well, I think it's scary!" replied Rachel tearfully. "Supposing we get stuck here, we don't even know how to get back."

"Yes we do, back through the tunnels! If the worst came to the worst, we could ride back on Rufus and Smokey!" said Gareth defiantly.

"I suppose so," said Rachel brightening up a bit. "But what about all the things Merlin said last night? He hasn't really explained anything yet."

"I don't know about that," answered Gareth, stepping down from the window. "I'd say he's dropped a fair few bombshells already! Starting with the fact that, Bronwyn is apparently our Mother, not that anyone has bothered to tell us up until now!"

"I know, I can't believe it, it's wonderful!" she answered.

"I'm glad you think so! Seems to me they kept an awful lot from us!" said Gareth dryly. "Makes you wonder what's coming next!"

"What do you mean?" she asked.

"Well, what else don't we know about?" he replied.

"An awful lot I'm afraid," came Merlin's voice as he swept into the room. "But by the time you leave here, you will know everything!"

His robes today were a bright emerald green with gold embroidery around the long pointed sleeves, with a golden tasselled belt around his waist.

"How did you sleep?" he continued. "I had a room prepared for you, but it seemed a shame to disturb you, you both fell asleep so quickly!"

"Very well, thank you," said Gareth automatically, with a slightly

161

sullen tone.

"Good! Isolde will be here with some breakfast for us soon," he continued brightly, ignoring Gareth's attitude. "I have brought you some fresh clothes; you'll just have time to change before we eat. There is a small room upstairs, where you can take turns to go and change," he said handing them both a neatly folded pile.

"I'm not wearing these!" said Gareth indignantly. "The shirt, I could just about live with, but I'm not wearing tights for anyone!" he finished holding up the offending tunic and hose.

Seeing the thick brown leggings, Rachel sniggered behind her hand at his horrified expression.

"Don't laugh it's not funny!" he said indignantly, as her snigger developed into a full blown laugh. "I am not wearing these!" he said adamantly waving them in front of them.

"You will wear the clothes I have given you," said Merlin firmly. "They may be strange to you, but they won't look strange to anyone else, these are the outfits that are worn here. You will arouse far too much interest wearing your own clothes."

"You can go first!" Gareth said sulkily to Rachel, realising he didn't have much say in the matter.

Rachel climbed up the narrow winding staircase into a small room. There was a big wooden bed in the middle, with a heavy looking, hand stitched cream cover. The room was simple, with a rustic feel to it, and apart from a couple of tapestries on the walls, and a small window overlooking the sea, the walls were bare. There was a small table by the window with a brown earthenware bowl and a big pitcher full of water. She poured some out and washed her face and hands. The water was cold and took her breath away as she splashed it on her face.

She inspected her bundle, to find it contained a long thick petticoat and a long cream coloured dress with a V-neck edged with beading, and long pointed sleeves. There was a long blue tasselled belt similar to Merlin's and a pair of soft leather pointed flat shoes. She would have been much more at home in her jeans and trainers, but the long dress was something of a novelty. She slipped it on and smoothed the long thick folds of the skirt down, wishing there was a large mirror to see what she looked like. There was a rough looking wooden brush on the dressing table, and she brushed her long golden hair with it.

She found it much more difficult going down the narrow staircase hampered by the heavy long skirt, and after, almost tripping over it, she held it up in a bunch in front of her, feeling her way down the steps in the soft strange slippers.

When she joined them downstairs again, she found Gareth tucking into a large chunk of bread and ham, with a goblet of milk.

"You look like one of those damsels!" he laughed, picking up an apple.

"Do I? Well it's your turn now, and I can't wait to see you in your tights!"

He scowled at her, which only made her find the concept even more amusing, and she grinned as she helped herself to some food from the tray, settling back on a large chair to eat it, as Gareth went off reluctantly to change.

He eventually reappeared wearing the same scowl and his new outfit, which consisted of a brown tunic reaching his knees, with a leather belt and the brown hose with a pair of laced pointed boots. Rachel put her hand to her mouth to stifle a giggle.

"One word and these are coming straight off!" he said angrily, as she looked hard at her plate trying not to laugh.

"You look splendid my boy!" replied Merlin, slapping him on the back. "Splendid, now, I'm sure you both are anxious to see the castle!"

Gareth perked up at this, his unfortunate attire temporarily forgotten in his desire to explore their new surroundings. They followed Merlin back down the stairs and into the busy sunlit courtyard, where no-one gave them a second glance as they walked across to the main castle doors.

It was quite apparent that Merlin was a much-respected figure, as everyone they passed gave a slight stiff bow, and the women all bobbed a small curtsey, as they went into the main building. The long stone corridor was dark and cool; its high vaulted ceiling had carvings at the corners of the stone ridges that decorated it. Merlin opened two heavy studded wooden doors at the end, and they both gasped as they entered.

This was obviously the room where the knights had met with King Arthur, as there, in the centre of the room sat the famous circular stone table.

There were twelve heavy, high-backed seats positioned equally round it, each with a carved, painted emblem on the back. Banners on long poles hung all around the hall with the same emblems, each with a small stone plaque underneath. Conical metal torch-holders lined the walls in abundance, although they were not necessary now as the light filtered in through the great arched windows, the shafts of light all meeting in the middle of the stone table.

"Wow, this is awesome!" breathed Gareth, reverently.

"The Great Hall in all its splendour!" answered Merlin. "Ah, I only wish you could see it as it used to be. That was a sight to be seen! All of the knights, gathered here with Arthur, every seat filled and this is where the new laws of truth, chivalry and honour were born, around this very table!" Merlin said passionately, his eyes misty with his memories.

The twins gazed around silently, in wonder, as the old man's words set a scene they could only imagine.

"Briton was a turbulent place, everyone fought for lands and power," the old wizard continued. "Women and children would be killed, and entire villages burnt to a cinder! The Romans invaded, but they brought only a temporary peace. They introduced their culture and built great cities and roads. When they left, the turmoil started again. Arthur wanted peace for his people and gradually others joined him; they were to become the Knights of the Round Table!"

"Wow!" breathed Gareth, "I can't believe I'm here! I read about the knights, didn't they have to make special promises and do something really brave to become one?"

"They did indeed," replied Merlin, laughing at his excitement. "They were a very elite group, and had to prove their worth before they were accepted. In fact if you go down to the far end of the hall you will see their oath, carved into a stone plaque."

"Ace!" exclaimed Gareth, as he made his way past the Round Table.

The back of the hall was much darker and as Gareth reached

the stone plaque, he was conscious of a shadow in the corner. He jumped as a dark figure moved quickly, disappearing behind a small door, which they shut firmly behind them.

"Whoa ... who was that?" Gareth asked, nervously.

"Mmm?" answered Merlin distractedly.

"There was someone there, they went through that door," he replied, pointing at the small arched doorway.

"I saw no-one," Merlin answered.

"This is brilliant," said Rachel, looking at the carved stone. "The Pledge of Chivalry and Honour," she read aloud. "I do solemnly swear to be true to God and loyal to the King!"

"Wow, what else does it say?" said Gareth, forgetting his previous fright almost immediately.

"It's a bit difficult to read," said Rachel. "Some of the words are strange."

"That's because it is written in old English, some of the words are spelled differently," explained Merlin, joining her. "This is the pledge that the knights would make before the assembly. It continues to say that the knight would fight only for truth, justice and honour. They would protect those in need and weaker than themselves, be courteous to women and loyal to their friends. They had to be true to their word, and agree to live a pure and noble life, in friendship and support of their fellow knights, and above all to defend their kinsman to the death!"

"They had to be really good with a sword as well, didn't they?" said Gareth in admiration.

"They did indeed, as they fought many battles," agreed Merlin. "After the Romans left, many reverted back to their old ways, taking whatever they wanted! The knights fought them to protect the villages, and the women and children, so they could be safe from the marauding villains. For that, Arthur eventually paid the price and died for his cause."

"That's so sad, after he did so much," said Rachel sympathetically, as she saw Merlin wipe his eyes on the corner of his beaded sleeve.

"Sad, no, not sad, but wonderful!" he answered resolutely. "There are not many men that can say that they have done so much in their lives: they are but a few!"

The twins fell silent as Merlin's eyes misted with the memories of the past.

"It seems awful that they had so many battles. A lot of people must have been killed!" said Rachel quietly, since she was generally opposed to any sort of violence.

"It was my dear, it was, and a great many lost their lives!" said Merlin sadly, "but you only have to read your history books to see that all of the battles through time, have all been fought to gain power in one way or another. This was what the knights were against. They fought for justice!"

Rachel and Gareth nodded, looking silently at the plaque, beginning to understand the old wizard's passionate words.

"These are things that I must tell you, as this is where your heritage began. When the Romans left Briton, to defend Rome they took their great armies with them and suddenly the Britons found they had no defence against any invaders. It was Roman might that had kept out the Gauls and Saxons."

"So what did they do?" asked Rachel.

"It was Arthur's plan to use his Roman military knowledge to teach the Britons to defend themselves by working together. Arthur himself had Roman blood in him, Artorius was his real name. The knights joined him in the cause – they were all from different regions and he taught them how to train their men into small armies. Their small numbers were insignificant on their own, but combined, they could present a formidable force, enough to protect the people of Devon and Cornwall."

"And it worked, didn't it!" said Gareth.

"It did indeed, but for many, it cost them their lives," said Merlin. "Lives they gave up gladly, to protect their families and their way of life! This is why I had to bring you here, to show you your heritage. A heritage that is a lot closer than you may think!"

The twins nodded solemnly again, not really understanding his last words.

"Come, now we shall resume our tour," said Merlin, brightly. "Enough history for the moment!" he concluded as he strode back through the hall.

As they passed back through the enormous doors back into the corridor, Merlin walked ahead and as they turned a corner, Gareth caught sight of a shadowy figure again out of the corner of his eye. He stopped and turned to look, but it dodged back out of sight again behind a pillar; this time he caught sight of a long black dress and a flash of a white apron as it disappeared out of view.

Somewhat unnerved, he rushed to catch up Rachel and Merlin, who were several paces ahead; and still hearing soft footsteps behind him, he wondered why they were being followed.

Chapter Fourteen
Tales of Times Gone By

Merlin may have earned his reputation in history as a great sorcerer, but he could also be classed as one of the greatest storytellers, as the twins soon found out. His accounts of the past left them with a lot to think about when they left the Great Hall, and as he took them on their tour of the castle, he recounted the legends and stories of the knights, his voice echoing in the vaulted stone corridors. They could imagine everything, as he told them about the events of long ago in the very setting it had all happened.

Gareth even stopped looking over his shoulder, as he became entranced by Merlin's tales and he hadn't heard any footsteps for quite a while. The corridors in this area were very busy and Gareth felt much more comfortable. Maybe he had imagined it after all, he thought. After all there were a lot of people in the castle, and why would they want to follow them anyway?

They entered a large kitchen, bustling with ladies working on long wooden tables, preparing a vast amount of vegetables. Others were tending to a large pig, roasting on a spit, or kneading dough into shapes, putting them on a shelf above the fire.

It was hot and smoky in there, and they paused as Merlin sampled a piece of bread, which was still warm. He nodded in appreciation to a small lady in a long dress, covered with a long white pinafore, who slapped his hand jovially as he reached for another piece, and several of the young girls laughed at her audacity.

"I've never seen so much food," said Rachel. "Surely they don't do this every day?"

"No, no," laughed Merlin. "They are preparing for tonight's feast!"

"Feast?" questioned Gareth, shifting uncomfortably, as one of the younger girls smiled coyly at him.

"Oh yes, there will be a great feast tonight, many of the knights are returning from a mission to restore peace in the villages at the far end of Cornwall. They will meet tonight to celebrate their success, before they go their separate ways. We always honour the knights and give thanks for their safe return, 'tis the way here and there will be many a hungry mouth to feed tonight!"

"That sounds brilliant, can we go?" asked Gareth.

"Most certainly, a feast is something not to be missed!" answered Merlin, as they left the kitchen.

"Oh I can't wait, will the knights really be there as well?" asked Gareth, hardly able to contain his excitement.

"They most certainly will, everyone will be there!" Merlin said with a smile. "I believe Kay, Bors, Gawain and Galahad arrived early this morning. Bedevere is on his way and so is Lamorak, they will be here later."

They left the tempting smell of food and the hot kitchen and continued through the castle and up to the top of the largest tower overlooking the sea. A small doorway led them out onto the battlements where the wind whipped at them as they stood looking out at the sea surrounding the castle where it perched at a great height, as though it were on its own rocky island.

"That is the wonderful thing about this castle; it's very position makes it virtually impenetrable," said Merlin, as the strong winds threatened to blow them from the battlements. "Look down below you, an enemy approaching from the sea would almost certainly be dashed onto the rocks. The sea here is rough and wild, and the tides are unpredictable."

They leaned over the edge and saw the waves dashing unmercifully against the black jagged rocks below them.

"They wouldn't stand much chance trying to bring a boat in there," remarked Gareth, as they watched a huge spray of foam cover the rocks as the waves crashed against them.

"Indeed, those that have been foolish enough to try have met their end on the rocks below," said Merlin proudly, as Rachel shivered at the thought of it.

"The only way in is across the causeway, the only strip of land that connects the castle, and they can guard it heavily, since the sea defends this side for them."

"It's brilliant!" said Gareth. "I bet no-one has ever got in here!"

"Not yet," said Merlin, "but there are always those who will try. This castle is a prize that many would love to win, and like any other, it has its own fair share of battle scars."

"So, there have been attacks on the castle, even with the rocks and sea protecting it?" asked Rachel.

"Oh yes," replied Merlin gazing steadfastly out to sea, "and there will always be, as long as it stands, and as long as it houses the remaining followers of the cause."

"So it's not just the castle they want, you mean they want to kill the knights?" she asked.

"The knights and what they stand for, the same as they did with Arthur," said Merlin sadly.

"The knights won't let them though will they? Surely they will always be able to protect it?" Gareth said, imaging them galloping out of the castle on their horses across the causeway with their lances and shields shining, seeing off anyone daring to penetrate their great fortress.

"Alas, Tintagyle will eventually fall, that will be its destiny, but although the castle will fall, the ideals wont, they will live on for many a year. Those remaining will struggle to keep it alive for as long as they can. One day another great leader will take the burden from them, and continue in the ways set here!"

"And they do!" said Rachel, suddenly looking excited. "They must do, because there are knights all through our history books. They start to wear suits of armour, and they go on crusades into other countries! I remember reading about it, they go with a King, but I can't remember his name!"

"It pleases me greatly to hear this," said Merlin, "to know that their work was not only continued, but remembered. It means Arthur's death was not in vain."

He grew silent, his faded blue eyes misted as he gazed out to sea, lost in his memories again. The twins stood silently watching the waves, dashing against the rocks below, realizing how important Arthur had been to the old wizard.

"You must miss him," Rachel said sympathetically.

"Miss him? Yes," Merlin nodded absentmindedly. "He was like my own son."

"Come now! I am forgetting myself," he said suddenly, breaking the awkward silence. "There is much to do, and still much to tell. We can continue round the battlements, to my tower rooms, plenty of fresh air this way, yes indeed, nothing like it!"

With that, the commanding emerald figure strode off, leaving them to follow, watching his bright gown swirl as the wind caught it and his long snowy white hair blow in disarray as they walked around towards the furthermost point of the castle.

On the other side, they paused for a moment to look down at a small beach, where the land rose sharply up towards the castle and the cliffs. They could see a small cave and a patch of stony beach, protected from the waves and the strong winds. For some reason Rachel felt drawn to it, she knew instinctively that there was some importance to this place, and paused to look at it.

A tall figure at the far end of the battlements disturbed her thoughts, as she realised he was watching her. He was a regal figure, with shoulder length hair and a long red cloak bearing a gold emblem, he smiled and nodded courteously to her. She smiled back uncertainly, suddenly realizing she had been left behind by the others and she turned with relief as Gareth shouted to her from a small wooden doorway in the tower.

She rushed over and followed him into the stairway looking back briefly over her shoulder, but the figure had gone. They navigated another winding staircase that led them downwards this time, back to Merlin's rooms.

"Come, make yourselves comfortable, as I have another long tale to tell," he said as they entered. "Make sure you shut that door firmly behind you, Gareth. These old castles are draughty, and one puff of wind through the door will have us picking up papers for the next ten minutes!"

Rachel looked around at the vast amounts of papers and parchments piled up on every surface and thought that it would probably take much longer than that, an hour at best!

There was a tray of food waiting for them on his big desk, and Merlin had wasted no time in loading up a plate, urging the twins to do the same.

"Isolde, bless her, such a treasure, everything waiting for us, even when they are so busy," he said, with a mouthful, making himself comfortable in his big cushioned chair, where he ate heartily, wiping his long beard periodically on a white napkin.

"Now, I still have much to tell you, but where to begin?" he mused, taking a bite of chicken leg.

"Well, you started to tell us about Valonia, last night," ventured Rachel. "You said it wasn't an ordinary place."

"No, it certainly isn't!" he agreed. "But we are starting half way through the story, and I need to start at the very beginning, for you to understand."

"So when exactly is the beginning of all this?" asked Gareth, rather impatiently.

"I have brought you back as close to the beginning as I can, into my time."

"This time thing is getting very confusing," Gareth replied.

"Forget time for a moment, it is but a dimension where we, as earthly beings live out our lives to eventually die, as is our destiny."

"I don't see how we can forget it, when we've just travelled back thousands of years," said Gareth flatly.

"Let me tell you the story from whence it began, long before Arthur's time. It will all become clear when I have finished," said Merlin, taking a long drink from his goblet thoughtfully, while the twins waited quietly, in anticipation.

"Long ago," he started. "A very small vestige of our creator's power was somehow left here, trapped, if you like. There were only a few, who knew about it, and they sought to protect it and kept it hidden. They knew enough to know that it was something special;

something they could not allow to fall into the ordinary man's hands. The ancient Briton's lived a simple life; they worshiped what they could see: the earth, the seasons, the moon, and the stars, things they understood. Mother Earth was their God. Fortunately there were those with an ancient wisdom that recognized that this power was something much more than anything they had previously understood. They learned from it, and sought to protect it at all costs, and for that, they became the Guardians of the Power. They became timeless ethereal beings, trapped in time with the very source they protected."

"Hang on," interrupted Rachel, looking horrified. "Aren't we supposed to be the new Keepers of this Power? That won't happen to us will it?"

"No, no, my dear, your part is entirely different."

"Thank goodness," said Rachel, breathing a sigh of relief.

"For hundreds of years the power lay protected and undisturbed until the time of Arthur. When he was quite young, Arthur was brought to me by his mother, for reasons I shall not disclose, but when he was old enough I sent him to join the Romans. He learnt their ways, ways much more sophisticated than our own at the time. He learnt how to fight with an army on horseback, with proper plans, executed with precision to their advantage."

"But I thought Arthur's parents were the king and queen here, why did he go with the Romans?" said Gareth, trying to remember the stories and films he had seen.

"Firstly, Briton didn't have one sole King or Queen that ruled the country. There were chieftains, leaders who had earned their lands in previous battles, who built great fortresses like this one. They would be considered as 'King' of their domain. Secondly, Arthur's early story has been kept a mystery, and I think it should remain so."

"So where does this Power fit into all of this then?" asked Gareth, realizing the old wizard was not going to disclose any secrets he knew about Arthur.

"Patience my dear boy let me continue. As I explained before, the Romans left us and as a high ranking officer, Arthur could have gone with them. He would have had many privileges in Rome, but he chose to stay and help the people of his birthright. The Saxons and Gauls knew of the Romans' departure and were waiting for the chance to invade and Arthur knew this."

"I still don't understand what the Power has to do with all this?" said Rachel, growing impatient with his lengthy explanations.

"It had a great deal to do with it," Merlin answered. "Arthur's vision to bring everyone together and build an army of their own, instead of every leader fighting against their neighbours, was at first difficult and it was hard to obtain the peoples' trust. He and a handful of knights were eventually faced with an impossible battle, without enough supporters, it looked as though they were doomed to fail. This was when the Power, despite its protection, suddenly unleashed itself in the form of Excalibur, the tales of which, quickly spread far and wide. Men came from the far corners of Devon and Cornwall to serve under Arthur and their mission began!"

"So that's how the Knights of the Round Table started," said Gareth in admiration.

"Indeed it was!" answered Merlin. "The stone table was made round for equality, so that no-one, not even Arthur sat at the head of the table. Everyone's efforts were equal, as they all fought under the same banner, even if their own men and homestead was fifty miles or more away!"

"That's so fantastic!" breathed Gareth.

"It was indeed, except that where there is success, there is also great jealousy, from others seeking power. Here the tale continues, Medraut was Arthur's step brother, he pretended to serve their cause and fought with them, but all the time he was consumed with jealousy and wanted everything that Arthur had."

"Who was Medraut?" asked Rachel.

"You would know him as Mordred: here he was Medraut, the Black Knight. He was to become Arthur's mortal enemy, a man he trusted as a fellow knight. Eventually at the battle of Camlann, fighting alongside Arthur, Medraut saw his chance to slay the one man who held everything he desired. There were a great many that died fighting the Saxons in that battle, and it is said that Arthur was one of them."

"But, you don't think he did?" asked Gareth. "Do you think this

174

Medraut killed him?"

"Oh, I do indeed. The losses were heavy on both sides, but Arthur still seen on horseback to lead his men up to the point where the battle was won. He raised his sword high as the enemy retreated. Medraut supposedly found him, and dutifully led his horse back, with Arthur's body draped across it, but I think it was his hand that slayed him!"

"Mordred tricked me into the quicksand in Valonia," said Rachel, "are you saying he's the same person that might have killed Arthur?"

"The very same!" said Merlin.

"But that was thousands of years ago, how could he be here and yet be the Lord of the manor in Valonia?" asked Gareth. "That's impossible!"

"Not so impossible when you consider that you are talking to someone who has been on this earth, even longer than you could ever imagine."

They grew silent, realizing that Merlin was referring to himself, and that seemed quite impossible as well.

At this point Gareth heard a slight noise behind him, as though there was someone at the door, he expected to hear a knock, but none came and he assumed that it must the wind rustling up the stairs as Merlin had predicted and returned with interest to his story.

"Mordred brought Arthur's horse and body back, but he carried Excalibur himself," continued Merlin. "To others, it was a selfless act that drew no attention, as it was their custom. I think he wanted the sword for himself, as he kept it for many a day, and only relinquished it when he was pressed to do so by the other knights. I think that during this time, a small amount of the sword's power may have rubbed off on him, as he has been able to do things that no other mortal, apart from myself, would be allowed to do."

"What sort of things?" asked Rachel.

"He has been able to travel through the passages to Valonia, into a time where he doesn't age! Time stands still for him there, in the same way it does for you, while you are here."

"Does it?" replied Gareth, in surprise.

"Indeed it does, if you have looked at your watch since you have

175

been here, you will find that it hasn't moved since you left Valonia," answered Merlin.

"No it hasn't, I noticed that," said Rachel, "but I just thought the battery had gone in mine!"

"No," laughed Merlin. "You will find it works perfectly, once you are back in your own time again!"

"So if we went back now, it would be as though we hadn't left?" asked Gareth.

"If you went back two years from now, the people would still be leaving the meeting in the cavern, as it was when you entered the passage of time with me!"

"And we wouldn't get any older, if we stayed here?" asked Rachel.

"No, and this is what happens to Medraut in Valonia, he becomes ageless, time has no effect on him as it is not a time he is supposed to be in!"

"This is where I really don't understand this time thing!" said Gareth, turning the conversation full circle.

"No, to understand that, you need to understand Valonia," Merlin answered. "Once the Power made itself known by releasing itself into Arthur's keeping, it became of our time, and part of it was unleashed into man's hands. This was all very well, while it was being used for good, but in the wrong hands there are no boundaries on the havoc it could wreak on mankind. The Guardians realised this problem and decided to take steps to prevent it. A special place was created and named Avalon. A place suspended in its own time, a time which moved at a much slower pace, totally out of synchronization with the continuing time here. Excalibur was hidden there, along with Arthur's body."

This time Gareth knew there was definitely a scuffling noise by the door and he looked round in time to see the door-knob turning. The door opened very slightly but again no-one knocked or entered. For a moment Gareth had the distinct impression that someone was listening to them, but before he could say anything a slight draught blew some papers off the cabinet next to the door.

"Oh dear, just as I said, draughts everywhere, did you not pull the door hard enough Gareth?" admonished Merlin. "Go back and

176

give it a good bang!"

"I did, I checked, it was shut fast!" answered Gareth as he got up to close it. As he approached, he heard footsteps running down the stairs. He paused to listen to them, and wondered if this was the same woman who he had thought was following them earlier, but then he realised that the footsteps were too heavy, they were those of a man.

"There was someone there! They were listening at the door," Gareth said in alarm. "I heard them running away!"

For a moment Merlin looked concerned and went to the door; he walked out and looked down over the winding staircase, but all was quiet.

"There is no-one there, I think you must be imagining things!" he said. "Maybe my tales are too much for you, maybe we should leave them for a while."

"No, no, we want to know!" said Rachel. "Anyway, it could just have been the man that was on the battlements with us, going back down the stairs."

"Man?" questioned Merlin. "We were alone up there! Dear me, what imaginations you two have."

"There was a man there – I saw him!" Rachel said, adamantly.

"And there really was someone at the door!" Gareth insisted.

"Well, now, I am sure there is a very reasonable explanation for all of this," said Merlin, thoughtfully stroking his beard. "Maybe I missed the man on the battlements and maybe that was him on the stairway. If he had opened the turret door, the wind would have whistled down the stairs and if it was not shut tight, my door would easily have blown open. There now, that must be the answer," he concluded with a satisfied smile.

Gareth was not so sure; he knew that the door had been shut and he knew that he had seen the door-knob turn, but before he could say any more, Merlin returned to his story.

"Now, I was telling you about Avalon, wasn't I?" he said

"So where is this Avalon, then?" asked Rachel who, unlike her brother, was quite happy with Merlin's deductions.

"It started out as Avalon, but later, the letters altered and it became known as Valonia," he answered. "The Guardians ensured that only a chosen few should pass into this time, those of the direct blood-line from Arthur, with their closest friends. The caverns of time were opened up and they were smuggled through into Avalon, into a time ahead of their own. This is where they buried Arthur and vowed to protect the Power."

"So Valonia is really Avalon! That explains why the place is so strange," interjected Gareth. "We thought we had stepped back in time when we got there!"

"You had, Valonia, is a sort of half-way place between the two worlds. It renders it safe from a visit from anyone from any other time, including yours, as your time has followed the true course, from this one here."

"That explains why I couldn't find it on the map, and why our phones wouldn't work and we couldn't get the radio!" said Gareth, excitedly.

"Exactly, because in your time, it's not really there," he answered.

"I'm sorry, but I don't get that bit at all," interrupted Rachel. "If the whole purpose of this place is to stop anyone from going there, how were we able to do it?"

"Because you are special, you belong there," explained Merlin. "As I was explaining, the people who went to Avalon were Arthur's immediate descendants. In Avalon, they became the protectors, and the Power passed to them for safe keeping, hence the title 'Keepers of the Power.' The other people were there to support and to continue the Ways there in secrecy, and for that, they earned the titles of Keepers of the Ways, or Keepers of the Knowledge."

"That explains the lettering on the plaques in the village and the books we found, with the gold letters, K.O.K. and K.O.W!" cried Gareth, and Merlin nodded in response.

"All of these people committed their lives to this village, to live separately from the rest of the world, in another dimension of time."

"But surely anyone could walk up the lanes from the station into the pass and walk down to the village, though?" asked Rachel, still unconvinced.

"No my dear, they couldn't, because the lane would not be there.

All of the pathways, the pass and the village are in a totally separate time. No one could take this route uninvited."

"Wow, that's just awesome!" said Gareth, ignoring his sister's worried look.

"The Keepers hold the Power; it passes to them for safekeeping," continued Merlin. "The Guardians decided that it should never pass to any one person. Since then it has been held by twins that have followed on directly from the blood-line of Arthur, one male and one female. For generations, this is how it has continued. As I said before, Mordred was still pursuing the Power and came through the tunnels of time, bringing his twin sister with him. He has waited for centuries, flitting from his own time to the one in Avalon, with time passing him by, hoping that eventually the line of twins would run out and the Power would pass to him."

"But it didn't, did it?" asked Gareth.

"No, and that is why he took matters into his own hands to eliminate the twins in succession, Geraint and Johnny. He thought that he had finally become Keeper himself and then killed his own sister Celia. What he didn't realise, was that the Power had already passed on to you."

"This is all very complicated!" said Rachel, with a large sigh. "What exactly does it mean for us?"

"That is not for me to decide. My role is to enlighten, guide, and inform you, nothing more. I have kept Bronwyn's secret since you were born, a secret that has now been taken out of my hands by those much greater than I. However I must tell you though, that with this Power comes a gift."

"What sort of gift?" asked Rachel dubiously.

"The male twin inherits great bravery and strength; the female inherits the wisdom and the sight."

"What do you mean by the sight?" asked Rachel, ignoring her brother's obvious enthusiasm at his gifts.

"The sight, my dear, means that you have the ability to see, predict, and understand things that most cannot."

"Well, that would explain a lot then!" said Gareth, sarcastically. "That would explain why you've always known things in advance, and why you've always been a bit weird!"

"I haven't been weird!" said Rachel tearfully. "I haven't got this sight thing!"

"You have my dear, you have already told me you saw me in a crystal ball," said Merlin gently. "This is a gift; it is not something to be frightened of. It is merely something that you don't understand yet."

"I don't want to understand it and I don't want to see things!" she announced woefully.

"Well, you've already been doing it for years, trust me!" said Gareth resolutely. "You know you have, the only difference is that now we know why!"

"No I haven't!" she said stubbornly.

"What about that grey bird you were on about for years? I never saw it until it attacked me and I fell off my bike!" he retorted quickly.

"Ah, now that is something different," intervened Merlin, as Rachel looked about to launch herself in fury on her brother. "I can explain your sightings of the bird, as it was in fact sent by Bronwyn."

"What?" they both chorused in astonishment.

"Bronwyn was so distraught at having to leave you both, that she used her powers as a Keeper to devise a way to watch you, check up on you, and make sure you were all right."

"Hold on a minute, you're telling us that Bronwyn was the bird!" said Gareth disbelievingly.

"Not exactly, she didn't actually fly there herself, you understand, she merely transported the form of the bird as her eyes. She used this form in desperation to stay close to you, her children."

For a moment, they both fell silent, deep in thought, reeling from the impact of the old wizard's words.

"So if Bronwyn could do that, what about the horrible black bird that watched us on the beach and forced me onto the quicksand? Was that something to do with Mordred? Did he do the same thing?" breathed Rachel in horror.

"I'm fairly sure he did, although again, these are not powers that he should have."

"So he was trying to kill me?" asked Rachel, even more

180

horrified.

"You and anyone else who has stood in his way," answered Merlin. "This is why you had to come back here; nothing is safe without you taking up your inherited roles. The past, the present, the future: Mordred has to be stopped before he does any more damage!"

The twins sat quietly again, still trying to digest the enormity of his words.

"Well, I think, that's enough for now," said Merlin kindly, "and we have a feast to prepare for. Forget Medraut, for tonight you will meet some of the great men who fought with Arthur, loyal, honourable men who were true to his cause!"

"The knights, right?" said Gareth, hopefully. "We'll meet the knights?"

"You will indeed, my boy!" he laughed. "Now Isolde will have left you some clothes in the room upstairs, I will come back for you later, and we shall join them all at the great feast!" he said proudly, as he made his way to the door, his gown swirling around him on the way out.

Chapter Fifteen
Speeches and Spectres

"So what do you make of all that then?" asked Gareth, as the door shut behind their elderly host.

"I dread to think!" Rachel answered resignedly.

"Well, you must admit that even if it sounds a bit far-fetched, it explains an awful lot!" he answered, feeling slightly annoyed at her reluctance to enter into the debate he was so keen to embark on.

"I suppose so!" she answered in a tired voice.

"Look, I know you don't like all of this," he started, slightly more sympathetically, "but I can't wait to meet the knights at the feast, it's just a shame that Arthur isn't here as well: it would have been so unbelievably fantastic to meet him too!"

"Well, since you're looking forward to it so much, you can go and change first then," replied his sister caustically.

"I'd forgotten about that bit!" Gareth replied, his former exuberance suddenly leaving him. "Oh no, I dread to think what he's going to have me wearing next!"

"Well, you'll soon find out won't you!" she answered unsympathetically.

Reluctantly, he climbed the small stairs to the bedroom. His patience had run out with Rachel, who he decided was being deliberately difficult, and if he knew anything at all, it was that there was no point trying to reason with her in her present mood! On inspecting his new attire, folded neatly on the bed, his worst fears were realised.

"Oh no! Fancy clothes now, this just gets worse!" he said aloud in disgust, as he held up a richly-embroidered tunic with matching bright blue hose, and if that wasn't bad enough, there was a matching pair of pointed blue slippers!

"I can't believe I'm doing this!" he said with a big sigh as he struggled into them.

He returned back down the stairs, still tugging at the hose. This time Rachel didn't bother to spare his feelings and laughed, until the tears rolled down her cheeks.

"It is almost worth putting up with all of this, just to see you dressed in that!" she said in between fits of giggles. "I would give anything to have a camera!"

"Well, I'm really pleased it's put a smile on your face!" he replied dryly. "No doubt you'll have some long girly dress that you'll be quite pleased with!"

"Well, whatever I've got, I'm not going to look as silly as you!" she replied unkindly, still giggling as she made her way up to the small room upstairs.

The sight of her brother's skinny legs in the bright blue hose had cheered her up no end, and she was still smiling as she inspected the dress left for her, a dress that wouldn't upset anyone. It was quite beautiful; she held it up and stroked the soft fabric, admiring the beads sewn along the edges of the sleeves, and all over the bodice in a deep V shape. The material was a silky cream colour, and the bodice was embroidered in fine silver threads around tiny silver beads.

She put it on and twirled round holding out the full skirt, deciding that maybe dressing up in these strange costumes was quite nice after all. She was disturbed by a knock at the door; she opened it to find a very shy Isolde, who immediately bobbed a curtsey.

"Merlin said I was to come and help you, miss! I am to do your hair," she said quietly, with her head down submissively, as though frightened to look at her.

"Oh, oh, all right then," said Rachel, equally unsure of herself, and totally unused to anyone 'doing her hair' for her!

"Do you have a brush, miss?" prompted the young girl.

"Oh ... yes ..." Rachel answered haltingly. "There's a brush on the dressing table."

She sat down uncomfortably while Isolde brushed her hair, braiding half of it into a coronet, leaving the rest cascading over her shoulders.

"There, miss, that looks lovely!" said the shy girl, obviously pleased with her efforts.

Rachel thanked her and she scuttled away quickly, curtseying again dutifully as she left.

After patting her hair, in the absence of a mirror, Rachel ventured downstairs to join Gareth, who was looking avidly out of the window, at the courtyard.

"Just as I expected!" he announced, looking at her. "I'm the only one that looks stupid!"

Taking his remark as the nearest she would ever get to a compliment from him, she felt slightly guilty as he tugged at the hem of his braided tunic.

"Well, at least it's a bit longer than the other one, and I'm sure they will all be dressed like that!" she said sympathetically.

"I don't care, I don't do tights!" he replied emphatically.

"They don't really look that bad," she ventured.

"Yes, they do! But never mind that, come over here and have a look, I've been watching all the people arriving, there must be hundreds!" he said excitedly, almost forgetting his attire. "There has been stream after stream of them on horses, coming over the causeway: they must be all the knight's men!"

Rachel joined him at the window to survey the ancient scene again, the busy courtyard now lit by flaming torches. The smell of food and strains of music drifted up on the night air, along with the voices of the many people congregating in the courtyard, and even Rachel began to join in her brother's enthusiasm.

Eventually Merlin arrived in another long gown, even more richly decorated than the others. This one was a deep purple, embroidered in silver, with stars and moons. On his head perched a rather strange looking hat, in a matching design. It looked as though its long point should have stood erect, like a traditional wizard's hat, but instead the long point fell over his left shoulder.

The old wizard complimented them on their appearance and admired Rachel's gown and hair, before leading them down towards the noise. They followed him rather nervously through the corridors down to the huge banqueting hall they had seen earlier that day. This time though the corridors were full of people, some standing talking, others making their way towards the feast. Everyone had obviously donned their best attire for the occasion, most of the men wore embroidered tunics similar to Gareth's, and all of the women had long dresses, with full skirts and decorated bodices.

When they entered through the huge wooden doors, Rachel thought she had never seen so many people in one room. The noise was almost deafening as they picked their way through the crowd to find seats at one of the over-laden, long wooden tables.

Their table was at the back of the hall next to the top table, where the knights were all sitting as guests of honour. Merlin sat in between Rachel and Gareth, who found himself next to a large rough-looking man and a lady with long black hair. Rachel's neighbours were younger, and much more interested in each other than in the new arrivals, although they both nodded courteously at Merlin as he took his seat.

In front of them was a heavy metal plate and a knife, and the table was full of platters containing large sides of pork, surrounded by whole carrots, parsnips, chunks of turnip, swede and large potatoes, cooked in their skins.

"Don't stand on ceremony here, fill your plate before it's all gone!" warned Merlin, carving off a chunk of pork with his knife.

The twins watched the other guests for a moment as they speared everything with their knives, dropping them on to their plates. They ate everything with their fingers, wiping the grease from the meat off afterwards, unceremoniously, on their clothes.

Heeding Merlin's warning the twins quickly did the same as the food was disappearing rapidly, as he had predicted. The pork was warm and tasted wonderful, even the vegetables had a flavour of their own, and they both nodded in appreciation, reaching for more. In between the platters were large pitchers of ale. Gareth reached towards one and was immediately reprimanded by Merlin, who took his large metal goblet and quickly filled it from another, containing water, much to Gareth's disappointment.

"You can have some mead for the toasts later," Merlin said, "but the ale is strong enough to lay the largest man here on his back after a few goblets!"

Most of the food had been consumed by now, and some jugglers in the middle of the room provided the entertainment for a short while, their finale creating a huge response from the large crowd, as they juggled with lighted batons that filled the room with their smoke. This was followed by several minstrels with strange sounding instruments, who sang lilting melodies as they passed amongst the tables.

Rachel glanced occasionally at the top table, at the knights, noticing that there was a high backed carved chair in the middle which was empty. She recognized Percivale, who had met them at the cave entrance with the horses and the young man with the dark hair, who she had seen on the white horse in the morning through the window. He seemed to have the attention of most of the ladies in the room, and for some reason she took an unfounded dislike to him.

The room fell silent as a large man on the knight's table stood up. The music died instantly, and all eyes turned towards him.

"Friends and fellow knights! We celebrate the safe return of our noble brothers!" He said as loud cheers and banging of fists echoed round the tables. He smiled and raised his hand, and the room fell silent again. "Vortigen's power is weakening. The Saxons have been driven out of Cornwall again, and Bedwyr's people are safe. There was many a good man though, that fell, aye, Richard of Caer Wise, and his son Marcus. Torrick and Myr, Rodrick, and Bowden from Ives, to name but a few. The fall was heavy, and there were many other brave men that met their fate in this battle. But not as many as those of the Saxons though! The Saxon loss was far greater than ours: 'twas their blood that stained the ground, with the remaining few fleeing for their lives, to the far corners of Cornwall. There they will be picked off, one by one, by our brothers in arms. So we toast the brave, who lost their lives for our cause, and may God protect their souls!" he said raising his goblet high.

"Aye, may God protect them!" resounded around the room as the heavy chairs scraped and they all stood raising their goblets in respect.

"And we thank God for our victory and the return of our own! Lamorak, Percivale, Kay, Bors, Owaine, Galahad and Bedwyr, our own knights, who still carry the fight to every corner of our lands against our enemies, our own knights still willing to fight for Arthur's cause, and carry on his work here!"

"Aye, thank God for their return! To the knights!" the crowd murmured, toasting again, raising their goblets in silent appreciation.

"And a toast to all of those, who are still willing to take up the sword against the Saxons and anyone else who dares to burn our villages and murder our kinsman," the large man continued passionately, swigging again from the goblet in his hand. "A toast to anyone prepared to join in the fight for our lands!"

"Aye! Aye! We will fight! We will fight!" the adamant responses resounded around the great stone walls, as the crowd grew louder each time in their support. Rachel glanced around nervously as the tension in the room built, and the men stood, goblets raised, shouting loudly.

"Let us not forget our cause! Let us not forget why we fight, and let us not forget our great leader!" said the large knight.

"Aye! Aye!" The response was quieter this time, more sombre.

"A leader we can no longer see," the knight continued, "But a leader whose spirit will always lead us into battle for his cause. Be assured that, against our enemies, he still fights with us! Not dead, not forgotten, but challenging us to continue, until the last enemy of our people has been slain!"

The room was completely silent as he turned to the empty chair in the middle of the banqueting table, raised his goblet and said, "To Arthur, our leader, our King!"

"To Arthur!" was the respectful response. All eyes were turned to the empty seat as they raised their goblets and drank, repeating his words.

The silent commitment in the room emphasized the deep respect that everyone there had, for their dead leader. The twins found it quite overwhelming and politely raised their own goblets towards the high-backed seat in the middle. As she did so, Rachel was astonished to see that it was no longer empty. It had been filled by the man she had seen in the rich clothes on the battlements earlier. This time he wore a golden crown over his dark wavy hair and nodded genially to his people as they drank their toast. His smile was the same as earlier, gentle and compassionate, and for a moment, it was directed at Rachel, as he raised his own goblet and saluted his people.

There was a loud scraping of chairs as everyone sat down and the noise resumed as everyone started talking and the minstrels struck up again. Rachel looked back at the place in the middle of the top table, but it was once again empty.

"Who was that man they were toasting?" she asked Merlin quietly.

"Which man?" Merlin asked cautiously.

"There was a man, sitting on the middle chair, while they were making the toasts!" answered Rachel, feeling sick as she knew what his answer would be, even before he said it. "He was the man I told you I saw on the battlements."

"It was him you saw, I had no idea!" Merlin said excitedly. "And tonight, you saw him again? That was Arthur, my dear," he said, patting her hand comfortingly. "I don't think you realise what an enormous privilege has been bestowed upon you; every man in this room would have given anything to see their leader again, but you and I were the only ones to see him!"

Privilege or not, Rachel didn't enjoy the rest of the banquet; instead she spent the rest of the evening casting fearful glances at the empty chair in the middle of the table, afraid that the imposing figure in the crown and robes would reappear.

To her relief, the seat remained empty, but even this didn't make her feel any better. Instead she managed to catch the eye of the dark, young knight several times, who obviously must have thought she was looking at him, like every other female in his vicinity. She caught his attention again and he smiled at her, and was treated to a frosty glare.

She wished she could just leave and go back to the safety of the tower room. Her brother on the other hand was in his element, especially when Bors and Kay, the two knights they had been toasting earlier, joined them to talk to Merlin. They recounted their battle story, which Rachel found almost as distressing as the apparition she had seen earlier.

"What's the matter with you?" asked Gareth, eventually noticing how quiet she was.

She shook her head and mumbled, "Tell you later." Gareth shrugged and his attention returned to the conversation of the knights. The room was even noisier now, the voices and laughter almost drowning out the music from the minstrels who were still resolutely playing and singing, despite their audience's lack of attention.

"Well, 'tis good to see your safe return, I am so glad that all turned out well, but I think we may now have to bid you goodnight," Merlin said to Kay and Bors. "It is time I looked after my two young charges here, and I am happy to go to my bed before this gets any livelier!"

"And livelier it will get, indeed, as there is still many a long hour to celebrate!" laughed Bors.

"Celebrations into the night that are far too long, for a man of my years!" returned Merlin.

The wizard politely said his goodbyes, the knights bowed low, and they left the Great Hall with Gareth still protesting loudly.

"Oh did we have to leave? It was just getting going! I'll bet it will get better and better!" said Gareth, annoyed that he was going to miss any of it.

"No I would say it will be all downhill from here, as the ale will be taking its effect on most that have downed many a flagon. No, it is time to leave, before it gets really raucous!" was his firm reply. "We have much to do tomorrow, yes much to do indeed!"

They followed Merlin's swirling purple gown as it swished away in front of them, back through the corridors to the spiral steps leading to his rooms. Once in the tower room the old wizard left them fairly quickly, and they watched out of the window for a while as the crowd in the courtyard below carried on the festivities. Eventually even Gareth had to admit defeat after his fourth rather large yawn, and they made their way to the room upstairs, and climbed into the huge bed.

Normally, Rachel would have been most indignant at having to sleep in the same bed as her brother, however big it was, but on this occasion she was almost grateful that she was not on her own, as she was still feeling very unnerved by her sighting of the late King Arthur.

"What a night! That was just so fantastic!" said Gareth as he jumped on the bed.

"To be honest I'm really glad it's over," she replied dismally.

"Why? I thought it was amazing!" he replied, pulling the bed-cover up to his neck. "There's something wrong with you! How could you not enjoy that?"

Reluctantly she told him about her visions of Arthur on the battlements, and at the feast.

"Wow, and you're complaining about it? I would have loved to have seen him!"

"Yes, but you didn't, did you!" she replied crossly. "It was only Merlin, and I! And even he didn't see him on the battlements!"

"So?" questioned Gareth.

"Gareth, you're completely missing the point here, he's dead!" said Rachel, sitting on the edge of the bed, while her brother slid down making himself comfortable. "I don't want to see dead people!"

"Well, if you think about it logically, they're all dead, aren't they! Think about it, everyone we've seen tonight, all died hundreds of years ago! So I don't see what your problem is," were her brother's final words, as he pulled the covers around him. He immediately dropped off into a heavy sleep, aided by the goblet of mead he had had earlier at the toasts.

Eventually Rachel managed to go to sleep, after tossing and turning on the lumpy bed, not comforted in the least by her brother's last remarks! It was a restless sleep, where she dreamed of men on horses fighting with great shining swords, against hundreds of rough looking men with helmets, wielding large axes.

She saw villages on fire with women clutching their children screaming, fleeing from men. They chased them, shouting in a strange guttural language, their axes swiping at anyone crossing their path. She watched almost like an observer, as they caught the

190

women and dragged them away, screaming even louder. She saw the wounded lying in pain, and the dying as they drew their last breath from fighting to save their families, and she felt their suffering as though it were her own.

In the distance, she saw horsemen with banners held high. Their long silver swords glinted as the light caught them and they galloped hard towards the smoke and mayhem. The swords clashed hard against the axes, and they were met with a ferocious defence. They continued to flood in from several directions, cornering the marauders, who, eventually were so confused, they disbanded and fled, rather than be left with their sudden unknown opponents. They headed towards the woods and hills, with the horsemen in pursuit.

An eerie stillness prevailed. A stillness that was almost as disturbing as the vicious fighting. A stillness where there was nothing left except smoke and the crackling sparks of fire as the last building fell, amongst the muffled cries of the remaining women. Fearfully they went towards the bodies strewn around the burning village, sinking to their knees crying as they found their husbands, fathers, or children on the rough ground, stained dark with blood.

The sound of the horses' hooves became fainter as the knights rode after the fleeing enemy, except for one remaining knight, who pulled up his horse on top of the hill and turned to survey the tragic scene below him.

He was young, and wore the battle dress of the knights, his dark brown wavy hair fell beneath his helmet and his deep-set dark eyes looked sad. For a moment he sat on his pure white horse with its silvery tail and mane, surveying the scene of destruction left behind them.

Rachel found herself standing next to him, looking at the remains of the village, as though she saw it through his eyes, and for a moment she felt his anger and disgust, followed by a deep sadness. Her eyes were still stinging from the smoke as she turned to look at the young knight and noticed the tears that ran freely down his face. Again she felt what he was feeling, and enormous waves of extreme sadness, guilt, and despair washed over her momentarily, turning quickly into a fierce hatred, which overwhelmed her completely.

The knight wiped the tears away with the back of his hand, and urged his horse forward in the direction the others had gone, looking backwards once more at the tragic scene, before he galloped off to join them.

Left alone on the hill, Rachel still felt a huge sadness, and she realised her own face was wet with tears. She looked back after the knight, who was barely visible now as his horse galloped headlong towards the woods.

She brushed her tears away and stood watching the scene below her, slightly puzzled as the intense pangs of grief and anger were gone. Instead she was left with a great emptiness as though she had no thoughts or feelings. She could feel the wind blowing her hair and she could smell the smoke as it filled the air. The sounds of grief below her grew louder, as more people ventured out to join the others already mourning their family's deaths. She wanted to close her eyes and put her hands over her ears to shut it all out, but she couldn't.

Chapter Sixteen
A Dark, Narrow Escape

"Rachel! Rachel! For goodness sake, wake up, will you!" she heard Gareth calling from a great distance.

Her eyes flew open, and she realised he was shaking her, but more importantly she was back in the lumpy bed at the castle.

"Thank goodness! I was beginning to think there was something wrong with you! You've been moaning and thrashing about for ages!" her brother said.

"I had the most dreadful nightmare!" she replied, sitting up and rubbing her eyes, still dazed.

"Sounded like it! Come on, you'd better get up! Merlin's downstairs and that girl brought us breakfast ages ago!"

Breakfast! The very thought of it brought a wave of nausea as Rachel sat up, struggling to rid herself of the lingering feelings of the nightmare.

"Come on, Merlin told me he's going to take us somewhere really special before we go back!"

"All right, I'll be down in a minute, and by the way Gareth, 'that girl' has a name. It's Isolde!" she said crossly.

"Okay, Isolde then, if it makes you feel better!" he replied, slightly puzzled by her angry reaction.

"It does," she answered, struggling up further against the solid pillows. "She might be a servant here, but I don't think we've got any idea what the people here have been through."

"Right, well, I just came to tell you that breakfast is downstairs!" he replied making his way towards the narrow staircase, deciding it was best to leave her since she was in such a strange mood.

Eventually Rachel made her way down to join them, still feeling slightly odd, and unable to shake off the depressing feelings of the dream.

"Ah, Rachel, we have saved you some breakfast," said Merlin as he handed her a plate. "Are you all right my dear, you look very pale?"

"She's had a nightmare," Gareth answered for her.

Merlin nodded, taking in her silence and white face.

"Well, now, I'm sure you will feel better once you have had a drink and some food, take your time my dear, take your time."

He was right, she did feel better once she had finished a goblet of milk and eaten some bread. She sat quietly listening to them discussing the banquet and the awful feelings the dream had left her with, started to diminish.

'It must just have been a nightmare after all,' she thought to herself, listening to her brother's excited voice recounting over and over again, the events of the night before.

"Now then, Gareth, maybe you could carry the trays down for Isolde. She has been kind enough to wait on us several times now and I'm sure she will be delighted to find she has one less trip up the stairs to make! Can you remember your way back to the kitchens?" asked Merlin.

"I think so," answered Gareth, slightly surprised at this request.

"Splendid," said Merlin, as he loaded him up with the trays and opened the door, shutting it rather unceremoniously behind him.

"I trust you are feeling a little better now, Rachel?" he enquired once they were alone.

Rachel nodded, realising Merlin had just sent Gareth on an errand so that he could talk to her.

"The nightmare you had, do you feel you could tell me about it now?" he ventured.

Although she had no desire to relive the dream, she recounted it, mainly out of politeness, shuddering as the powerful feelings came back to her. Merlin nodded, saying nothing until she had finished.

"It was so real, it wasn't like a dream, it was as though I was really there," she said with a sob. "I have never seen anything like that before in my life, and I don't ever want to again. It was ... it was barbaric!" she finished.

"There have been many events here that one could only describe as barbaric. The memories linger on in those who experienced them and you have picked up on this, and witnessed them in your dream."

"You mean it was real? It's something that really happened?"

"Most certainly," Merlin replied. "Any visions that you have, will be shown to you for a reason."

"Well, that's even worse then! I don't want visions and I don't want to see things like that!"

"I know it distresses you because you are not used to it, but this is a great gift and a part of your inheritance. I know you do not understand it, but there will always be a connection or a reason why you see certain things."

"I don't care, I didn't ask for a gift, or an inheritance and I don't want one," she answered resolutely.

"Do not distress yourself; anything you see will always become apparent in its own time. Eventually you will learn to trust your visions and learn from them," he said, patting her hand sympathetically.

Meanwhile, Gareth had made his way down to the kitchen. He couldn't see Isolde and put the trays down hastily on the nearest surface he could find, escaping quickly as several girls noticed him and giggled behind their hands, reminding him sharply of the way his sister's friends behaved in his company.

He left shaking his head, deciding that girls were obviously girls, wherever they came from, when a small doorway opened and an old lady in a long black dress and white apron, appeared in front of him.

"'Tis you, I knew it was! Oh let me look at you!" she said advancing towards him.

"I saw you in the Great Hall yesterday, and I knew it was you, come back to us! I shall not let them take you away again, oh no, this time I will hide you. Come, come with me," she said, her hand gripping his wrist surprisingly firmly.

"I'm sorry, but I think you must be mistaking me for someone else," Gareth said worriedly, trying to stand his ground. Frantically the woman pulled at him, becoming more and more agitated as he resisted. She called out and a man appeared, a strange looking person, his face almost lopsided, with long wispy hair, straggling around it. He limped badly as he came out of the doorway and joined them.

"Oh Alfrick, see who it is, he has come back to us!" she said, "but we must not let them know he is here, or they will take him again for sure!"

The lopsided man screwed up his face and peered at Gareth.

"Aye 'tis him, no doubt about it, 'tis him all right!" he answered, revealing a toothless grin.

"Look I don't know who you think I am, but I can assure you I'm not them!" said Gareth in alarm, realising he had been right all along and they had been followed the day before by the old woman.

"Alfrick, you must help me get him away from them, you know what we must do!" she whispered confidentially to the strange man, her bony fingers digging into Gareth's arm.

At that moment a large black bird flew towards the open window and settled on the stone sill, its beady eyes watching them. It looked at the old woman and edged nearer, its claws hooking on to the inside of the sill as it cocked its head to one side as though it were listening intently. Gareth looked at it in shock as he recognised it instantly as the bird they had seen in Valonia.

"'Tis him, 'tis him!" panicked the old woman, shooing at the bird with her apron. "'Tis the Black Knight himself, he watches him; he knows who he is and that he has come back to us! Quickly, get him into the passage and shut the door, where he cannot see him!"

She tugged frantically at Gareth's arm, still looking fearfully at the bird and the lopsided man joined her. The bird swooped at them, its wings outstretched and its beak heading straight for the old woman.

"Quickly, Alfrick, quickly," she screamed as she fought off the huge black bird.

Gareth ducked as it mounted a second attack, and before he

196

could do anything a rough hand was clapped over his mouth, and his arm was forced up his back, as Alfrick propelled him towards the doorway.

The bird hissed loudly, and flapped its wings angrily, swooping again as Alfrick forced Gareth into the doorway and the old woman banged the door behind them. Gareth panicked and struggled against them, finding the lopsided Alfrick much stronger than he looked. However hard he struggled, it made no difference and he found himself pushed into a dark passageway with the door barred firmly.

"Do not worry, he cannot see you now. I will never let Medraut know where you are. He shall not know our secret," she continued in a slightly deranged fashion. "He has always suspected, he has watched, he has listened, but he has never been able to find you!"

Gareth struggled again, choking at the strong pungent smell of dirt and grime coming from the hand at his mouth, and found his arm forced further up his back as Alfrick pushed him forwards.

"I will never let him know who you really are, and I will not let the others take you away again. I will hide you, you will be safe with us!" she crooned, as they continued down the dark passage.

Gareth's shouts of fury were muffled by Alfrick's hand, still clapped firmly across his mouth, and he struggled desperately against his lopsided captor.

"Oh if you knew what pain it caused me to have both of my beautiful boys taken away!" she continued, as they pushed him firmly down the passage. "'Twas not your fault, they did not understand you as I did, but do not worry, we will look after you, just as we always did. We will hide you away from prying eyes and none shall know you are here, just as it was before!"

The fear mounted in Gareth as he tried again to get away from the surprisingly strong man. He drew his arm forward and elbowed Alfrick heavily in the stomach.

"No!" he shouted, eventually wriggling free after delivering a hefty kick on what must have been Alfrick's bad leg. "Let me go! I don't know who you think I am, but I'm telling you, you've made a mistake!"

Gareth lunged at Alfrick, who was still clutching his leg and howling with pain. The lunge knocked him backwards and he fell heavily against the wall. He gave the old woman a shove that sent her tumbling against her accomplice and ran as fast as he could down the maze of passages that wove their way underneath the castle. He ran on and on, turning left and right into other smaller stone corridors, until he was completely out of breath. He stopped by a small doorway where the door was ajar. He looked in cautiously to make sure it was empty before he went in and shut the wooden door behind him. He pulled a heavy latch down so that no-one could follow him and leant back in relief against the wall, his heart pounding in his chest.

There was a candle burning in a small holder on a wooden table, which gave him just enough light to see he was in a small square room with no windows. It was furnished spartanly with rough wooden furniture. He began to get his breath back, and listened at the door. He couldn't hear anyone, but no doubt they would be looking for him, he thought glumly. His relief was rapidly diminishing, as he realised he must be deep under the castle somewhere, and he had no idea how to get back.

Gareth stood deliberating as to whether he should attempt the corridors again and try to find his way out, or stay there for a while in the hope that they would give up looking for him. Another thought suddenly struck him, since there was a candle burning in the room he was hiding in, might the person who had lit it be returning?

As if that someone had heard his thoughts, a door creaked slowly open in the furthest corner of the room and Gareth rushed to unlatch the door he was standing by.

"It's all right, don't be afraid, I have come to help you," he heard a young boy say.

"Don't open the door, Alfrick is still scouring the passages for you."

Gareth left the latch and turned to look suspiciously at the boy, wondering if he should trust him.

"If you come this way, I can take you through the tunnels that no-one ever uses, most here do not even know of their existence. I will lead you back to Merlin's rooms," said the boy.

"How do I know you're not going to take me back to Alfrick and that awful old woman?" asked Gareth.

"You have my word," replied the boy, looking assured that this would make all the difference.

"Oh ... what the heck ..." said Gareth, he couldn't stay in there for ever and he had no idea where he was, so he decided to go with the boy. "Thanks, I'd be glad if you could take me back."

Still unsure of whether he was doing the right thing, Gareth followed him through the door into another room. The boy went to the corner and lifted up a trap door. He lit a conical torch and went down a small wooden ladder into a narrow dark tunnel.

"Come, do not be frightened, I know all the passages here well, these will lead us to the north tower where you can go up and across the battlements to the stairway that will lead you to Merlin's rooms."

"Oh, I think I know that bit, we were up there yesterday."

"You were," said the boy, in a matter of fact tone.

"Oh, I don't remember seeing you," said Gareth surprised.

"No you wouldn't have done," replied the boy.

Gareth half expected an explanation of some sort to follow this statement but none came, so he decided to ask another question instead.

"Who is that old woman and who did she think I was, do you know?" he tried.

"Her name is Gwelliant, you must not think badly of her. She is very old and her mind wanders. She mistook you for someone she was nursemaid to a long time ago."

"Who?" asked Gareth intrigued.

"A boy she was very close to, she looked after him well. She has always been a faithful servant," he replied.

"She said she had two boys, and they were taken away from her," said Gareth.

"Yes at one time she did," he answered. "We are nearly there now; I will take you up the tower on to the battlements where you will be safe to continue on your own."

"Oh right, thanks," said Gareth, as they went up a steep flight of stone steps and emerged out of the dark tunnel underneath the stairwell of the tower. He could hear voices and noises from the kitchen and corridors as they swiftly made their way straight up the stairs.

"There was something else I thought strange," said Gareth, determined to get at least one satisfactory answer from the boy. "They both got really jittery when a nasty looking black bird came in the window. They seemed to think it was watching and they called it the 'Black Knight'. That's when they decided to shove me into the tunnel." The boy's reaction was immediate; he stopped and looked at Gareth. "Even stranger, I've seen that bird before and it wasn't here!" he finished.

The boy didn't answer and carried on to the top, where the wind blasted through the open doorway to the battlements.

"You will be safe from here," he said.

"Thanks, thanks a lot," said Gareth, assuming he wasn't going to get any more information.

"Wait, a warning my friend," said the boy. "I know this bird you speak of, and if you have seen it several times, then Medraut is watching you, be very careful. If you see the bird, speak of nothing as the bird is the eyes and ears of Medraut."

"I just don't understand," said Gareth. "It's reasonable that someone can train a bird to do things for them, but how can it pass on information?"

"You may see the form of a bird, but in fact it is whatever that person wants you to see. It is either the person themselves or just a guise they are using, to watching and listen to you. Be very careful!"

"Right... I will ... well thanks," said Gareth, completely shocked by this explanation.

"There are a great many things here that you will not understand. Whatever Merlin has told you so far cannot possibly explain everything here and there are a great many secrets that none shall ever know. Stay with your sister always while you are here and stay close to Merlin, he can protect you."

"Right ... well, I will then .... thanks," said Gareth, aware he was repeating himself but was too stunned to think of anything else to say.

"I have to ask something of you in return."

"Yes, yes of course," mumbled Gareth, completely thrown by the boy's warning.

"All I ask is that you tell no-one you have met me, especially Merlin."

"Okay, if that's what you want, I won't."

"Thank you, and good luck!" the boy said, clasping his arm in the same way he had seen the knights do.

"Thanks," replied Gareth as he stepped through the doorway. "I'm sorry, I don't even know your name," he said, turning back, but there was no-one to answer him, as the stairway was empty. The boy had gone. He went back in and looked down the stairs, but there was no-one there and no sound of anyone running back down the stairs.

Gareth made his way quickly across the battlements towards the next tower, which he knew led to Merlin's rooms, puzzling as to how the boy had disappeared so quickly and without a sound. He thought about his warning about the bird, and he remembered their earlier experience on the beach with the quicksand. It made him shiver and quicken his pace even more. He rushed down the stairs to Merlin's door, anxious to be back in the safety of his room.

"You've been a long time," said Rachel accusingly.

"Have I?" he answered lamely.

"I take it you found your way all right?" Merlin asked, "I was getting a bit concerned, I was beginning think you might be lost."

"Oh, er ... yes, I did get a bit lost on the way back, but er ... yes, I found it all right," said Gareth. "There are still a lot of people here though; the kitchen was really busy, I didn't see Isolde, I just put the stuff down on the table. I did see some of the knights though; I think they're leaving today. Anyway, you said we were going somewhere special, I haven't missed it, have I?" he finished, aware that he was gabbling.

"No, no, you haven't missed anything," replied Merlin, looking at Gareth slightly suspiciously, as though he knew that he wasn't telling him everything. "I do have someone very special I want you to meet before you leave."

"Is it Arthur?" asked Gareth, doing his best to act naturally and not give anything away.

"You're obsessed with him," retorted his sister. "He's dead, remember!"

"Well, it didn't stop you seeing him, did it?"

"Now, now," butted in Merlin, firmly. "No, it isn't Arthur, sadly, but it is none the less a very important person of an entirely different nature. After we have made our visit, Percivale will meet us with the horses and we will make our way back to the tunnels where you will be able to return to Valonia.

"I will go and fetch my cloak. I would suggest that you both do the same as there is a strong wind blowing out there," said Merlin as he went towards the door. "And I'm sure you will want to get your breath back before we leave Gareth. You might want to take a drink as well. Although I am surprised to see that the stairs have taken such a toll on such a strong, healthy boy," he said as he left.

"What did he mean by that?" asked Rachel, "he didn't look very pleased with you either."

"Quick, while he's out the room, you won't believe what happened to me!" said Gareth, and told her as fast as he could about his experience. "The boy said I wasn't to tell anyone, so I'm only telling you because we're in this together, but we mustn't tell Merlin!"

"Why ever not?" she asked.

"I don't know, but there must be some big secret to do with this Gwelliant and whoever it was she'd been nursemaid to. It was obvious that he didn't want to tell me who it was and she was convinced I was someone else!"

"We'd better get our cloaks, or he'll know we've been talking about something," said Rachel, and they went up the stairs into the small room.

"This business about the bird is really scary as well. He was actually telling me that the bird was Mordred, and the woman said it was the 'Black Knight' watching me!"

"Why do you think it attacked?" asked Rachel. "Do you think it could have been helping you, like the other one did?"

"Oh no, it was hissing and spitting furiously, it didn't look as though it was in any mood to be helping anyone, it seemed angry. Actually it was sitting quietly just looking, until she said it was him!"

"Maybe that's what made him angry, after all Mordred wouldn't want us to know that the bird was him, or even 'his eyes and ears' would he?" she answered.

"No, I think you could be right."

"What did the boy look like?" asked Rachel.

"Like all the others I suppose, I was so frightened I didn't pay that much attention at the time and it was really dark in the tunnels," he answered, thinking hard, trying to visualise him again. "Come to think of it, he wasn't dressed like all the others that are running around outside, his clothes were quite fancy. He had a dark red tunic, but there were gold bits all around the edges, and there was a big gold emblem on the front and the back."

"That sounds a bit like the ones I saw on King Arthur's cloak, and on his tunic at the feast!" she replied, turning as she heard a noise.

"Merlin's back, we'd better go down, and don't say anything, we'll keep it to ourselves," said Gareth.

Rachel nodded and they both put their cloaks on and went down to join the old wizard.

Chapter Seventeen
Nightmares and Mist

They joined Merlin and made their way down the tower stairs into the busy courtyard. There were obviously a great many people still left after the feast, as it was even busier than the day before. There were groups of men talking, some standing with their horses as though ready to leave. The blacksmith had several customers waiting and his hammer could be heard clinking as he secured a metal horseshoe onto the stallion he was shoeing as they passed. The scruffily dressed children were playing games, dodging in an out of the groups of ladies in their long gowns as they chatted sociably to the knights. There seemed to be a general attitude of good feeling, no-one appeared to be working apart from the blacksmith as it was obviously still an occasion there.

They made their way through the throng towards the arched gateway, where they recognised Percivale standing with a group of men talking. Another man stood nearby holding their horses reins as though they were about to leave.

As they drew nearer to the group of men, two of the many stray geese took to following them. One taking a fancy to the trailing hem of Rachel's dress, pecked at it, squawking loudly. She turned and tried to shoo it away as its beak made contact with her ankle. She let out a shriek and flapped her hands at it, but the goose stood its ground, spreading out its wings, hissing angrily. She stopped flapping, and took several nervous steps backwards, as it hissed again.

One of the men stepped forward and came to her rescue, getting rid of her unwelcome follower in a second.

"Thank you," she said with relief.

"'Tis my pleasure," was the answer, and she could hear the amusement in the voice.

She looked up to see that her rescuer was the dark young knight, whose glance she had kept meeting by mistake at the feast.

Her cheeks burned with embarrassment, as his grin turned into a laugh, showing a neat set of white teeth. His dark hair waved in an unruly fashion on to his shoulders, and his outfit was plain and unassuming compared to the elaborate attire of the knights at the feast. His open necked shirt and trousers were loose fitting, with a dark plain waistcoat.

It was obvious that he found her plight highly amusing, and before she could regain some dignity, the goose slipped unnoticed round the back of her and launched another hissing attack on her trailing dress. She shrieked loudly, and hid behind the young knight, who gallantly made sure the offending goose was frightened away permanently. He shooed it firmly away until it gave up and waddled back to the rest of the gaggle at the far end of the courtyard.

He returned still laughing, and feeling even more stupid, Rachel found herself thanking him again, whereupon he bent low in an exaggerated mock bow. "At your service," he said pretending to be serious, only to be given away by the twinkling mirth in his blue eyes.

"For heaven's sake, stop teasing my young charge, Galahad!" Merlin intervened. "Save your impudent gestures for the girls of the castle, at least they are used to your roguish ways!"

"Merlin, my apologies to you, and to your charge," he said with another bow. "I meant no offence," he added humbly, although his eyes still twinkled and Rachel felt sure he was still making fun of her.

"None taken, my boy, none taken!" laughed Merlin, slapping him on the back. "So you ride with Kay today then?"

"Aye, we ride to Caer Wise to return the bodies of Richard and Torrick that fell in the battle," the young knight answered, his smile vanishing.

"A noble deed my boy, a noble deed! 'Tis a sobering duty to return the dead to their kin! May God keep you both safe on your way!"

"Aye, 'tis a lesson to us all!" he replied quietly. "There were many of our own that fell! Many more battles like that one and there won't be enough of us left to keep up the cause, 'tis a sobering thought indeed."

"God's speed!" said Merlin, clasping his arm, placing his other hand on his shoulder, in a supportive gesture.

Percivale brought two horses forward and Kay and the young knight mounted them. Another man passed them the reins of two horses with the bodies of the dead men draped over them, wrapped in richly decorated cloths.

Rachel stepped back hastily as soon as she noticed the bodies, even though she couldn't see them as they were completely swathed in the rich cloths. Nevertheless the mere thought of it sent a shiver down her spine and a terrible image of a battlefield briefly invaded her thoughts. Gareth however looked on curiously, unaware of her distress.

Galahad thanked Merlin for his words and wished them well, as the procession walked in a stately fashion, through the arched gate towards the causeway. As soon as the dark young knight mounted and rode through the gateway on a pure white horse with a long silvery tail, Rachel recognised him and her dream flooded back to her. She knew instantly that this was the knight that she had seen in her nightmare.

They watched the small party pick its way carefully across the causeway and the sight of him on the striking white horse, looking sad and sombre as they led the horses carrying their dead, left her in no doubt that she was right. She knew that it was his feelings that she had somehow intercepted and felt, with all the horror of the past event that she had witnessed in her dream.

"It saddens the heart to watch this, two brave men, taken back to their loved ones, and many more, whose bodies won't find their way back to their kinsfolk!" Merlin said shaking his head in despair, as they watched them reach the end of the causeway. "But now, we must not dwell on this because there was a victory: yes indeed a great victory that these poor souls gave up their lives for!"

They nodded in silence, Gareth because he was feeling the enormity of the whole situation, and Rachel because she was still reeling in shock that she had just identified the person in her awful dream.

"Now then, we have our own important business to attend to!" Merlin announced resolutely. "Let us not forget our own mission! No indeed, we shall make haste, we have a bit of an uncomfortable climb ahead of us, but I'm sure you won't mind that!" he said, leading them through the arched gate on to the causeway.

They followed him and the huge gates were shut behind them, but instead of walking over the causeway he led them to the left, towards the cliffs on the other side of the castle.

"Merlin, who was that knight?" asked Rachel, "the one on the white horse?"

"That's young Galahad, most of the girls take a fancy to him, the same as they did with his father," laughed Merlin.

"I did notice that at the feast! But that wasn't why I asked!" she replied indignantly.

"So why the interest?" asked Merlin, noticing her sharp response.

"He was the man in my nightmare, I recognised him as soon as I saw him on that horse."

Merlin stopped and looked seriously at her.

"I had my suspicions when you told me about it, and now you have confirmed it. The scene that you dreamt about was the burning of Galahad's village, where the people he grew up with were slaughtered by the Saxons. They rode back to help them, but were too late."

"You said he's like his father, was he killed there as well?" asked Gareth.

"No, no, Galahad is Lancelot's son."

"Wow, Lancelot from the stories of Arthur and Guinevere? Is he really his father?"

"Was," corrected Merlin. "Lancelot died shortly after his treachery with Arthur's wife. Not a very loyal or courageous act on his part," the old man said flatly.

"That's why he was so sad!" said Rachel quietly.

"Yes, Galahad suffered a great loss, but he is young, and now he fights with a passion against the Saxons, and anything else that threatens his people. Don't be fooled by his flippancy, he has a torment burning inside him that he cannot escape, and sometimes, I think he is still as deeply troubled as ever."

"The awful feelings I had, they were his, weren't they?"

"I think they were my dear."

"But why? Why would I dream about it, I don't even know him?" Rachel asked.

"As I explained earlier, your visions are always shown to you for a reason!"

"Excuse me for butting in, but didn't you say we were meeting someone?" asked Gareth, slightly peeved by the way his exuberance about Lancelot had been firmly crushed, and almost annoyed by the fact that he had no idea what they were talking about.

"We most certainly will be," Merlin answered as they reached the edge of the cliff. They looked down on a steep pathway that led onto the cliff face, below which, was the small shingle beach they had seen from the battlements the day before. It nestled in between the high rocks the castle perched on, and the steep cliffs the other side. The small winding pathway down to it looked none too inviting.

"I'm not sure about this," said Rachel, looking down fearfully at the sheer drop on the other side of the steep pathway.

"Nonsense," replied Merlin. "Come along, if I can do this at my great age, I'm sure you can!"

Gareth followed him quite confidently, heights had never bothered him anyway, and Rachel was left to follow them. Her long skirts hampered her as the wind caught them and she tried hard not to look down at the rocks below. The path hugged the cliff and was narrow in places, it sloped downwards steeply, and she followed them feeling slightly sick and giddy. She tried to hold onto the rocks at the side of her with one hand, and clutch the folds of her dress in the other, while the wind threatened to use her dress as a sail and lift her away. She was so relieved when they reached the small beach she felt like crying.

"There now, that wasn't too bad was it," said Merlin, and she glared at them both for not realising her fear.

A strong breeze was blowing off the sea, and the waves foamed onto the shingle beach with a watery crash. This was closely followed by the sound of the shingle shifting, before another great wave rolled in. The noise was quite deafening along with the wind. To their right was a cave entrance, which Merlin was already striding towards, quite unperturbed by the wind and the waves dashing at the rocks only a short distance away.

They entered the darkness of the cave and Merlin picked up a wooden torch from further inside. He passed his hand over it, and a dim glow gradually began to illuminate their surroundings, just enough for them to see where they were going. He led them deep into the cave, stooping through narrowing openings as they went deeper and deeper into the cliff. Pointed rocks hung down from the ceiling in places as the caves went on and on. Eventually they came to the smallest opening and almost had to crawl through, bent double, to find they had entered into a large domed cave.

There was an eerie green glow and as they went in further they could see a large underground lake stretching right across the cavern. A strange misty vapour clung to its surface, making it difficult to see exactly where it ended or began.

The temperature had dropped dramatically compared to the sheltered warmth of the passageways, and Rachel gave an involuntary shiver. They didn't need the torch now as the green glow from the lake dimly illuminated the cave. As they walked on the vapours drifted around their legs as it floated across the ground. The water was still and had a strange emerald hue about it, but the hovering mist moved gently, like clouds floating in a soft breeze, except that there was no breeze in the airless cavern.

Merlin walked to the edge of the lake but the twins didn't follow, there was something strange and unreal about the place that made them both feel uneasy.

"Merlin, what are we doing here?" asked Gareth.

"Sh!" Merlin sharply silenced him, turning back to the lake.

"Argante, Argante!" he said, as though speaking to the eerie green water. "Argante!"

The mist appeared to move and swirl and ripples appeared in the water. Rachel stepped back several paces and grabbed her brother's arm. A voice came out of the mist, or was it from the water? Or was it from somewhere else in the cave? They couldn't really tell.

"Who speaks my name?" asked the scornful, condescending voice of a woman. "Who dares to call me?"

Rachel clutched Gareth even harder, as the mist floated rapidly from left to right in a most unnatural way. It swirled as though it was moved by the wind, but there was no wind in the eerie cave and they both stepped back again quickly, peering into the mist for the owner of the voice.

"Argante! It is I, Merlin! Has it been so long that you do not recognise my voice?"

"Merlin?" questioned the voice, "My druid friend?"

"A very old friend, Great Lady, that humbly seeks an audience with you."

"Wise wanderer of the forests, pray tell me what is so important that you would make this request?" asked the cold musical voice that seemed to come from all around them.

"Argante, Great Lady of the Lake. I bring you news, and I bring you the new Keepers of the Power!"

The mist swirled again, and Rachel and Gareth watched in fascinated horror, as the figure of a woman rose from the lake, and drifted towards them with the mist swirling around her protectively. It was difficult to see whether she came across the water or out of it, as the whole substance of water and mist became one as she materialised in front of them.

The mist cleared slightly as she came nearer, revealing a pale unreal looking figure of great beauty, in a pure white dress adorned with pearls and gold beading. Her red-gold hair cascaded down to her waist in thick waves, framing a face that could have been carved out of marble, with translucent white skin, high cheek bones and piercing emerald green eyes, with long dark lashes. On her head she wore a small coronet of delicate flowers and interwoven leaves, which matched the threads of gold leaves around her neck. Her appearance was one of exquisiteness and although her costume was breathtakingly simple, it had a subtle ornate elegance about it at the same time.

"Argante, Great Lady, it is good to see you again," said Merlin bowing low.

"It has been a long time," she answered, her cold face softening slightly.

"Indeed, a very long time, my Lady!"

"I trust the years have treated you well my wise friend?" enquired the musical voice, now pleasant.

"They have indeed, and I am honoured by your concern, Great Spirit!" Merlin answered, bowing again.

"And what is this news that you bring me after so long, pray tell?"

"Forgive me for disturbing you, Great Lady, but there have been events that I feel I must tell you about!"

"Events, I am sure there must have been many events," she answered, her voice becoming hard and cold. "What are these events, that are so important, pray tell?"

"I have with me the new Keepers of the Power."

"Why do you feel the need to involve me in this matter, this is not of my choosing," she said, glancing at Rachel and Gareth disdainfully. "It was not my decision to hand the Power to mere mortals. There have been many Keepers, why should you wish to seek an audience with me, with these?"

"These Keepers are different, they are not from Valonia."

"Not from Valonia?" she said sharply. "How can this be?"

"They are of the line, their mother was a Keeper, but she married in another time to a man from the new world."

"In another time, what other time?" she said angrily, the mist quivering around her.

"The future my Lady," he answered rather hesitantly.

"Do you dare to come here and tell me that the Power has passed out of Valonia, into the future, the very place we have kept it from?" she fired at him angrily. They felt the temperature in the cave drop dramatically and they both shivered.

"No, no, my Lady, the Power had been kept in Valonia. It was

Medraut who interrupted the course of things by destroying the Keepers. That is why their mother kept them hidden in her new world, safe with their father. They knew nothing about this place or Valonia until we brought them here. They were brought back, as they were the only ones who could stop Medraut, as the true inheritors."

The mist stopped quivering and the cold, beautiful woman seemed to search Merlin's face. An unnatural silence filled the cave, but the freezing chill seemed to gradually lift.

"I will trust your wisdom, my old friend," she said finally, tossing the thick mane of red-gold hair haughtily. "What of Medraut, has he been destroyed?"

"Not destroyed my Lady, but thwarted, his powers have diminished and the power is safe again with its rightful keepers."

Argante didn't answer, instead, she raised her eyes to the cavern ceiling, motionless, breathing deeply, as though in a trance. Then with another swish of her hair she looked back at Merlin.

"Medraut may be thwarted, but 'tis only temporary, he still has power. He will come again! He will not come with an army of men. He will come with great sorcery. He will use great cunning and deception. He must be destroyed; death is the only end to Medraut's powers. As long as he lives, the Power will never be safe. He and his line will pursue it until their final end."

"We heed your warning, Great Lady!" Merlin bowed again.

"These Keepers from another world, how can they protect the Power, pray tell? Have they learnt the ways, have they the magic, or the knowledge?"

"No my Lady, they have none of this yet."

"Then how are they to be of any use, pray tell? And how can it be that they have no knowledge? Have they no interest in their duties?"

"As I said my Lady," continued Merlin patiently. "Their mother shielded them from all of this to keep them safe, but they are the true descendants, and certain things have been passed to them without them knowing. They need to learn how to use these gifts that they have so recently discovered. We need to be patient and teach them. They know nothing of sorcery, magic or even the basic knowledge of fighting with a sword and shield."

"How so?" her voice was sounding almost angry again. "How can they not know this?"

"Because, in their world, their time, they have no need of this," replied Merlin, defending them. "I have been privileged to have an insight into this time where they live in peace; they have no battles to fight."

"What of our invaders, what of the Angles, the Jutes, the Saxons?"

"All live in harmony, my Lady. They have great leaders that they all follow, there are no warlords. They have had battles my Lady, fierce battles, so bad that we could not even imagine them, but Briton's shores have remained safe for centuries!"

A smile lit up the beautiful face and she nodded slowly, digesting this news from a world she would never see; the future.

"This pleases me greatly, this news you bring! This is good news, indeed! So it will come to pass that there will be no warlords! There will be no invasions, the Britons will be safe! I am so pleased with this news, which my wise friend brings from another world: greatly pleased!"

"Well, thank goodness for that!" whispered Gareth to Rachel.

"Shh! She'll hear you, you idiot!" Rachel replied, glancing fearfully at the beautiful translucent figure. Too late, the emerald eyes fixed upon them and her face was as cold as marble.

"Do you dare to mock me?" asked the haughty spirit.

Gareth shook his head, as the green eyes bore into them, in a look of complete contempt.

"You may be from another world, but mock me, and you mock all of those who have gone before you! Be careful with your audacity, no mortal being has ever mocked me and lived."

The temperature dropped again, even colder than before, and the green eyes glaring at them were hard, cold and contemptuous.

A chilling frostiness began to creep through them, rendering them both immobile. Rachel saw her brothers lips turn blue and his face drain of all colour as the cold in turn passed through her body, making her limbs feel like stone, devoid of all feeling. It crept slowly upwards numbing her brain, until it was an effort to breathe, or even think. She felt herself trying to fight it, and was vaguely aware of Merlin stepping in front of them as she finally lost consciousness.

Chapter Eighteen
The Prophecy

Merlin stood in between Argante and the twins, holding his cloak out each side of him to shield them from her icy glare.

"Great Lady I beseech you, do them no harm! The boy is foolhardy, but he meant no offence! Please take into account their ignorance of our ways."

As Argante's petrifying glare was broken the warmth rushed back to Rachel and Gareth, as though they had just emerged from a freezing pool, and they both gasped for air behind Merlin.

"Please, Great Lady, give them a chance, they are, after all, the inheritors," the wizard pleaded.

"Inheritors they may be, but are they worthy? What use are they to us without the knowledge of centuries?"

"Argante, they may not have this, but they have the same powers as all the Keepers, even though they have only the little knowledge that I have this far given them."

Argante looked at the twins sternly, but also with curiosity this time.

"I have always trusted your judgment Merlin, and as a favour to an old, wise friend of the forests, you may show me these Keepers." Argante said haughtily, tossing her beautiful head. "Bring them forward!"

Neither of them moved: neither of them wanted to get any closer to her as the fear still remained with them from their last experience. Argante looked annoyed again, she was used to having her commands executed in an instant, and these strange children were trying her patience, despite Merlin's fond words of them.

"This boy, is he as brave as he is foolish?" she asked.

"He is indeed my Lady. It was his hand that defeated Medraut. He took up the sword against him to protect his sister. The sword Excalibur released itself and aided him in this task."

Her face remained cold but her eyebrows rose at this, as though in surprise, and she looked at them with even more interest. Merlin pushed them both forward slightly.

"The girl, is she a seer?" she asked, her gaze falling on Rachel, much to her discomfort.

"She is, Great Lady, she has seen but a few things, but her visions are true."

"What has she seen?"

"She has seen the slaughter of Galahad's people at Malmesbury, and she has seen Arthur himself!"

Argante looked at Rachel with interest, as she tried to edge backwards, away from the searching green eyes, only to be pushed forwards again by Merlin.

"Come hither, girl!" she commanded, beckoning to her. Her pale outstretched hand revealed long silvery nails, the fingers adorned with heavy, jewelled rings. Rachel looked at Merlin in panic, as she had no desire to move from the safety of his side. He ignored her and gently pushed her forward.

"Closer! Come closer: come to the edge of the lake where I may look at you!" Although it was a command, her voice had softened and she smiled as Rachel stood trembling at the edge of the lake.

"There is no mistake that you are a descendant, you have the look of all those gone before you," she said kindly.

Argante raised her pale hand again and placed it on Rachel's forehead. Her touch was icy cold, but instead of the awful chill that Rachel had felt previously, the coldness gently rippled through her head, and she had strange sensations of beautiful swirling colours. Again she became unaware of her surroundings, and instead saw pictures of her life, flashing in front of her. She saw her friends, her school, her father, Bronwyn, even the gypsy at the fair and Mordred by the quicksand. The pictures went on: she saw the feast, King Arthur and the dream of Galahad looking back to his village in ashes and lastly that of a young boy in a dark red tunic with gold emblems.

Argante removed her hand and the colours drifted away. Rachel found herself coming to, held by the piercing, emerald green eyes, as though Argante had been examining her very soul.

"You have the Powers within you to become a truly gifted seer, but it frightens you and you deny it, you have seen many things, but you have ignored them, have you not?"

Rachel nodded, still shaking.

"This is because you have not yet understood your heritage. You must not be frightened by it: this gift has been given to you to use for great good. There are those who have much less power than you, and strive to gain more to use for destruction and evil. You will not do this, you haven't the nature. What is your name, girl?"

"Rachel," she answered faintly.

"It will not be easy for you, Rachel. Your destiny has been mapped out, caught between two worlds. You will continue to deny your gift, but there will come a time when you will ask for it. You will wish you had learnt and developed it as the others gone before you have done. You will ask to see! Until this time your full powers will never be released, and until then you will not see much more unless there is danger or you have a calling. You must not be frightened by this; you must listen to it and trust it. It is there for your guidance."

Rachel gulped nervously and nodded.

Argante smiled as she looked at the frightened girl before her, and the cave lit up as though warm sunshine had suddenly entered. Her smile lit up her cold face, transforming it completely. Colour warmed the pale cheeks, and her green eyes gleamed brighter than ever, this time with a warm brilliance against the jet black lashes. Her hair glowed in a flaming red cascade, against her white gown. Rachel thought for a moment that she had never seen anyone so beautiful in her life, even in a film.

216

"Fair Rachel, you will grow into a very beautiful woman," she continued, this time her voice soft and low, as though in confidence. "There will be many to court your favour, but there will much heartache for you. Your life will become torn between two worlds and you will have difficult decisions to make because of this."

"Thank you," Rachel stuttered, not knowing what else to say, and curtsied as she had seen Isolde do, thinking it might show respect.

Argante smiled again, but this time her look held sympathy. She waved her hand and looked at Gareth, her face resuming her previous coldness.

"You boy, come forward!" she commanded, as Rachel returned to Merlin in relief.

Any bravado Gareth may have had earlier, had left him completely now, as he walked nervously to the edge of the lake.

"Look I'm… I'm really sorry about before!" he mumbled, too frightened to look at her. "I didn't mean you to hear … I mean I didn't…."

"Silence!" came the sharp answer, and Gareth shut up immediately. "What are you called?"

"Gareth, ma'am," he said in an attempt to be respectful.

"You bear the name of one who has gone before you, a brave and noble knight who gave his life to protect others. To honour this name you have much to live up to! You will not forget this and you will respect his memory!"

He nodded, not taking his eyes off her.

"You will have your own calling. You will need great bravery, more than you can imagine, for yours is the hand that must destroy Medraut," she continued, ignoring the look of shock that crossed his face. "He will be as much your mortal enemy, as he was Arthur's. Do not underestimate him or his seed. You must destroy, or be destroyed. You are the last in the line of keepers, if you do not do this, Medraut will lay claim to the Power and the world you come from will be no longer. Medraut must never be allowed to have the Power, do you understand?"

"I think so?" said Gareth not entirely sure how he was supposed to do this.

"You will take up the sword, you will take up the lance and you will fight as your forefathers did. You will do whatever it takes to accomplish this. Do I make myself clear?"

"Um, yes," mumbled Gareth.

"And above all, you will grow up and learn to be a man. There are knights who have gone before you, much younger than you, that would have already fought their first battle. They recognised their duties to their families and their King. They would not dare to stand before me and mock!"

"I'm really sorry," said Gareth again, glancing briefly at Rachel who grimaced sympathetically, feeling sorry for him as he endured his dressing down.

Argante looked hard at him, the green eyes fixed on his.

"You have great spirit, and your calling will not be easy. There will be times when you will feel useless and powerless to do what you need to do, but you will overcome this. You will show great determination, and you will make sure you acquire the skills you need. I have seen a glimpse of your future and I have confidence in you!" she finished to his surprise. "You will trust your sister's judgement and listen to her. She will be your wisdom and guidance, as it is with the Keepers of the Power. You will become a man and a knight and follow their code as your forefathers did before you. Kneel!"

Gareth looked stunned at her last command and looked at Merlin apprehensively.

"Kneel!" she repeated, rather sharply, her second command sending him down quickly onto the hard rough floor, where the sharp stones dug into his knees.

Rachel gasped as she watched her draw a long sword out of the misty water and lay its blade on her brother's shoulder.

"I name you Sir Gareth, a Knight of the Holy Order. You will follow the code and fight for the order that has been set down by King Arthur. May God protect and watch over you in your duties!" Argante lifted the sword from one shoulder to the other and as the heavy shining blade crossed in front of him, Gareth instantly recognised it as Excalibur, the same sword he had held in his own hand in the cavern facing Mordred. For a moment he wondered how it could have got there, since Merlin had returned it to the stone it had come from.

"Arise Sir Gareth," she commanded, the heavy sword at her side.

"Thank you," he said completely stunned by his knighthood and scrambled up rather shakily.

"And now you will both return to your own time, but you will be back, and it will be of your own choice. You will tell no-one of this meeting, in this time or any other," Argante said finally.

The twins shook their heads, "No, no we won't, we promise."

"Merlin," she said turning to him, the warm smile lighting her face again. "I thank you, I have learned much from this meeting. I have had an insight into the future and can find my own torment bearable in the knowledge that everything we have done here has not been in vain, and I thank you for that again."

"It is my pleasure, Great Lady," he said bowing again as he spoke.

"I have great faith in you and your ancient wisdom. You will teach them all they need to know, and you will guide them, for they will not be able to do what is ahead of them without you."

"It is a great honour to have your trust. I will not fail you!" replied Merlin.

"I do not doubt that! You have never failed me, my druid friend. You have done well, but there is much danger ahead for these new Keepers, and their path between the different worlds will make containing this secret even more difficult."

"I thank you, Great Spirit, for your words, and if I may make so bold as to ask a favour, one more request."

"You may," she answered regally.

"I am old and sometimes even my magic is not what it was. There may come a time when I may not be able to help these Keepers, can I ask that they may come to you if their need is really great?"

"They may," she answered, "and you are right, this time will come, but it will not be death that will keep you from your duty to them. I think you have seen this time have you not?"

"I have My Lady, and it is good to have that assurance."

"Now, I must say farewell to my old, wise friend. It may be a very long time before we meet again, if in fact ever," she said almost sadly. As she turned away from them she was shrouded by the mist, wrapping itself around her protectively until she vanished from sight.

"Farewell," said Merlin into the mist that was already diminishing into eerie wisps.

Suddenly the cave felt very empty and still. Merlin turned away from the lake, and started back toward the small entrance.

"Come!" he said rather sharply. "Our business here is finished," and with that he set off back the way they had come, without even waiting for them.

Rachel and Gareth quickly followed, surprised at his abruptness.

"Do you think he's angry with me for upsetting her?" Gareth whispered.

"I don't know, I shouldn't think so, he defended you enough! Maybe he's got his own reasons for being like that, he did look really sad when she left."

"Maybe you're right, he did," said Gareth, as they entered the last cave and could see the daylight flooding in from the beach. "We'd better stop talking about it; I don't want to get caught out again!"

The sea air hit them as they emerged back on to the small beach, where the waves seemed even closer than before. Merlin was sitting on a large rock waiting for them, and he smiled as they joined him. He seemed cheerful enough, although his usual exuberance was missing.

"You did well, both of you, although I think you need to learn to curb that tongue of yours young man!" he said looking at Gareth disapprovingly.

"I'm really sorry; I didn't think she could hear me."

"Argante wouldn't need to hear you, she would know your thoughts as they entered your head," he answered, wryly. "But no matter, there was no damage done, although subjected to a few more minutes of her anger like that, would have left you there, carved in stone!"

"She would have turned us into stone?" said Rachel in horror.

"In the blink of an eye, if she had a mind to," Merlin answered. "Argante is a very powerful Spirit, not someone you would want to upset, but maybe I should have warned you."

"Who is she?" asked Rachel.

"Argante is the Lady of the Lake, Earth Mother and Guardian of the Power," he replied. "Some say she is the Power, but I think she represents it in spirit form."

"So she isn't real then, if she is a spirit?" asked Rachel slightly confused.

"Oh no, she's real, she is both a living woman and a spirit, she is immortal and she will remain here forever."

"Why did she keep calling you a wanderer of the forests?" asked Rachel as they started to climb back up the cliff steps.

"My story is a long one, and far too complicated to tell half way up a cliff," answered Merlin, puffing slightly as the incline steepened. "But I will try. In short, I was a seer like you and I knew I had a destiny, but I had to search for mine. I knew it wasn't to be found in the castles or the people in them. I knew that my knowledge had to be found from somewhere else. It led me to the fields, the forests, the lakes and shores. I wandered for many a long year. I listened to the birds, the trees, the wind, and I learned a great many things. My search led me here to this cave where I met Argante. She appeared to me from the lake as she did today and told me what my destiny was."

"What was it? Your destiny I mean?" asked Gareth, as he desperately tried to keep up with the conversation from behind.

"I was brought here for Arthur, and for yourselves and for all of those who have been involved with the Power. It was on this very beach that Arthur's mother gave me her tiny baby, so that his destiny might be fulfilled: a destiny that you already know about."

"Argante said we have a destiny as well, what did she mean?" asked Rachel as they finally reached the top. "And you said I'm a seer, what's that?'

"That is the name we use for someone who has visions, or the sight, someone who sees things that others don't," he answered. "But Argante also said that you won't see anything until it is your time to do so, and that you will ask to see."

"I can't imagine ever doing that!" she answered resolutely.

"You may not think so now my dear, but obviously you will!" Merlin nodded wisely. "Argante has given you glimpses of your future, with her prophesy."

"Prophesy?" said Gareth as he climbed up the last bit of the path to join them. "Do you mean all that stuff she said will really happen?"

"Argante has told you what is in store for you if you follow the path ahead of you at this moment. But everyone makes their own destiny by the choices they make, so this is not set in stone, it is up to you."

"So, am I really a knight then as well?" asked Gareth.

"Argante has given you this honour, yes," replied Merlin, "although the title of Sir Gareth will probably not extend into your own time!"

"Imagine that at school!" laughed Rachel. "Have you done your homework, Sir Gareth?"

"Exactly!" chuckled Merlin. "But here, you are now a knight of the order as she said."

"Wow ...." breathed Gareth proudly.

They followed the small pathway back onto the causeway, where they saw Percivale waiting for them with Smokey, Rufus and two more horses.

"And now it is time for you to return home," said Merlin as he mounted his horse. Percivale helped Rachel up into the saddle as he had on the night they arrived and soon they were following the two men across the causeway with the castle getting further away behind them.

Gareth looked back at it wistfully over his shoulder. "I wonder if we will ever see it again."

"I hope we don't, if what that woman said is true!" Rachel answered firmly.

"You can't mean that!" said Gareth. "You must admit it was fantastic staying there."

"Oh I do mean it; I don't think I would ever want to go through all of that again!"

They dismounted at the entrance to the tunnel and Merlin handed the horse's reins to Percivale and asked him to wait for him. They thanked Percivale and said goodbye as Merlin started into the tunnel.

"Wait a minute, what about Rufus? We can't leave him here!"

said Rachel in dismay.

"Don't you worry about him," smiled Merlin. "He will be in the same place that he was when you left, best not to alter anything: you arrived here on foot and that is how you shall go back."

They entered the tunnels and the pattern was the same as their original journey, with the torches lighting up and going out behind them. Their footsteps echoed and they both felt quite subdued, the last few days had given them a lot to reflect on and it seemed as though their visit had been much longer than it actually was.

Half way through the tunnel they suddenly felt a strong wind blowing towards them, the nearer they got, the stronger it became. It was so strong they had to battle to stand up; it felt as though it was lifting them off their feet and yet they could still feel the ground they were walking on. It was a strange sensation and then suddenly it was gone!

"Wow, we're back in our own clothes: how did that happen?" shouted Gareth, looking down at his jeans and favourite trainers. Rachel's long dress had been replaced as well, by the clothes she had been wearing when they had left Valonia. Only Merlin's clothes were the same.

"How did that happen without us even noticing?" she asked, looking around behind her, half expecting to see their garments scattered around the floor.

Merlin laughed. "You have just passed through the tunnel of time. I didn't think you would want to arrive back in the clothes that offended you so much while you were there Gareth, so I arranged for your others to be provided!"

"Too right, I'm glad to see the back of those tights!" he agreed.

"Hose!" corrected his sister.

"Well, whatever they were, I'm still glad to be out of them!"

Merlin and Rachel laughed at him and they carried on down the tunnel and into the cavern by the stone platform, where Gareth noticed that the stone was empty and the sword was gone. They heard a shout from the benches in front and saw Bronwyn rushing towards them, stopping rather hesitantly in front of them.

"Don't look so worried my dear, all is well," smiled Merlin. "They have learnt a great deal on their visit with me, enough I think to explain everything they need to know for now."

"Oh thank you Merlin, I knew you would take care of them, it wasn't that, I was just worried how .... well, how they would take things."

"There will be a great many things you will want to discuss, now that they know the truth. My job here is done so I will leave you all and go back to Percivale."

Rachel hugged Merlin as they said goodbye, with a tear in her eye. She had become quite fond of the old sorcerer.

"There, there, my dear, I will be seeing you again!" Merlin looked quite touched by her display of affection. "And you my boy, look after your sister and your mother now."

"Yes sir, I will!" answered Gareth, shaking the old man's hand solemnly.

"I have enjoyed this time we have spent together, yes indeed, it has been most enjoyable!" Merlin said as he waved.

"Thank you, Merlin, so did we!" returned Gareth and they waved until he was out of sight. It all suddenly felt rather flat as they made their way up the cavern steps to the tunnel.

"I take it that Merlin has told you everything?" said Bronwyn hesitantly.

"If you mean that you're our mother, yes he did," answered Gareth.

"And how do you feel about that?" Bronwyn asked, rather timidly.

"Well, it's going to take a bit of getting used to," replied Gareth rather flatly.

"Well, I think it's wonderful!" said Rachel, hugging her. "Does that mean you'll come and live with us?"

"I don't know, that will depend on your father, but at least it isn't a secret now and I will be able to see so much more of you!"

"Oh I do hope so!" said Rachel, hugging her again.

They came up through the glowing torches to the cave entrance and the twins were surprised to see it was dark.

"What time is it? It can't be night already?" said Gareth. "It must have only been about two o'clock in the afternoon when we left."

"Where you were it probably was, but here time has almost stood still for you," answered Bronwyn. "Once you reached the other side of the tunnels and passed through time. It stopped moving on for you here."

"Merlin did tell us that but I'd forgotten all about it," said Gareth. "How weird is that going to be?"

"How long have we been gone then?" asked Rachel noticing that Bronwyn was dressed in the same hooded cloak she had on when they left her.

"About an hour, I think," she answered.

"That's amazing!" said Gareth. "That must have been how long it took us to get through the tunnels with Merlin before we went back in time!"

"It would be," answered Bronwyn as they walked back through the empty cavern. "Catherine has just gone to take Betsy's family home and she will bring the cart back for us, she won't be long."

They waited by the cavern entrance, where the torches still blazed brightly and soon they could see the cart making its way up the hill, pulled by the big, black carthorse Rufus.

"Now that's even stranger!" said Gareth as they climbed into the cart. "Not long ago he was standing with Smokey, all geared up in those fancy trappings! Now he's here, all harnessed up as though nothing ever happened!"

"I know, it's a bit strange all this magic!" agreed his sister.

Catherine made the fatal mistake of asking Gareth if he had enjoyed the castle, which started him off on a never-ending account of the knights, the feast and every detail about the castle he could possibly remember. It lasted all the way back down to the cottage and continued well into their second mug of cocoa! Eventually he ran out of things to say, after he recounted Rachel's unfortunate episode with the goose, and he looked at his sister knowingly, as he deliberately missed out his meeting with the boy who had helped him and their visit to the cave and encounter with Argante as they had promised.

"Well, I am glad you enjoyed it!" said Bronwyn yawning. "It's very late and we must get to bed as you have the journey home tomorrow."

They all went up to bed and surprisingly enough, the twins were quite tired even though it was not really bed time for them as they had been in a completely different time zone.

"I wonder if you get jet lag going through time!" said Gareth, as he reached his bedroom door.

"Don't be silly, we weren't on a jet!" answered Rachel.

"I know, but it's the same sort of thing though isn't it?"

"Goodnight Gareth!" was his sister's reply as she shut her door, glad to be away from his incessant chattering.

When they woke in the morning, there was a rush to pack and get ready to go. Bronwyn had decided to go back with them to explain things to their father. Catherine took them so far in the cart, and they left her and walked down to the station. As they waited on the platform for the train Gareth's attention was drawn to a sign on the wall, advertising Tintagel castle.

"Have you ever been?" he asked Bronwyn, and she replied that she had a long time ago.

"We pass Tintagel on the way home," said Gareth. "We passed the signs on the way down, I remember them. Could we stop off and just have one last look?"

"It won't be the same," answered Bronwyn. "There is nothing much left of it now."

"Oh go on Bronwyn, please, just one last look before we go," pleaded Gareth.

By the time they boarded the train, Bronwyn had reluctantly given in to Gareth's demands to see the castle one more time before they left. They got off the train at the nearest station and caught a small bus, which took them through the winding country lanes back to Tintagel.

When they reached Tintagel, though, they couldn't believe the sight before them. They walked down a high street with gift shops and tearooms, looking nothing like the area they had been in the day before.

"This can't be the same place!" said Gareth. "It's spelled differently as well. Look!"

He was pointing to a sign saying 'Tintagel Castle this way'.

"It is the right place. I did try to warn you," said Bronwyn. "You saw it spelled the way it would have been hundreds of years ago!"

"Well, we'll see the castle at least!" said Gareth as he dashed off down the long pathway that had been made for the tourists to gain easier access.

They reached a vantage point at the back of a small car park, where the castle should be seen against the skyline. Instead they saw the outline of a ruin. Hardly any of the great fortress remained. Part of the archway was still there, but most of the surrounding walls and all of the towers and battlements were gone. The causeway was still there, connecting the castle to the paths made for the tourists, and the rocky island it stood on still jutted into the sea, but even that looked smaller, as parts had eroded away.

"I don't understand, it can't all be gone, we were only there yesterday!" said a disappointed Gareth. "I can't believe it looks like this now!"

"You have to remember, you saw it as it was when the knights inhabited it. I know you're disappointed, but just think, none of these tourists will ever know what it was really like!" said Bronwyn. "You must remember it the way you saw it."

"I suppose so," Gareth nodded.

"Now I really think we need to head for home. I am going to have a hard enough time explaining all of this to your father, without having him standing at the station, wondering why we're so late. If we hurry we can catch the next train."

They walked back into the car park and before they turned the corner, something made Rachel stop and look back at the castle ruin. For a moment she thought she saw a figure in a long white dress, with long red hair streaming in the wind, standing on the edge of the cliff where the main castle walls would have been. A woman's unmistakable commanding voice drifted on the wind towards her, barely audible, and for a moment she thought she heard the words.

"You will be back, it is your calling."

coming soon...

THE GOLDEN CASKET
AND THE SPECTRES OF LIGHT

late 2009

Katie Paterson

Katie Paterson, of Scottish descent, has lived most of her life in the Midlands.

As a mother of two grown-up children herself, she has an ambition to help keep reading 'alive' for children, and was inspired to write The Chronicles of Valonia by a lifelong fasination with the Arthurian period and legends.

Other titles from
The Chronicles of Valonia

The Golden Casket and The Spectres of Light

ISBN   978-1-906873-11-0
late 2009

The Battle of The Underworld

ISBN   978-1-906873-24-0
Due 2010

The Quest for The Immortal Walker

ISBN   978-1-906873-25-7
Due 2011